Highlander's Redemption

Books by Emma Prince

The Sinclair Brothers Trilogy:

Highlander's Ransom (Book 1)

Highlander's Redemption (Book 2)

Highlander's Return (Bonus Novella, Book 2.5)

Highlander's Reckoning (Book 3)

Viking Lore Series:

Enthralled (Viking Lore, Book 1)

Other Books:

Wish upon a Winter Solstice (A Highland Novella)

Highlander's Redemption

The Sinclair Brothers Trilogy

Book Two

By

Emma Prince

Highlander's Redemption (The Sinclair Brothers Trilogy, Book Two)

Copyright © 2014 by Emma Prince.
Print Edition

All rights reserved. No part of this publication may be reproduced, distributed, or transmitted in any form or by any means, or stored in a database or retrieval system, without the prior written permission of the author except in the case of brief quotations embodied in critical articles and reviews.
For more information, contact emmaprincebooks@gmail.com.

This is a work of fiction. Names, characters, organizations, places, events, and incidents are the products of the author's imagination or are used fictitiously. Any resemblance to actual events or persons, living or dead, is entirely coincidental.

For Scott. Always.

Chapter One

Scottish Borderlands
Late June, 1307

"I leave on the morrow for Cumberland."

Jossalyn's breath caught in her throat, but she kept her eyes downcast and her tongue still. She sensed her brother was already in a foul mood, and her questions always seemed to annoy him. She had learned over the years how to avoid his rage—or at least she had become better at it. Lord Raef Warren was as unpredictable as the weather here in the Borderlands.

She waited, her hands clasped in front of her, while her brother moved to the other side of his huge oak desk and shuffled the papers that lay strewn across it. Finally, he continued.

"The King is believed to be ill, which means that I may be able to leverage a Barony at last."

This had her snapping her head up. Despite the years of practice biting her tongue, she opened her mouth without thinking. "I could help! I could try to heal—"

His hand slammed against the top of the desk, rattling his ink pot and causing her to jump.

"Silence! How dare you insinuate that you could help the King, and with your little herbs, no less!"

She had done it now. His rage would boil over, and he would take it out on her. She tensed, waiting for him to dart like lightning from behind the desk and strike her.

Instead, he smoothed back his sandy blond hair with one hand, inhaling through his nose to try to calm himself. "The only reason I called you here was to let you know that I would be away and to warn you not to disobey me." He stepped back around the desk toward her, his glaring eyes locked on hers. "But if you defy me one more time, sister, I will name you a witch and have you burned alive, blood relation be damned." His voice was calm, but deadly so.

Jossalyn lowered her head once more, giving her brother what he wanted—her utter submission. But if she had met his stare, her eyes would have revealed her defiance. She was not broken or cowed, no matter what Raef might think.

A little piece of her heart squeezed at the thought. She had been sneaking to the village outside Dunbraes Castle for years, tending to the people unfortunate enough to be under the rule of her power-hungry brother. Yes, she had been discovered a few times—and had borne his rages, insults, and even his fists—but it was worth it to help people, to save lives with her healing abilities.

"Perhaps this visit to the traveling court will give me the opportunity to marry you off as well. Then you'll be someone else's problem," he said coolly. "Who knows, it may even help me toward my Barony. I hear the Earl of Suffolk is looking for a new bride. Someone young."

Her stomach twisted, but she forced herself not to react. Her brother had made mention of arranging for her marriage before—after all, she had just turned twenty—but his threat about the Earl made her nauseated. The Earl of Suffolk had visited Dunbraes several months ago to discuss the mounting war between England and Scotland. He was old enough to be her grandfather, and had already worn through three wives. The first night of his visit, he had become so drunk on the castle's store of fine wine that he had tried to grab Jossalyn. When she had twisted out of his clawing hands, he proceeded to vomit on her slippers.

She swallowed. "How long will you be gone?"

He grabbed her chin, forcing her eyes to meet his. "Likely only two weeks, but it depends if the King dies or not," he said bluntly. "And don't get any ideas about making one of your little trips to the village, sister. I will have you watched and followed. I can't have my best bargaining chip with the Earl getting into anything…unseemly."

Her heart sank, but she didn't let the mask of

meekness slip from her face. His hazel eyes bore into her for a moment longer, seemingly trying to reinforce his threats. He didn't need to, though. Jossalyn knew from years of experience that her brother wouldn't hesitate to punish her, should she defy him.

"That is all," he said finally, releasing her chin and turning his back on her.

She curtsied despite the fact that he couldn't see her then silently crept out of his study and toward her chamber. As she walked up the stone steps toward her door, she felt a shadow following her and glanced over her shoulder. One of her brother's soldiers, Gordon, trailed her from several feet back. He stopped when she did but merely stared back at her, his coarse face and dull eyes flat in his obedience to Raef's order to follow her.

So this was to be her hound while her brother was away. Gordon was hulking and imposing, but at least he wasn't particularly bright. Perhaps she could still find a way to do her work in the village while Raef was in Cumberland. It would probably have to involve some discomfort for Gordon, unfortunately.

She turned back up the stairs toward her chamber, her mind running over her most potent herbal laxatives.

Chapter Two

You are to stay no longer than a week, collecting as much intelligence as you can.

The words burned into Garrick's mind, along with his older brother Robert's serious tone as he had said them. Garrick had been chewing on his Laird's words like a bitter cud for the entirety of the week-long journey from the Sinclair clan holdings at Roslin in the farthest northeast corner of Scotland all the way to the Borderlands. Despite Garrick's protestations, Robert thought it best to send him to the border to conduct a covert information gathering mission—along with Robert's right-hand man, Burke Sinclair.

But Garrick worked alone.

He always had, and except for this mission, he always would. If Robert hadn't invoked his authority as Laird of the Sinclairs, Garrick would have rejected the mission outright. He was needed elsewhere. Then again, his King, Robert the Bruce, had also agreed to lend Garrick for the operation, and he couldn't very well go against his Laird *and* his King. So here he was, stuck with Burke, a distant cousin and clansman, a mere day's ride from Raef Warren's Borderland holding at Dunbraes.

He spat over the neck of his large warhorse as they continued to move quietly through the dense forest. It wasn't that he didn't want to help the Scottish cause for independence. In fact, he had devoted his life to it. He had fought in every major battle of the last ten years, and in quite a few minor ones as well, first with his brother defending Sinclair lands, and later, alongside Robert the Bruce. It was more the idea that he could *only* collect information. He had to "blend in," as his brother had ordered, and talk with locals about what they were hearing.

Blend in. Talk. Him. He would rather have his bow in his hand, sending arrows into the throats of his enemies, Raef Warren included.

Burke was the man for the job. He was charming and handsome—or so the lasses seemed to think—and had a strange way of putting people at ease whenever he talked with them. Of course, Burke was also a highly trained and skilled warrior, wielding his great sword better than most men in the Highlands. But he was even more skilled when it came to interacting with people.

Unlike Garrick. He had worked alone for too long. His skill with his bow had allowed him to enter the Bruce's army, but because he excelled at precision shooting, he had risen quickly out of the mass ranks to become the Bruce's most trusted shot.

This meant that he was sent out on solo missions, waiting for hours and sometimes days at a time hidden in underbrush or tree foliage before his target came into view. He knew how to wait. He knew how to kill. Aye, he could go unnoticed anywhere in the Highlands, but he'd be damned if he could "blend in" within an English-held Borderland village, casually chatting with the locals about the English army's movements.

Resisting the urge to spit again, Garrick instead moved his horse slightly to the right, taking them farther into the woods and away from the road. Burke did the same without comment. Both men had fallen into a sullen silence shortly after departing from Roslin Castle the week before. Neither wanted to be here, but that didn't change anything. Their Laird had given the orders, and they both had to obey.

Thankfully, Robert was familiar enough with the area from his own days of raiding and information gathering that he had been able to give them instructions on how to find a safe house a day's journey northwest of Warren's holding. There, they would stash their warhorses, weapons, and armor, all of which would have made them stand out starkly—and draw dangerous attention.

They would also need to borrow a cart and draft horse and the clothing of English commoners. Nothing could be done about their Scottish accents besides trying their best to soften them to the Lowlanders' lesser bur. The Borderlands had become so fluid these days that many Scots and English lived together, especially surrounding the larger castles that kept changing hands. Dunbraes had been under Warren's control for several years, but it was surrounded by Scotsmen and their farmlands, so there was no avoiding interaction between the two nationalities.

Garrick and Burke had agreed that their cover story would be that they were two blacksmiths from a village farther north. They were looking for temporary work, and so had decided to try to find employment at the largest nearby holding—Dunbraes Castle and its village. Smithing would explain both men's large, muscular frames. It was dangerous to look too much like a warrior these days.

It grated to have to pretend to be supporters of English rule over Scotland, or at best act neutral, but times were too volatile to walk into a powerful English holding wearing kilts and speaking with a Highlander's brogue.

Garrick urged Fletch, his chestnut warhorse, forward a little faster. The sooner they reached the safe house, the sooner they could move on to the village, and the sooner this damned mission would be over. Garrick wanted nothing more than to return to the Bruce's side and do what he did best—fight. This week was sure to be tedious, but at least it would be over soon. Aye, this was bound to be the most boring week of his life.

Chapter Three

Jossalyn peeked behind her shoulder once again, but she knew without looking that Gordon wouldn't be behind her.

A smile itched at the corners of her mouth. She didn't relish the suffering he currently experienced, but she could barely contain her excitement to be going into the village—and only two days after her brother had left for Cumberland!

Besides, Gordon would be just fine, though he would likely be glued to the garderobe or his chamber pot for the next few days. Such were the effects of a little buckthorn bark steeped in water. Of course, as soon as his symptoms showed themselves, she had ordered that he be given a tea of chamomile to soothe his innards and keep him hydrated, which eased her conscience further.

Not minding the basket under her arm, she nearly skipped through the yard in the middle of the castle in her excitement. The portcullis was drawn up along the outer curtain wall, and both villagers and residents of the castle moved in and out freely on this particularly fine summer day. Perhaps she would even be able to stroll to the outskirts of the forest near the village to collect herbs before seeing to some of the villagers.

The combination of sunshine, fresh air, and freedom were surely going to her head, she thought giddily. She walked under the portcullis and wound her way toward the village, which sat just south and slightly lower than the castle a few hundred yards away.

She weaved her way around the west side of the village, swinging her basket and humming a tune. Yes, the forest would be perfect on this warm afternoon. She had heard from one of the castle's servants that a villager named Laura had a colicky baby, but she was running low on fennel, which would treat the colic.

When she reached a likely looking spot on the edge of the forest, she plopped her basket on the ground and began searching for the distinctive yellow flowers. She couldn't remember the last time she had felt so free. Even when she had been able to get away from her brother and the castle in the past, she always had to be looking over her shoulder, and she knew she would catch hell from him if he found out what she had been up to. But with Raef gone, and his lackey incapacitated for the time being, she felt like she could fly. She hadn't felt this way since—since before their parents had died.

Though it had happened almost seven years ago, the thought of her parents' death cut dully into her joy. It had been some sort of fever. Meg, the village healer back at her childhood home in England, had done all she could, but death's grasp had been too strong. Jossalyn's girlish screams still rang in her own ears. She had begged Meg to heal them, not understanding the limits of a medicine woman.

Once the initial shock had worn off, she had begged the healer for a second time, but instead of asking for the impossible, she had pleaded with Meg to teach her everything she could about the art of healing. The old woman had resisted at first, but quickly noticed an unusual aptitude in Jossalyn for identifying plants and their uses, and her gentleness with the sick and ailing. Meg had called it a gift. Jossalyn just wanted to help, and if this was her way, then so be it.

A few years later, when Raef had been entrusted to hold Dunbraes against the Scottish, she had found another friend and teacher in Vera, the old Scottish wisewoman and healer of the village. Vera was more than willing to have an eager and knowledgeable apprentice, despite the fact that she was also the sister of the Lord of Dunbraes Castle, a very unusual arrangement.

The only person who seemed to mind, however, was her brother. As the years went on, he set himself more and more against her work as a healer. At first, he only warned her that it wasn't proper for a lady to move around the village so freely. Then, he told her she couldn't continue with her work. When she did anyway, he took to screaming at her, shoving her, and even hitting her.

Though he claimed that it was merely a problem of propriety, Jossalyn suspected that it went deeper than that. Her brother had changed, albeit slowly, since their parents' death.

He had always been concerned with order, even as a child. But now he seemed poisoned with it, and with his desire for power. Perhaps he saw illness as the ultimate powerlessness, the ultimate intrusion onto order and control. He couldn't save his parents, nor could a healer, and that had frightened him. While Jossalyn had turned to healing as a way of dealing with their loss, he had turned to rage. And she had seen him shudder at the sight of her after one of her trips to the village, as if illness clung to her, followed her, and threatened to sink its claws into him as well.

Something happened in the last few months to make his rage even worse, too. Jossalyn had heard rumors that he was to wed an English lady, yet nothing had come of it. And the English army seemed to be mobilizing for a great attack on Scotland any day now, which had everyone on edge.

Jossalyn pushed the dark thoughts from her mind. She had chewed on them so much lately and was tired of them poisoning her just as they poisoned her older brother. She would enjoy this day, and even when her brother returned and forced her to stay inside the castle walls, she would have the memory of the warm sunshine on her hair and back, the smell of soil and plants on her hands, and—

Suddenly, a faint reverberation vibrated through her slippers. The ground was rumbling—and it was growing stronger.

Her eyes shot from her feet to her right, back up the faint, overgrown path she had walked along to reach the edge of the forest.

All of a sudden, an enormous draft horse pulling a wagon crashed through the underbrush only a few yards away. She jumped back in surprise but tripped over her basket, which still sat on the ground next to her. She tumbled backward, landing on her bottom in the low bushes she had been scouring a moment before.

"Whoa!" A commanding male voice shouted from the wagon, drawing the draft horse to a halt mere feet away from where Jossalyn had been standing.

She quickly tried to get herself upright and give the rude wagoners a piece of her mind, but her skirt tangled in the brambles of the underbrush, and her thrashing only made it worse. Embarrassment mixed with ire, and a warm flush moved up her neck.

Just then, she glanced up as the driver of the wagon leapt from his seat and strode toward her. Her thrashing stilled, and her jaw slackened. Walking—no, gliding, and with deadly grace—toward her was the most dangerously handsome man she had ever seen.

His frame was large but lean, his broad shoulders tapering into a trim waist and long legs. He wore a pair of simple breeches and a white shirt, but due to the day's warmth, he had the sleeves rolled back, revealing bronzed and muscular forearms. His dark brown hair was held back at his neck, and a day's growth of beard shadowed the hard line of his jaw.

She nearly gasped when she caught a glimpse of his eyes, though. They were almost black, and bored into her intensely. His brow furrowed as he took her in, which gave him an even darker, more intimidating look. He finally reached her, looming so large from her position on the ground that he blocked out the sun.

"Are you all right, lass?"

If it was possible, her eyes grew even wider. He spoke with a soft lilt. A Scotsman.

Chapter Four

Burke had warned him not to try to skirt the village on the west side, for the path was nearly overgrown by the forest. But Garrick had insisted that they would be less likely to be spotted, and so had forced their horse and wagon down the almost invisible path. It would look better for them to enter the village from the south, he had insisted, so that it would appear like they had already spend time in the area and weren't coming straight from Scotland.

He had gritted his teeth at the conditions of the path, if it could even be called that, and silently dared Burke to make a comment so that he would have an excuse to unleash his annoyance on his cousin. It wasn't Burke's fault, of course, but Garrick was strung tighter than his bow—which he had been forced to leave back at the safe house—and anxious to get this entire mission over with.

He had been so distracted in his thoughts, however, that he failed to see the lass until it was almost too late. Luckily, his reflexes were sharp enough that at the first flash of golden hair and dark green skirts, he pulled up hard on the reins, forcing their enormous draft horse and cumbersome wagon to a halt before they squashed the lass like a bug.

As it was, she looked squashed anyway. She had crumpled into a bush and was struggling to right herself. Feeling like an arse for not paying attention, and dreading having to beg apology from this lass he had nearly run over, Garrick swung out of the wagon and strode toward her. Her hair, which sparkled like gold in the sunlight, had slipped from its braid and partially obscured her face, but her eyes followed him as he moved.

"Are you all right, lass?" he said in his least-Scottish sounding voice, coming to a halt in front of her.

She shoved her golden hair out of her face with one hand to reveal flawless strawberries-and-cream cheeks. Her eyes widened, and Garrick suddenly found himself swimming in their emerald depths. Maybe drowning was more like it.

His eyes traveled down to her berry-red lips, which were parted in a surprised O, and his mind went instantly to thoughts of how soft and sweet they might taste.

He viciously ripped his mind away from such idling. He wasn't here to seek pleasure with a Borderlands lass—no matter how incredibly enticing she was. And yet, there he stood, staring down at her like a dumbfounded lad. For some reason he couldn't get his tongue to work. All he could seem to do was drink in the sight of her on the ground, rumpled, surprised, and just as speechless as he was.

Burke cleared his throat from where he stood behind Garrick, which caused him to snap his head up, breaking the spell.

"Our apologies, my lady. We are unfamiliar with these paths. Are you hurt?" Burke said smoothly, hiding his brogue far better than Garrick had.

Burke's words made Garrick feel even more like an arse. Here he was, enraptured by this lass's finely formed face while she was toppled over in a bush, struggling to get to her feet. He quickly extended his hand to her. She shifted her glance between the two of them, seeming to weigh Burke's good manners against his poor ones.

Finally, she placed her delicate hand inside his. He wrapped his other hand around her upper arm and hauled her out of the brambly bush she had fallen into. But he overestimated the force required, and ended up yanking her clear off her feet. She screeched as she came hurdling upward and toward him, but the sound died when she bumped into his large chest.

Christ, this wasn't going well, he thought with annoyance at himself.

Thankfully, she bounced off his chest and landed on her feet, though she wobbled a bit. Placing his hands on her shoulders to steady her, he took a step back so as not to intimidate the lass—or inflict any more of his "help" on her.

"I apologize for startling you, my lady, and for, er—for flinging you," he said through gritted teeth. Damn, but he did feel like a lad—one who had been caught with his hand in the honey pot.

The lass seemed to be gathering whatever shred of dignity and level-headedness she had left. She smoothed her dark green skirts with her slim hands, which Garrick noticed trembled ever so slightly.

"Yes, well. You should drive more slowly on these overgrown paths," she said. Her voice was strained, but her English accent was clear. So, she wasn't from the Borderlands as he had initially thought. He felt himself grow slightly more guarded.

"Again, we deeply apologize, my lady, and beg your forgiveness," Burke said with a regal bow. "As I mentioned, we aren't from here, and were trying to find our way to the village at Dunbraes."

"Ah, well, you are nearly there. The village is a stone's throw from here," she replied, then hesitated for a beat before going on. "May I ask what your business is? You see, I know the village and its people well, and could perhaps point you toward what you seek."

That sounded innocent enough, but Garrick suspected that his stronger Scottish accent was making the lass curious at best—or worse, suspicious.

"How fortuitous!" Burke said, plastering a smile on his face, though his thoughts likely ran in the same direction as Garrick's. "We are blacksmiths from a small village farther north. Though we were both apprenticed with our uncle with the aim of taking his place, he has stayed on as the head blacksmith back home, and sadly there wasn't enough work to keep us employed. We were hoping to find more work in a larger village."

Some of the tension went out of the lass's shoulders. Burke had managed to easily explain both their accents and their large, muscular frames, all while keeping a friendly smile on his face. Damn, he was good.

"Hmm, John may welcome the extra help." Her brow furrowed slightly as she thought. "In fact, he should be giving his bad hip a rest anyway." Seeming to decide something, she gave a little nod. "I can show you where our village smithy is and make an introduction. I need to check on him anyway."

Garrick felt his own curiosity pique. Without thinking, he said softly, "*Check* on him?"

The lass blushed prettily and lowered her eyes under his gaze. "Yes, I am—I am a healer." Though she tried to steady her voice, it nevertheless faltered. Now it was Garrick's turn to furrow his brow. What would cause the lass to feel embarrassed to name herself a healer? What was she hiding?

Perhaps he had spent too long alone in the field. Here he was, growing suspicious of a lass just because she blushed under his hard stare. He was likely scaring the wits out of her. Even without his kilt, metal-studded leather vest, sword, knives, and bow and arrow, he probably didn't look like the friendly villagers she was used to seeing.

"May we offer you a ride back to the village, my lady?" Burke said. "At least then you'll know you won't be run down by a few country bumpkins like us!"

Country bumpkins? Even in their simple English clothes, Garrick doubted they could pass for bumpkins. But despite his skepticism, Burke's charm worked yet again. The lass cracked a small smile, and his stomach pinched. Her green eyes danced and those rosy, supple lips arched into the perfect curve.

"I suppose I could accept a ride. But not from strangers," she said.

Burke matched her smile and swept another gallant bow. "I am Burke Ferguson, and this is my cousin, Garrick Ferguson." They had decided to use their first names to avoid any dangerous slip-ups, but had chosen a nice, safe Lowlander surname, despite how ridiculous their names now sounded to his ears.

She bobbed a curtsy to them. "And I am Jossalyn W-Williams."

Garrick didn't miss her little hitch—the second one in mere minutes. Now he was suspicious. Good thing his mission was to ask questions around the village and gather information. He would have to keep a special eye on this lass—not that such a task would be hard.

After she had collected her basket full of herbs, the three of them walked over to the wagon. Before Burke could prove himself a gentleman and make Garrick look like a bumbling arse again, though, Garrick wrapped his hands around the lass's slim waist and lifted her onto the bench at the front of the wagon. Then he swung himself into the driver's seat, leaving Burke to take up a perch in the back of the wagon, which was mostly empty except for some supplies to give the appearance that they had traveled from a nearby village.

As Garrick took the reins in his hands, he was acutely aware of the lass's presence next to him, in no small part because she smelled incredible—like sunshine and wildflowers. He gripped the reins hard, trying to get his hands to stop tingling from the memory of the feel of her trim waist and that perfect spot where it flared gently toward her hips.

Aye, he would be staying close to Jossalyn Williams—for the mission, he told himself firmly.

Chapter Five

Jossalyn tried to still her racing heart, but it hadn't stopped pounding wildly since she had laid eyes on the two Scotsmen—well, only one of them had her chest hammering, actually.

Even now, as the one named Garrick turned the wagon down the cart road that ran through the middle of Dunbraes village, she couldn't quite seem to catch her breath or think straight.

It was because she had nearly been run over, she told herself for the umpteenth time.

It was because he had wrapped his large, strong hands around her waist and lifted her like a feather. Men simply didn't touch her like that; she was Raef Warren's sister after all, and a lady.

It was because she had nearly let her name slip, then lied badly to cover up a mistake that would have likely ended her forbidden foray into the village to see to the ailing.

But a little voice inside whispered that the uncontrollable fluttering in her chest was actually because the man sitting mere inches from her in the wagon was the most stunningly, strikingly, dangerously handsome man she had ever seen.

His eyes—which had appeared nearly black at first, but had revealed themselves to be a steely gray—cut into her like a knife. He seemed to be able to see directly into her, knowing her lies and understanding her girlish blushes. And his body—he was built like stone but moved like silk. She had seen muscular men before—after all, Dunbraes was one of the central gathering points for English troops before they advanced into Scotland. But something about his build sent shivers through her like no other. It made sense that he was a blacksmith, for nothing but warfare or smithing could hone such a physique.

Something tickled her mind about such a thought, though. Why hadn't these two brawny, able-bodied men in their prime been drafted into either the English army or the Scottish resistance?

Perhaps it was because they were Borderlanders. These unfortunate people in whose midst she lived had suffered the worst of the conflict. They often got hammered by both sides, and had to maintain fluid alliances just to survive. Jossalyn could understand not wanting to join the fight and risk everything if—or rather, when—the tide turned to one side and then the other. She had seen enough of the cruel treatment by the English against the peaceful farmers and villagers in the Borderlands to know just how dangerous it was to be Scottish, let alone a supporter of the Scottish cause for independence, in these times.

These two men were likely just trying to survive, even if it meant working in an English-held region. Plenty of other Lowlanders had done the same, so why did she keep feeling that tickle in the back of her mind? Something about these two—and particularly Garrick—made her curious. She had a hard time picturing him as a simple blacksmith from a small village. He seemed too—dangerous.

So lost in her thoughts was she that she nearly forgot to instruct Garrick to stop as they approached John's smithy. Without thinking she gripped his forearm as she pointed to the smithy and told him where to guide the wagon so that it would be out of the way. His hard muscles flexed under her touch, and his skin was warm and smooth where her fingers brushed past his rolled up sleeve. She jerked back as if burned, but he didn't seem to notice—or at least he pretended not to for her benefit.

Garrick pulled the draft horse to a halt where she had indicated, then swung out from his seat. Before she could begin her own descent, though, he moved like lightning to her side of the wagon, extending those large hands toward her to help her down. She placed her hands on top of his shoulders, feeling the ripple of his muscles as he tensed under her touch. Then those hands were on her waist again, sending waves of heat from where they firmly gripped her. She could feel another blush creeping up her neck and willed it away, but to no avail.

As if she weighed next to nothing, he lifted her first up so that her feet would clear the wagon's bench, then down until her feet gently touched ground. For some reason, though, she felt like she was still floating in the air. His hands lingered for a moment, and his steel-gray eyes collided with hers. His look was unreadable, but there was something fierce in it, though she didn't know why.

A quiet cough from Burke, who had already started walking toward the smithy, snapped both of their eyes away. Garrick's hands instantly left her waist. She could still feel where they had been, though, as if she had two large handprints branded into her now.

Garrick gestured for her to lead the way, and she grabbed her basket and moved past him, trying to keep her chin level and her cheeks from flaming again. Crossing the wagon road, she tapped on the smithy door lightly. When she heard John's bellow to come in, she pushed the door open.

Despite the brightness and warmth of the summer day outside, the interior of the smithy was dim and roasting hot. A large fireplace with several tools sticking out of it dominated the back wall, and except for a few tables strewn with more tools, the only other feature of the room was the huge anvil in the middle, where John was currently working.

John squinted into the light of the open door, his bald head dripping sweat. When he recognized

Jossalyn, he tossed his tools down immediately. "My lady! What brings you here today?" He gave a quick bow, then straightened, moving around the anvil toward her. She took note of the slight limp and the way he was favoring his right hip.

"I've come to make an introduction. John Elliot, these two men are here to inquire about work. This is Burke and Garrick Ferguson, from a village to the north." She stepped aside to let each of the large Scotsmen enter the smithy. John removed one of his gloves and extended his hand to each man, then grunted in satisfaction.

"Well, you've got enough hand strength to work for me, and that's a start," he said with a nod.

As Burke explained their circumstances and their desire for work, Jossalyn began digging in her basket. Though most of her attention was taken trying to find the comfrey root that would ease John's hip pain, she could feel Garrick's eyes on her, following her movements. Her fingers fumbled slightly, but she took in a steadying breath. It must be the heat from the fireplace that was making her cheeks feel so warm.

Burke concluded and the smithy fell silent as John considered them, one hand rubbing his square chin. Finally, he spoke. "I've had a few jobs piling up ever since this old hip of mine has kept me from working like I used to. It won't be permanent, mind you, but I suppose you lads could help me get caught up."

"That sounds fair enough. We'd be much obliged,

even if it's only for a few days or a week," Burke replied.

"Now that that's settled, I have one more matter of business with you, John," Jossalyn said firmly, putting on her most serious face. She handed him the comfrey root. "Boil this in water until it turns into a thick paste. Then soak a cloth in it and wrap the cloth around your hip. That should ease the pain, especially when the fogs start to roll in."

She turned and nearly ran into Garrick's broad chest. She hadn't realized it, but he had taken a step closer toward her as she had been speaking.

"I—I have to go," she managed to get out as she quickly skirted around his towering frame and toward the door. "I have other patients to see. Good luck with your work." She didn't know who these last words were directed at, but she felt so flustered in such close proximity to Garrick that she rushed toward the door, longing for the fresh air outside.

"How would you lads like to get started right now?" She could hear John's deep voice behind her as she passed through the doorway. She felt Garrick's eyes following her, the sensation burning into her back even as she hustled down the road.

Hours later, when she was on the other side of the village in Laura's small but cozy hut to administer a fennel tea to Laura's colicky baby, she could still feel those hard gray eyes boring into her, searching her, flickering with—something like heat.

Chapter Six

Morning light crept in around the furs covering Jossalyn's chamber window, but it was early still. In the summer months, the sun rose earlier here in the northern Borderlands than it had in her childhood home in lower England. She normally relished the longer days in the summer, but for some reason, she felt like lingering in bed today.

It wasn't just "some reason," she chided herself and she rubbed her eyes. She knew very well why she was dragging her feet. She was a coward. She had gone two whole days without seeing Garrick, fear and shyness keeping her well away from the smithy even though she had been in the village both days to visit her patients. How could she simultaneously long to see him and be terrified at the power he seemed to have over her?

Last night, she had resolved to straighten her spine and face him. Even the thought of being in his presence twisted her stomach into knots and made her feel foolish and clumsy, but he might not be here very much longer—perhaps only a few more days—and she knew she would regret not seeing him again.

There was no point in denying, especially to herself, that she was drawn to him, attracted to him. She wanted to know more about him, to simply feel the intensity of his presence.

And in order to do that, she had to stop being such a ninny. She had to get out of bed, go to the village, and stop avoiding the smithy like a skittish cat. Besides, from the look of the yellow light coming in behind the furs, it would likely shape up to be another beautiful summer day. She only had a few more days until Gordon was well enough to resume his watch over her, and even though sneaking around like a snake wasn't ideal, at least she had freedom from her brother for a while yet.

With that thought, she flung off the covers and scurried to the armoire, selecting a simple blue dress for the day's work ahead. She quickly scrubbed her face in the cold water left in the pitcher from the night before, but took extra time to plait her hair, making two smaller braids going back from her temples and feeding them into a larger braid that swung down her back.

She breezed through the kitchen on her way to the yard, tossing an apple and a few heels of bread into her herb basket. Then she was across the yard and past the large stone walls of the keep. The sun was already climbing in the bright blue sky, and the air, though cool and fresh now, promised another warm day ahead.

Before going to the smithy, she would check on just one patient, Laura's brother Thomas, who had been suffering a toothache. It was on the way anyway. She wasn't stalling, she told herself stoutly.

Thomas was already doing much better, so there wasn't much for her to do besides give him some more lemon balm. Then it was time. She wound her way out of Thomas's hut and through the back alleys toward the smithy. Perhaps if she approached from the alley rather than the main village road, she would be able to see if there was any activity going on in the workspace behind the building before having to knock on the door.

Lost in her thoughts and trying to rein in her nerves, she nearly walked right by the backside of the smithy. She jerked to a halt and looked up, only to nearly gasp in shock.

There in the small uncovered yard behind the smithy, Garrick was working in the morning sun. Shirtless.

The rippling planes of his torso glistened and twisted in the light as he brought a hammer down with a steady rhythm onto the horseshoe he was shaping. Her eyes widened as she took in every honed muscle, every perfect, sweat-covered line. His broad shoulders and wide chest narrowed into a trim but muscular waist. His rhythm was hypnotic, and she probably would have kept staring open-mouthed at his unbelievably strong and honed body, but then suddenly, as if sensing her eyes on him, he looked up and locked his stare on her.

She nearly bolted, overcome by her own longing to drink him in with her eyes, and the embarrassment of getting caught doing so. This wasn't going according to plan. Taking a steadying breath, she forced herself to close her mouth and take a step toward him.

He could feel eyes on him. He wished he had his bow, a knife, anything to reach for, since being seen usually meant being dead in his line of work. At least he had a giant hammer in his hands. Tensing slightly, he allowed himself to look up.

He nearly dropped the hammer on his foot.

Standing like a statue in the alley a few yards away was the impossibly enticing healer lass again. Jossalyn. Her green eyes were wide and those pert, berry-red lips were parted once more in surprise. A ray of morning light was hitting her from behind, illuminating her hair like polished gold, and highlighting her shape—rounded breasts, narrow waist, and slightly curving hips, all covered in a fitted blue gown. She looked like a goddess of the dawn, or like the morning sky itself.

She seemed to give herself a little shake and began walking toward him. He lowered his hammer and drew the back of his forearm over his forehead, though both were sweaty.

"Good morning. I came to check on John and to

see—" she faltered but recovered, "to see how you and your cousin were getting on."

As if on cue, Burke pushed through the back door of the smithy, but halted abruptly at the sight of Jossalyn standing in the small open area.

"We are fine, thank you," Garrick said, more curtly than he had intended. He couldn't seem to think straight whenever the lass was nearby.

"How thoughtful of you, my lady," Burke said smoothly, covering Garrick's brusqueness. "We have settled right in and have helped John tackle these languishing jobs. You'll also likely be pleased to know that John has been able to rest a bit more with us around to help. He said this morning that his hip is feeling better, and he has gone to deliver some of his work to his customers."

"That is indeed good news!" the lass said brightly, but then stood there moving her slippered toe in the dirt of the smithy yard for several more moments.

The silence stretched. She clearly wanted to stay, but Garrick wasn't sure why.

"Perhaps your visit to check on John won't be a complete waste," Burke said, jumping into the silence. "Garrick, haven't you been complaining of a sore shoulder lately?"

Garrick started to object, but caught the sharp look Burke was shooting at him.

They had already spoken to several villagers, casually chatting about the weather, this year's harvest, and then slipping into questions about the activity of the English army, the visitors at Dunbraes, and speculations about just when war might break out. So far they had learned that Raef Warren was away visiting Longshanks, which didn't bode well. Warren had grown increasingly powerful of late. If he had the King's ear, he was poised to launch a major attack on Scotland, especially considering his ideal position in the Borderlands. Other villagers had mentioned that the castle's men-at-arms had been training more that usual lately—another bad sign.

Jossalyn seemed well-connected throughout the village, yet she had disappeared after that first day. Perhaps now was his chance to probe her for information. Besides, Garrick thought grudgingly, he could think of worse ways to pass the morning that spending it with a pretty lass.

"Yes, my shoulder. It's...sore," he said, rolling his right shoulder a few times for emphasis.

"Why don't you two go into the smithy while I finish up this horseshoe," Burke said as he moved to take the hammer from Garrick. As he released the hammer into Burke's hand, he gave the other man a glare in return for his earlier sharp look. Burke was being rather heavy-handed in insisting that the two talk alone. Did he have other intentions besides creating an opportunity for Garrick to gather information? And why did he lift the corner of his mouth at Garrick like a damn sly cat?

Not wanting to draw attention to their silent conflict, Garrick let it go and instead turned and pulled open the door to the smithy. As Jossalyn glided through the door ahead of him, he caught that smell again—wildflowers and sunshine. Damn, but why did the lass have to smell so good?

The smithy was warm, as usual, but the shutters were pulled back from the windows, letting more of the morning light in.

"Why don't you sit here while I examine you," Jossalyn said, gesturing toward a footstool near one of the windows.

He obliged, sinking down on the low stool. As she approached, he realized that her breasts were on a level with his face. Damn. It was one thing to go a while without enjoying the company of a lass. It was quite another form of torture to have a strikingly beautiful lass's perfectly rounded breasts shoved in his face while he was working a covert operation and couldn't get involved.

She bit her lower lip as she approached him nervously. Perhaps his still-naked torso made her maidenly sensibilities squirm. For some reason, he liked that thought.

"Show me where it hurts," she said, a little shakily.

He rolled his right shoulder again. "It hurts when I...move it a lot," he said lamely.

She furrowed her brow and placed her fingertips on his shoulder lightly. Even the soft contact made him twitch. His muscles flexed involuntarily under her touch. Christ, he was acting like an untried lad!

She poked and prodded him, telling him to say when it hurt. At random intervals, he would say, "That" or "There," trying to guess how to fake an injury. As she worked, she leaned over him, and her golden braid swung over her shoulder, the tail of it brushing against his bare stomach. He gritted his teeth, resisting the urge to wrap that blonde braid around his fist and pull her down onto his lap.

She didn't seem to notice how she tortured him, or perhaps she just thought that his twitching jaw was an indication of the pain his shoulder was causing him. Either way, his thoughts didn't seem to penetrate her concentration. Her nervousness dissipated as she focused on his shoulder. He could see from the absorbed look on her face that she was lost in thoughts about how to heal the imaginary injury.

"Have you ever hurt it before?" she said softly, her breath brushing his exposed skin.

"Nay," he gritted out, not caring that he had slipped into a thicker Scottish accent.

Finally, she turned away from him and toward her basket of herbs, which she had deposited on one of the smithy's tables. Trying to remind himself of what he was supposed to be doing—which was not to stare at her curved bottom—he cleared his throat.

"I'm curious—why does John bow to you?" To be honest, that question had less to do with their mission and more to do with his own suspicion that the lass was more that she seemed.

She spun around, her eyes wide, but then she casually waved her hand as if brushing away his question. "Oh, you know. I suppose he feels grateful to me for easing his pain. I am the village healer, and many of the people I treat do that." She spun back around to dig furiously in her basket. What was she hiding?

Trying to shake his suspicion, he forced his mind back on topic. "I suppose you've had to do a lot of extra healing lately, what with more soldiers moving through Dunbraes, and the increasing number of skirmishes here in the Borderlands," he said, summoning all of Burke's smoothness he could muster.

"Yes, there are far more war wounds now, though my brother doesn't let me—" She stiffened suddenly.

"Your brother?" Garrick said lightly, sensing a moment to strike.

"Um, yes, my brother. Ranald Williams. He worries about me, that is all. He doesn't like me to come too close to the war, even though I could help."

Garrick could hear the strain in her voice, sensing a lie, or at least an omission, but he could also hear the pain there.

"So he forbids you to use your skills?"

She turned around, holding a brownish-looking root. "He...doesn't approve." She moved to the fire, which burned cheerily in the back wall, and tossed the root into the caldron that hung there. Then, using the bucket next to the fireplace, she poured water into the caldron over the root.

"But you are clearly very talented."

She shot him a wide-eyed glance, but quickly averted her eyes, and he could see that sweet pink blush creeping to her cheeks again. "Perhaps you shouldn't say such things until *after* I have administered my remedy to your shoulder," she said, her eyes still shifting away from his but a smile quirking the corners of her mouth.

He very nearly smiled himself, which shocked him. He couldn't remember the last time he had felt happy or carefree enough to indulge in a smile, let alone a laugh. Forcing his thoughts away from the lass's comely curved lips, he tried a new angle.

"Have you lived here long? In the Borderlands, I mean." Perhaps she would have English relatives who might know something about the temperament of the country.

"Oh yes, years now. We moved to…find work, like you. I trained with the former healer of Dunbraes, and my brother…works in the castle." She paused and stirred the brew she was making in the caldron. "I haven't seen England since we moved here. I know this may sound strange coming from and Englishwoman, but I think of Scotland as more of my home than England now."

That surprised him. An Englishwoman who cared enough about Scotland to call it her home? He wouldn't push the issue, though. Allegiance in the Borderlands, and during times of war especially, was a sticky subject, one that could offend at best and end with a hanging for treason at worst.

Instead, he watched in silence as she rolled up the sleeves of her dress and reached for a wooden spoon to continue stirring the contents of the caldron. Something on her forearm caught his eye, though. Several marks, fading from purple to yellow, marred her creamy skin. A handprint.

Suddenly he bolted up from the footstool and crossed to her in front of the fire. She jumped at his lightning-fast movement, but he wrapped his hand around her wrist delicately, holding her in place.

"What is this, Jossalyn?"

Chapter Seven

His touch on her wrist was light, but his voice was dark with anger, and his gray eyes were stormy as they bore down on her. She nearly flinched under the weight of his stare and his question.

"It's nothing. I just…it's just an old bruise." She hated the sound of the lie in her voice, but what was the alternative? Tell this strange Scotsman that her brother, Raef Warren, Lord of Dunbraes, had squeezed her arm so hard a week ago that the mark was still visible?

His eyes searched her face, seeming to see right through her, lies and all. "Your brother?"

She inhaled sharply, suddenly frightened that he knew too much. But she had told him that her brother disapproved of her healing. Lowering her eyes, she simply nodded, not wishing to either lie more, or worse, reveal the truth.

"He is so against you helping people that he uses force against you?" The incredulity and rage in his voice made her feel—safer, surprisingly. This stranger seemed to have more decency and regard for women than her own brother did.

She nodded again, but pulled her wrist back, breaking their light connection. She turned back to the caldron, where the comfrey root was turning into a paste the right consistency to apply to Garrick's shoulder. Hopefully the same remedy that had John feeling young and spry again would work on Garrick as well.

"Jossalyn."

The sound of her name on his deep voice sent a shiver up her spine. "Yes?"

"You don't have to stay with your brother. Where I'm from, your gift for healing would be valued, and the people there would treat you as you deserve. People would…care for you."

Her hand stilled in its stirring. Was she hearing him right? Was he suggesting…? No, he hadn't said that *he* cared for her, or that she should leave with him. But the seriousness in his voice told her that he did want better for her. And she wanted better for herself.

She had always let herself fantasize when she was collecting herbs or roots in the forest next to the village that perhaps someday she would escape her brother. This had often involved imagining getting married to some honorable English knight and living in the countryside where she had grown up.

But with her brother's recent threats to use her marriage to forge an alliance for his benefit, those dreams of wedded bliss had been quashed. And even setting aside the nauseating thought of marrying some old lecher for her brother's gain, she was no longer sure she wanted to move south back into England. She had never been farther north than the Borderlands, but she had become enraptured by the more rugged, wild country that she now inhabited. The longer summer days and the colder, snowier winter nights, the towering mountains in the distance, the violent storms and the tranquil lochs—these were the things that moved her, that made her feel alive.

And then there were the people. The village was a constantly changing hodgepodge of Englishmen, Borderlanders, and Scottish Lowlanders, most of whom were simply trying to keep their heads down and survive. No one would speak directly about it, but Jossalyn had been in enough backrooms and marketplaces to hear talk of the desire for Scottish independence. These people, on whose lands she was living, had been hammered by her countrymen, just as King Edward had set out to do. They sought their freedom—freedom from oppression, freedom to worship, to keep up their traditions, to live in peace—yet her King and countrymen had to have more, had to be in control.

Though she had never voiced such thoughts to anyone before, she had often felt a kindred struggle for her own freedom. She understood perfectly the value of independence and liberty from tyranny. She didn't want to live under her brother's control for the rest of her life, and certainly wouldn't be married off to some cradle-robbing English nobleman, so what was left?

She had always pushed away the whispers inside her head, but now they were clear and loud: she should escape, move north, leave behind England and its constant quest to make Scotland come to heel.

If she were free, she could work as a healer—a real healer, not just one who could only see patients when her brother wasn't paying attention. She could help more people. She could live as she pleased, marry whom she pleased. Perhaps she could even marry a man like Garrick.

Her heart pounded furiously at the thought. Of course, she hardly knew him, so she wouldn't let her mind rush to thoughts of a life with him, but maybe she could find someone who was as kind, or who would accept her as a skilled healer, or who stirred her and made her stomach flutter, the way the mere sight of him did.

Yes, the man standing behind her moved her in ways she didn't even understand, but this wasn't about him—it was about her freedom. But perhaps he could help her.

Letting that thought simmer for the moment, she turned back to face Garrick. He loomed over her, his naked torso dominating her field of vision. He was a patient at the moment, she reminded herself as she tried to keep her eyes from roving all over him.

She failed. She couldn't help but drink in the sight of all those contours and muscular planes. Something hitched in the back of her mind, though. She had noticed it before when she was checking his shoulder, but hadn't registered it.

"How did you get these scars? I would have expected to see burn marks on a blacksmith, not so many healed cuts."

His eyes flashed, and he paused for a moment before answering her. "My brothers and I roughhoused with each other a lot. When we were children, we fancied ourselves knights."

"Jousting and sword fights and all that?" she said with a wry smile.

"Yes, something like that," he replied, one corner of his mouth quirking into something resembling mirth. "But we grew out of it," he continued, more serious suddenly. Something dark lay behind his words, but she didn't want to pry.

"If you'll sit again, I'll wrap your shoulder, which should ease the pain."

He obliged, and she dipped a strip of cloth from her basket into the paste bubbling over the fire. She approached him, blowing gently on the paste-covered cloth to cool it enough to apply it to his skin. After placing the strip across his shoulder, she returned to the caldron, repeating the steps until his shoulder was covered in comfrey-soaked cloth.

As she finished arranging the last of the strips, his hands suddenly came up and wrapped around her waist. Before she could get out a gasp of surprise, he had pulled her down onto his lap, and placed a kiss on her surprise-parted lips.

He hadn't meant for it to happen, but he damn well didn't regret it either.

Her nearness was intoxicating him, making it hard for him to think straight. He didn't plan on getting involved, but hearing the strain in her voice when she mentioned her lowlife of a brother had made him furious—and protective, for some reason. This lass was none of his concern, but then why was his blood boiling at the thought of her brother laying a hand on her in anger? And why was he so intrigued at her apparently strong feelings of connection with Scotland? And why had his cock stirred when he had held her delicate wrist in his hand and inhaled the scent of her?

When she had pursed those plump red lips and blown on the cloth, however, that was his undoing. His mind had flown unbidden to thoughts of what else those lips might do, and he had nearly lost his battle to control his cock. It was all he could do to stop from pulling her to him right then, but he had managed to resist.

It wasn't until the last piece of cloth had been placed on his shoulder and her hands drew back that he lost his battle. He wanted more of her touch, wanted to feel her fingertips grazing across his skin again, to feel just how soft and sweet her lips actually were.

It was even better than he could have hoped. Her

surprise melted almost instantly into soft tentativeness. He forced himself to keep the kiss light, just a brush of his lips against hers. His hands stayed around her waist, and hers rested between them against his bare chest. Just when he was about to break off the relatively innocent kiss, she leaned into him a little, pressing her lips more firmly against his and slightly curling her fingers into his skin.

He tilted his head to deepen the kiss. Their lips melded more firmly together. She made a little noise like a sigh, and he took the opportunity to brush his tongue against her slightly-parted lips. She inhaled with surprise as his tongue gently teased the inside of her mouth, but she melted even further into him, moving her hands from his chest to wind around his neck.

Slowly at first, then with more confidence, she matched the movements of his tongue, caressing, teasing, and intertwining. Heat shot to his cock, which was pressed against her bottom. He gripped her hips, pressing her more firmly into his lap, even though he was only increasing the exquisite, pleasurable torture.

"Ahem."

Jossalyn shot like a spooked cat out of his lap and onto her feet at the sound of Burke's voice in the doorway.

"Am I interrupting?" Burke asked innocently, though his raised eyebrow and quirked mouth said he had seen enough to know the answer to his question.

"No, no, I was just...I'm all finished here," Jossalyn

stammered out, her cheeks flaming red.

"What do you want, Burke?" Garrick ground out through gritted teeth. Damn his cousin's bad timing—or was it good timing? How far would he and Jossalyn have gone? And what would have been the consequences to his mission? Christ, he had let his cock do his thinking for him.

"I finished up with that horseshoe and came in to see how it was going in here. Garrick, you look like you feel better already," Burke replied, his smile widening.

"I should go," Jossalyn said in a small voice. She snatched her basket from the table and hurried to the back door, pushing past Burke with her head down.

"Jossalyn, wait!" Garrick strode after her, pausing only to say out of the side of his mouth to Burke, "You'll pay for embarrassing her like that." Burke only grinned wider in response.

Garrick caught up with her in the alleyway leading off the smithy's backyard. He moved in front of her to stop her hurried steps, but she kept her head down, not meeting his eyes.

"Jossalyn, pay no heed to Burke's teasing. He only meant to aim it at me."

"But we shouldn't have—I shouldn't—"

He placed a finger under her chin and lifted it so that her eyes met his. Their emerald depths were clouded over with embarrassment. He struggled to find the words that would ease her shame, to express to her how much that one kiss had stirred him. He couldn't even believe he was chasing after her; normally, he let the lasses come and go, enjoying their company but nothing more. But with Jossalyn, he longed for more—more contact, more kisses, more conversations.

"I want to see you again," he finally managed.

"But you will likely leave in a few days' time when John is caught up on his orders, and I—I wouldn't be able to come and see you even if you stayed."

Her fragmented and cryptic speech brought a question to his mind, but he pushed it aside for the time being. He had to convince her somehow to see him again, for he didn't know what he would do if he never laid eyes on her again.

Damn his brother and this mission. He hadn't wanted to go on an information gathering operation in the first place, and now that he was here in the Borderlands with this remarkable lass, he had to leave. Burke was clever in letting it be known that they would be moving on shortly. It would rouse less suspicion if they had only planned on staying a short while from the beginning, but he had never foreseen becoming so enthralled with an English lass.

"Please, Jossalyn, I have to see you again," he said simply, unable to explain the situation to her, and not fully understanding his strong desire for her either.

She bit her lower lip, a look of frustration crossing her face. Finally, she said, "All right. I will visit you again. But," she said seriously, "we cannot...behave so intimately again. We must be friends, and no more."

He felt his face grow dark. Why would she deny the passion that clearly crackled like lightning between them? Why would she push him away like this?

Then it dawned on him. She was protecting herself. She was keeping her distance so that she wouldn't get overly involved, knowing as she did that he would be leaving soon. She had the strength to do what he was too weak to attempt. He wanted any time he could get with her, but wouldn't that make his departure harder on both of them?

He considered her demand that they act as friends. Would it even be possible? Based on his body's reaction to their kiss, it wasn't likely. But then again, he would rather see her again, if only for a few days, than not at all.

"Very well. Will you come by the smithy tomorrow?"

She nodded, her green eyes clearing slightly. "Yes. I'll come check on your shoulder."

He let his hand fall from under her chin and stepped back from her. She scrutinized him for a moment longer, her expression somewhere between quizzical and decisive. Seeming to have come to some sort of conclusion, she gave another little nod and walked around him and down the alley.

He waited until she was out of sight, then barreled back toward the smithy with one intention. He found Burke still smiling and leaning against the frame of the smithy's back door. Without ado, Garrick marched up to him and plowed his fist into his stomach. Burke immediately doubled over with a loud grunt.

"What was that for?" he wheezed when he could finally speak.

"You know."

"Well, someone had to bring you back down to earth, Garrick," he replied, straightening slowly. "How does making googly eyes at a pretty lass and then kissing her senseless help our mission again?"

Garrick gritted his teeth. Unfortunately, Burke had a point. "She seems somewhat sympathetic to the Scottish cause. I was hoping to learn whether or not she had heard of any seeds of rebellion within the village." That was close enough to the truth. Burke didn't need to know that Garrick hadn't felt this drawn to a lass since—well, ever.

"We should likely only stay a day or two longer. I heard from the baker this morning that there are rumors that Longshanks is ill."

Garrick sobered suddenly, his anger at Burke and his desire for Jossalyn pushed aside at such serious news. "Those rumors have been floating around for months. What makes them different this time?"

"Apparently Warren isn't the only one in Cumberland. Several of the aristocracy have gathered there and are said to be attending Edward's bedside."

This could be it then, the true start or end to the wars for Scottish independence, once and for all. Edward wasn't called the "Hammer of the Scots" for nothing—he had made it his personal mission to eradicate not only Scottish culture and sovereignty, but the very people themselves. His death could either be the rallying call for the entire English army, or it could be the swan song of English efforts to control Scotland.

"I have to get to the Bruce," Garrick said softly. He needed to report to his King, and prepare for the fallout from Edward's illness and possible death.

"We need to get to your brother, remember?" Burke said just as softly. "He is our Laird, and he is the one who sent us on this mission."

"My brother and the Bruce *both* sent me here, and the Bruce is our *King*."

"We can decide on the way north, but either way, we should be going soon."

Garrick ran a hand through his hair. "Aye, you're right."

"Tomorrow evening." Burke said simply. Garrick shot him a look, but Burke had an apologetic expression on his face. "That way you'll at least get to say goodbye to the lass."

"Aye. Thank you for that."

Burke nodded and moved into the smithy to continue his work. Garrick was left standing in the yard by himself, contemplating how to say goodbye.

Chapter Eight

Jossalyn was being vain. But she wanted her hair to be just right today. She had selected her brightest green dress, the one she knew brought out her eyes to their best effect. Now it was just a matter of taming her blonde locks into the intricate plaiting pattern she used for special occasions.

She had barely been able to sleep last night, but it wasn't just because her mind had tumbled relentlessly over her kiss with Garrick.

Her first kiss. Yes, she had pecked a few stable lads on the lips when she had been a girl, but she had never experienced a real adult kiss between a man and a woman. It wasn't at all what she thought it would be like. She had seen others kiss, but never with their tongues involved, and besides, seeing someone else was entirely different that experiencing the rush of sensation for herself.

Despite the long and sleepless night that had stretched since that kiss, she could still perfectly remember the soft heat of his mouth, his firm hands on her waist and hips—and something else that was also quite firm in his lap. She blushed for the umpteenth time at the thought, and at the memory of Burke's knowing smile when he had barged in on them.

Pushing her embarrassment aside, she tightened the green ribbon on the end of her plaited hair. She had more important things to think about now than her girlish blushes and that wondrous kiss.

She was going to escape—her brother, the castle, some grandfatherly husband, everything.

She didn't know how yet, but she would. Something about yesterday had caused a shift inside her. She could no longer live under the thumb of her brother, stifled and useless behind the walls of Dunbraes Castle. She had felt stuck for so long, unable to live as she wished, but unable to do anything about it either. She had bought into her brother's manipulation, thinking that things must be as he wished them to be. But now, she suddenly saw a new door cracking open, revealing a future of her choosing.

Certainly, Garrick's sudden entrance into her life had facilitated this, but she wasn't pinning all her hopes on him to rescue her. That was why she had insisted that they act as friends for the remainder of his time in the village. She still barely knew him, and both he and his cousin would likely be leaving the village soon anyway. It would be naïve at best, and dangerous at worst, to continue allowing their passion to overwhelm them. Soon, he would be gone, and if she weren't careful to separate her feelings for him from her desire for freedom, she could end up at the whims of fate yet again, instead of in control of her future.

But she had to admit, he had awakened something in her, shown her what life could be like if she were in charge of it. She could live in a place where her healing skills were valued, where people cared for her, where, perhaps, she could even be loved for who she was. He had shown her what passion was, and she wanted more.

So she would leave and start life over someplace new. Just the thought sent shivers of excitement and anticipation coursing through her. Suddenly she had a brighter future, even though the path to get to it was still unknown.

This newfound energy and confidence surged through her as she made her way toward the village. She would make her rounds to check on her patients, and then swing by the smithy to see how Garrick's shoulder and John's hip were doing. By the time she got back to the castle that evening, Gordon would likely be taking his first solid food in several days. She wouldn't have many more days like this, sneaking to the village and dodging her brother's lackey.

Before yesterday, she would have felt deep grief for the ending of this brief reprieve from her older brother's control. Now, she welcomed the end of the need to hide and lie about what she was doing. Soon enough, once she worked out the details, she would no longer have to risk punishment for doing what she loved.

Her joy must have been evident, for everyone she passed as she moved about the village smiled back at her, some even commenting on the beautiful summer day or how hale and hearty she was looking. She breezed through her visits as if she were the warm summer wind itself. By late afternoon, she had finished all her house calls and errands and headed toward the smithy.

She approached from the alley again, but no one was working there this time, so she went to the back door and knocked lightly before entering.

Instantly, she felt like she was intruding on something private and important, and her good mood faltered for a fraction of a second. Burke and Garrick were sitting across from one another at one of John's large tables, both leaning on their elbows with their heads close together. Both heads whipped around when she entered, and their eyes, Burke's dark blue and Garrick's steel gray, bore into her with intensity.

"I'm sorry. I was just stopping by to check…Where is John?"

Burke seemed to recover first and transformed smoothly into the jovial, chivalric man he always was around her. "Ah, mistress Jossalyn, what a pleasant surprise! John has gone out again, but he should be back later this evening. Is there anything we can do for you in the meantime?"

Her eyes moved between the two men. She could

feel a slight crease forming between her brows. "Is something wrong?"

"No, of course not, my lady! It is just that…" Burke shifted his eyes to Garrick and waited, an expectant look on his face.

Finally, Garrick broke the silence. "We leave this evening," he said flatly.

"Oh, so…so soon?" She sounded small and deflated even to her own ears.

"Yes, John is all caught up with his work and is feeling much better now. Besides, we got word that our uncle may be ailing. Nothing serious, I'm sure, but we will be headed north tonight," Burke said, not a crack showing in his veneer.

"Yes, of course," she said vaguely, her eyes drifting around the room, looking at the ceiling, the floor—anywhere but at Garrick. She could feel his intense gaze on her, nevertheless.

"I wish you both a safe journey," she said, suddenly anxious to get out of the too-warm smithy. She spun around quickly and exited through the door. Before she had gone three steps, however, she felt a large hand wrap around her upper arm, gently pulling her to a halt.

"Jossalyn…" Garrick swam in her vision as tears welled in her eyes.

"No, no, it's all right," she said airily with a wave of her hand. "I knew you were leaving. I just thought…that perhaps we would have a few more days to spend together…as friends."

Who was she kidding? Certainly not herself. She could never be friends with this man. She was friends with John and Laura from the village, and had been friends with Meg and Vera, her old teachers in the arts of healing. But Garrick was different. She didn't have *friendly* feelings toward him—she longed for him, dreamed of his kiss, felt her stomach flip every time she saw him or drew near to his large, muscular frame.

"I don't want to be your friend, lass," he said quietly.

Her heart jumped at his words, for his meaning was apparent. Could he feel the same way that she did?

But then he went on. "But…I have to go. I am duty- and honor-bound to return to my home and take up the work I was born to do." A dark shadow settled over his face, and for some reason, he seemed to be speaking about more than his job as a blacksmith, but Jossalyn didn't know why. All she could do was nod, for she didn't trust her voice not to break.

Ever so gently, he took her hand into his much larger one and raised it slowly to his lips. He placed a soft kiss on the back of her hand, and it felt like a hot brand.

She couldn't take it. She was going to crack to pieces right here if she had to say goodbye to him like this. Without thinking, she pulled her hand free of his grasp and away from his lips, then turned and ran back up the alley. She no longer cared that tears streamed freely down her cheeks.

Garrick watched her go with a stone wedged in his chest. His feet longed to give chase, but his head kept him rooted in place. This was how it had to be. She was just one lass, and he had a job to do. What did the feelings of two people matter when it came to the fate of an entire nation?

He scrubbed a hand over his face, trying to get the image of Jossalyn's emerald-green eyes, which had shimmered with tears, out of his head. He had a feeling no matter how many times he rubbed his face, the lass would stay with him long after this war was decided once and for all.

Forcing himself to turn back to the smithy, he caught Burke watching him from the doorway. His cousin didn't bother offering condolences or try to lighten the mood. Instead, he gave him a slight but resolute nod, waiting for Garrick's word.

"Let us prepare. We move tonight."

Chapter Nine

It would have to be tonight, then, Jossalyn thought as she opened the wooden door to her armoire. She had indulged in enough tears throughout the late afternoon and evening, bolting her chamber door and refusing to join the rest of the castle in the evening meal. Now, it was time to clear her head and make a plan.

She had already decided to escape Dunbraes sometime in the near future, but she hadn't anticipated that it would be *quite* so soon. But she couldn't deny that this was as good a time as any—better, probably, since her brother was still away and Gordon hadn't fully recovered yet from her dose of laxative tea. She wouldn't be watched from the castle. The only problem that had remained was how to put enough distance between herself and Dunbraes so that she wouldn't be traceable.

Garrick and Burke provided the solution, but she had to move—now. They were heading north, far enough that it would take at least a full day's worth of travelling, if she remembered their vague comments about their village right. And they had a large wagon with a loose canvas covering to protect their minimal personal effects.

Now, the only thing she needed to do was pack, sneak back out of the castle, find their wagon, stow away inside of it, and spend the long night ahead bumping and jostling toward freedom. It would be easy enough...wouldn't it?

When she ran through all the steps mentally, and all the things that would have to go right, she nearly gave up. If anyone in the castle, especially Gordon, spotted her leaving, they would send several guards after her—for "protection," they would say.

And what if Garrick and Burke had removed their canvas covering or filled the wagon with supplies? Or what if they discovered her before she could surreptitiously slip from the wagon as they passed through one of the many small towns to the north? Would they be angry with her? Would Garrick think she was crazy? What if he thought she was thrusting herself on him, despite the fact that he had made it clear that he was leaving and they would likely never see each other again?

This last worry sent ice into her stomach. She was using him, yes, but only as a means to secure her own freedom. She didn't expect anything from him. She was leaving of her own free will and with her own goals in mind, not to chase after him or force herself into his life. That was why she had decided that she would slip from the wagon before they reached their home village. She would start from scratch on her own, not latch onto him in hopes that he would save her.

She pushed away the lingering feel of his large, warm hand engulfing hers. Yes, she could admit to herself she wanted to be with him. But forcing herself on him was no way to start a life together. Perhaps someday, if she could ever be truly free of her brother and her past as an English lady of Dunbraes, she would be able to find him again, to start fresh, to meet on equal ground.

For now, though, she had to focus on her life—without him. She needed to be a healer, and to have control over her life. If she could somehow manage to find happiness with a man—she wouldn't let herself think of only Garrick—then all the better.

Despite the stretch of warm summer days of late, Jossalyn pulled out her thickest winter cloak from the back of the armoire. There was no telling what kind of conditions she might face in the coming weeks and months, and besides, it would help if she had to sleep on the ground. She found a satchel near the back as well and stuffed another chemise and dress inside, along with a few other small items.

She turned to her herb basket. This part of packing was more difficult. She would have to leave many of her supplies and plants, but she could always gather more. She could take only the rarer items from her basket, leaving things like blackberry leaves and dandelions, knowing she could find them again easily.

When her satchel was nearly full, she forced herself to sit on the edge of her bed and wait. She would need to go through the kitchen for at least a few scraps of food to take with her, but it would still be bustling from the cleanup of the evening meal. The sun was approaching the horizon, though. She would likely have a small window when the kitchen would be quieter but enough residual light remained in the sky for her to find Garrick and Burke's wagon.

When the sun had finally sunk below the horizon and the air began to turn pale blue, she eased her chamber door open and slipped through the stairwells and corridors to the kitchen. Just as she had hoped, the kitchen was now quiet and empty. She moved on silent, slippered feet toward one of the pantries and rummaged in the dim light until she found a few apples, a loaf of bread, a hunk of cheese, and several slabs of dried meat. She wrapped them all in a kerchief and stuffed them into her satchel, along with a half-full waterskin.

Now came the hard part. She would have to somehow slip from the castle without been seen or questioned. Luckily, the portcullis tended to stay open on these long summer evenings, allowing villagers to sell their wares to the castle's inhabitants. She held her breath as she approached the castle yard, praying to see the portcullis up and enough traffic moving in and out to provide her cover.

As the entrance came into view, she exhaled raggedly. It was open. But it looked like the guards atop the curtain wall were just getting ready to close it. The lingering villagers in the yard were making their way toward the castle's entrance, some pulling donkeys or carrying baskets as they made their way home.

Jossalyn surreptitiously pulled up the hood of her cloak despite the balmy evening air. Keeping her head down, she forced her feet to move at the wearied pace at which the other villagers were ambling toward the entrance. Altering her path slightly, she angled herself to the far side of a group of three villagers with a mule in tow.

"Have you seen Lady Jossalyn pass through to the village?"

Jossalyn's heart nearly exploded at the sound of Gordon's voice talking with one of the guards on the curtain wall overhead. She was nearly through the portcullis and almost bolted as if just being on the other side of the spiked grate would somehow make her safe from detection.

"She returned several hours ago. The lady is likely in her chamber," the guard replied.

"I knocked, but she didn't answer. Warren will have my bollocks if he hears that she was in the village while he was away," Gordon grumbled. "You're sure she came back?"

"Of course I'm sure. That tasty little morsel's not easy to miss, or forget." The men shared a knowing laugh.

Jossalyn swallowed the bile in her throat. It was no surprise that the met-at-arms of Dunbraes Castle would speak of their mistress in such a foul way. They all saw how her brother treated her—like nothing, like a mat on which to wipe his boots. Why wouldn't they do the same?

"I'll check on her in the morning. The little minx is likely counting her dresses or organizing her ribbons or some such bullshite. But what's this about your adventures with Lucy in the stables the other night? One of the lads told me…"

Jossalyn didn't catch the rest, for she was through the portcullis and beyond the thick curtain walls now. Forever.

She wove her way through the last few clumps of villagers on the road from the castle to the village, and then ducked down one of the dark alleys. She kept the hood of her cloak up, though, fearing the light of the nearly-full moon would reflect off her pale hair.

Just as she was about to turn the last corner before the main road in front of the smithy, she heard deep male voices and skidded to a halt. It was Garrick and Burke, talking quietly in front of the smithy. Her heart leapt at the sound of Garrick's voice, barely audible even though she was mere yards away from the two men.

"…with the rest of it in the wagon. We needn't tell John anything."

Burke didn't respond, but then she heard a rustling even closer to her and realized he had walked to the wagon, which was just around the corner on Jossalyn's side of the road. She heard him toss something into the wagon, and then caught the sound of rustling canvas as he covered the wagon's contents. Straining, she thought she could hear him walk back to the smithy, but she couldn't be sure, for both men moved unusually quietly.

She took a deep breath to brace herself. She couldn't wait any longer. It was time to act.

As quick as she could, she darted her head around the corner and back behind it again, but in the fraction of a second of sight she had given herself, the street had been quiet and empty. Neither Burke nor Garrick was in sight in front of the smithy. They must be inside. Taking another fortifying breath, she eased herself around the corner.

Blessedly, the wagon was mere feet from where she had been hiding. She darted behind it, squeezing herself between it and the building opposite the smithy. Then she threw one leg over the side, and pushed her foot underneath the canvas cover, which was loosely strewn over what looked like several dark lumps.

As she eased her weight in and began to pull her other leg over the side, the large draft horse, which was already hitched up, turned its head in the growing darkness of the night and looked at her.

She froze, her blood running cold, praying the horse didn't snort or give any other indication of its load increasing. Instead, it merely stared for a moment, then turned its head back forward as if it were bored by the sight of her stowing away in the back of the wagon.

Nearly witless and exhausted with the strain and fear holding her taut, Jossalyn eased the rest of her body into the wagon and shimmied under the canvas. She managed to wedge herself between the wall of the wagon and a few of the lumps of supplies she had seen earlier. Thankfully, the supplies made higher mounds than her body did, so the canvas draped smoothly several inches above her between the supplies and the side of the wagon. Her shape wouldn't be detected, even in daylight.

Just as she settled in, she heard the faint sound of the door to the smithy swing open and closed. A moment later, the wagon rocked gently from side to side as the two men swung into the bench at the front. Neither spoke, but Jossalyn heard the slight snap of the reins on the draft horse's rump, and the wagon began to roll. She was off.

Chapter Ten

At first, the hours had stretched uncomfortably for Jossalyn. The road seemed extra bumpy—were they even on a road? But why would the two men take one of the barely-used, faint dirt paths to travel north when there was such a fine road leading from Dunbraes?

Whatever the answer, Jossalyn had endured all the bumps and jostles she could stand not long after the wagon had started moving. But sometime several hours into their journey, either their path smoothed considerably or her weariness finally won out, for she dozed for a while.

She wasn't sure how long she rested, for she moved in and out of a light sleep. The wagon never stopped, despite the fact that they traveled through the entire night. Eventually, the total darkness underneath the canvas began to lighten to first a dim gray, and then a pale blue.

She dared to use one finger to lift the canvas ever so slightly, creating a tiny gap between it and the side of the wagon. She could see the early morning sky in the sliver of space. She guessed that they had been on the move for six or seven hours.

Not long after she had checked the sky, the wagon rolled to a halt. She held her breath, suddenly unsure of what to do. She had planned on slipping out of the back of the wagon during a stop for the men to rest or stretch their legs, but there hadn't been any such occasions. Could they already have reached the two men's homeland? If so, she would need to not only slip out unseen, but also would have some walking ahead of her to avoid plopping herself down in the middle of their lives—or, more precisely, in the middle of Garrick's life.

As she lay motionless, considering her options, she heard the quiet whisper of a blade being drawn. That was all the warning she had before the canvas was yanked back.

Something wasn't right, Garrick was sure of it. He couldn't put his finger on what was different, but his senses were screaming at him to be on high alert. They had traveled through the night, stopping for nothing. Nevertheless, he felt like a sitting duck in this damned wagon. They were moving too slowly, were too visible, even though they had stayed off the main roads nearly the entire journey.

Now that they had reached the uninhabited safe house, he should feel more relaxed. They could ditch the wagon here, and move much faster and more inconspicuously on their two horses rather than in this hulking, awkward wagon.

And most importantly, he would have his bow back in his hands. This last week had been excruciating without it. He had felt like he was missing a limb, like he was constantly exposed and unprepared. But not anymore. He would have Fletch underneath him, his bow and quiver on his back, and the Sinclair plaid around his hips and shoulder, where it belonged.

Then why couldn't he shake the feeling that something was off? As he pulled the draft horse to a stop, he motioned for Burke to go ahead to the safe house's barn to retrieve their horses and gear. As Burke moved away, the sounds of his footfalls faded, and Garrick was left straining to discern what had him on edge. He listened. Birds of varying species called in the distance. The draft horse snorted in exhaustion. And then he heard it.

Breathing. It wasn't his, it wasn't the horse's, and it certainly wasn't Burke's. He closed his eyes to concentrate, as he often did just before letting his arrow fly at a mark. Yes, it was there, though it was extremely faint—or muffled.

His eyes flew open and darted in every direction, but all he could see was the forest all around. As he turned his head over his shoulder, he could hear the breathing slightly more clearly. Could it be…coming from within the wagon itself?

Even as the blood surged in his veins, he forced

himself to move slowly, silently. He eased himself out of the front seat of the wagon and placed one foot and then the other on the loamy forest floor. He bent and placed one hand on the small dagger he kept in his boot to cut the fletching for his arrows, extending the other hand toward the canvas that covered the wagon. Then as smoothly as he could, he yanked free his dagger and jerked the canvas back.

The sight that met his eyes nearly caused him to stumble backward, but he kept his footing. Gazing up at him, wide-eyes and mouth agape, was Jossalyn. She lay on her side, wrapped in a cloak, but with her head turned up at him.

"What...how did you..." The gears in his mind ground together slowly as he tried to comprehend what he was seeing.

"Garrick! I...I was just..."

"Christ, what have you done?" He registered vaguely somewhere that he had shouted that, but the confusion and frustration were turning to anger quickly. She had not only endangered herself, but she was threatening their mission—and all of their lives. If she found out who they really were or what they had been sent to do, they could be hanged for treason—and maybe she could be too, for she had gone willingly with them. His mind raced, trying to figure out how much she could possibly know at this point.

Burke must have heard their voices for he was racing toward the wagon from the barn. "What is it?" he said, his voice tight with fear.

Jossalyn slowly lifted her head up and over the side of the wagon so that Burke could see her. Burke cursed under his breath, and Jossalyn flinched.

"Let me explain," she began shakily.

Garrick exchanged a dark look with Burke. Burke's normally controlled and gallant affect had slipped, and he was frowning deeply.

"I couldn't stay at Dunbraes any longer. My brother...he will be very angry with me for working in the village, and I wanted to be free to use my skills, and I am more needed here in Scotland, where I could actually help people, than I am sitting on my hands in some English garrison, and you were headed north and I needed a way to travel, so..." The flood of her words seemed to finally run dry, and she shifted her eyes between Burke and him, a pleading look on her face.

Garrick scrubbed a hand over his face. "And what was the rest of your plan, lass? Follow us around Scotland like a lost puppy?"

His words came out harsher than he had intended, but damn the lass for her foolhardy plan, and for endangering them all. Even as he tried to justify his harshness, he cursed himself for the stricken look she gave him now, her eyes wide and glistening, her lips turned down and trembling slightly.

"No, I w-wasn't going to follow you. I just wanted to get far enough away that I would have the freedom to..." She swallowed hard and tried to gather herself. "I was planning to slip out of the wagon in some smaller village on the way to your town. Then I could either travel onward from there, or set up a new life for myself—on my own."

"Garrick, may I speak to you for a moment?" Burke had regained some of his composure, and was now looking calmer.

Garrick turned from Jossalyn and followed Burke to the barn, where their warhorses, weapons, and gear awaited them. Once inside, Burke turned and said quietly, "All is not yet lost, Garrick. The lass doesn't know who we are."

For some reason Burke's rationality grated on him. "Aye, but what are we going to do with her? We can't leave her here at the safe house, and we damn well can't take her with us!"

He forced himself to lower his voice to a whisper again. "We don't have time to deal with this, Burke. The Bruce needs to know about the rumors of Longshanks's illness as soon as possible. The entire rebellion could rely on it!"

"Aye, I know that, and your brother needs to hear of it too. But as you said, we can't very well leave the lass in the middle of the forest right next to a secret safe house for Scottish rebels. We only have one option. We have to take her back to Dunbraes."

"That will put us back by at least sixteen hours of hard riding," he said exasperatedly. "Even if we could do another two legs of eight hours of travel on top of the nightlong ride we just had, what about the horses? And how are we supposed to keep our identities concealed from the lass if we are riding with our weapons strapped to our animals?"

"I don't know, but we can't take the wagon. It will only slow us down further. We will just have to avoid the lass's questions and get this over with as fast as possible."

"Shite, what a mess," Garrick said through gritted teeth.

This entire mission had been a mistake. He shouldn't be in the Lowlands gathering intelligence, he should be at the Bruce's side, fighting with his bow. If it weren't for his damned older brother, who had somehow convinced the Bruce that it was in both of their interests to monitor Raef Warren's holding, he wouldn't be in this debacle.

But if he hadn't been sent on this mission, he wouldn't have gotten to meet and share a kiss with Jossalyn Williams, the most beautiful and intriguing woman he had ever met.

He pushed the though aside harshly, though; right now, Jossalyn was only contributing to this disastrous situation. If she hadn't thrown herself in his path, they would be on their way to the Bruce's camp in northeast Scotland right now.

But, he reminded himself, she hadn't thrown herself in their path—he had nearly run her over. That's when the troubles with the lass began, and he had only made it harder on both of them by kissing her senseless and then leaving her the next day.

Either way, she had stowed away in their wagon and was now dangerously close to realizing they weren't who they said they were. She was setting them back by at least a day's worth of travel, not to mention the extra wear and tear on them and their animals.

This disgruntled thought came from the angry, stubborn part of him that didn't like to deal with people and their inconveniences. But the lass hadn't known they lied to her about who they were and where they were going. He couldn't hold it against her that she believed them, and he certainly couldn't blame her for wanting to get away from a brother who stifled her dreams and used force against her. In fact, if he set aside his stubbornness for a moment, he actually admired the lass's bravery in seeking out her freedom and trying to make a new life for herself.

He exhaled and ran a hand through his hair. Burke was waiting for him to agree that they only had one course of action. After one last futile attempt to search his brain for an alternative, which yielded nothing, Garrick grudgingly nodded.

"I'll hide our gear as well as I can and get the horses ready. You'd better speak to the lass," Burke said.

Chapter Eleven

Jossalyn fumbled with the tie on her cloak as she watched the sun creep upward through the trees. She still sat in the wagon, waiting for Burke and Garrick to emerge from the barn a few dozen yards away. Occasionally, she could hear their voices rise, but she couldn't make out what they were saying.

A knot had formed in her stomach despite her best efforts to calm herself. These were good men, she reasoned. Even though they weren't happy about her hiding in their wagon, they wouldn't hurt her…would they?

Her mind ran wild with speculation, all of the oddities about the two flooding back—how Garrick's voice sometimes slipped into a thicker Scottish accent, as it had when he had discovered her in the wagon, or how Garrick had been covered in scarred-over cuts rather than burns, as a blacksmith should have been, or how they had traveled all the way to Dunbraes looking for work but had known they would only stay for a week. And now here she was, in the middle of the wilderness with just the two of them, and they seemed overly jumpy, overly angry with her.

She forced herself to stop the spiral of these thoughts. She was being foolish, reading more into things than she should. And besides, why wouldn't they be furious with her? She had deceived them, and not just about hiding in their wagon. She had lied to them about her last name, her station, and who her brother was. If she wasn't careful, she might let something slip, and then she really would be in trouble, no matter how good these men were. If they found out that her brother was Lord Raef Warren, they would feel compelled to deliver her to him to avoid punishment for "kidnapping" a lady. And if her brother found out that she had not only been working in the village, but had tried to escape with two strange men…. She wasn't sure what he would do, and that's what frightened her.

She tried to gather her thoughts so she could at least present her case coherently to Burke and Garrick when they returned. She had been so surprised when Garrick had ripped the canvas off the wagon and the two of them had glared down at her that she hadn't explained it well at all.

Just then she saw Garrick storming out of the barn. His eyes locked with hers, and she felt a chill go through her at their cold steeliness. She bit her lower lip to keep it from trembling again and willed herself to keep her wits about her in the face of his intensity. He halted in front of her, his eyes still boring into her.

"Garrick, let me explain," she said again, and was relieved that her voice didn't shake as much as before. "I know it was wrong of me to use you this way, but I wanted—"

He held up a hand to silence her, and she couldn't help but flinch backward. He furrowed his brow in confusion, then looked at his hand and seemed to realize something.

"Lass, I'm not going to hurt you. I am not such a spineless man that I would strike you or force you to obey me. I'm not like your brother."

She felt her eyes widen in shock at his words. How did he understand so well?

He went on. "I think I understand why you would want to leave Dunbraes and start a new life somewhere else. But I cannot be part of it." This last was said through gritted teeth, as if it pained him.

"I don't expect you to just let me insert myself into your life!" She had to make him understand this, for it had never been her plan to merely latch herself onto him and hope he would save her. She was saving herself, regardless of him. "I would never assume that. I wanted to do this on my own. You were just a means of transportation."

That came out wrong. She knew it even before she saw his face darken at the insult. "What I mean is, I don't…expect anything from you. I know it was wrong to use you to get me out of Dunbraes, but I couldn't think of any other way, and time is running out before…before my brother finds out what I have been up to."

"Jossalyn, we have to take you back to Dunbraes."

"What? Why?"

He reached over the edge of the wagon and took her hand in his. Even through the shock of hearing that he was going to take her back to the castle, to her hellish life, a spark ignited in her stomach at his touch.

"Because you cannot come with us, and we cannot just leave you here. No matter how much of a bastard your brother is, it is not our place to be complicit in your escape." Despite his soft tone, his words bit into her.

"Why can't I just go on with you a little farther to the nearest village? I promise I'll never speak of you. No one will ever know of your part in this. Or you could just leave me! I can find my way to the road and hitch a ride with someone else!"

He shook his head. "Then I would feel responsible if something were to happen to you. It isn't safe for a lass like you to be traveling alone in the Borderlands right now."

"Please. Please don't take me back there." Her voice cracked with pleading, but she didn't care. Garrick's handsome but resolute face wobbled in front of her through the tears welling in her eyes.

He turned away from her and cursed, dragging a hand through his dark hair, which was coming loose from its tie at the back of his neck.

"I'm sorry, lass," he finally said, still not meeting her eyes, "but this is the way it has to be. I have to follow my duty."

Her heart sank, hearing the finality in his voice. Part of her wanted to scream at him, to beg him, to tell him that he and his duty could go to hell. But she knew that none of it would work. Besides, he was right—she had put him in this situation, and now that he had to deal with it, he had to follow his own sense of right and wrong. She couldn't expect him not to get a say in her using him to escape, and then also have to go along with her plan to deal with the situation now that he knew about it. He was involved now, and he had to act dutifully or risk her brother's punishment.

Even as she struggled to accept all this, she felt the tears overflowing. She had failed. She would be back to her brother's castle in less than a day, and she would have to face the consequences of her actions. This didn't mean that she would go back to being the frightened and submissive girl she was before; no, she would attempt to escape again and would resist her brother and his control over her as much as she could. But her hopes to start a new life for herself right away were now faded and distant.

She nodded and tried to swallow the lump in her throat, but it wouldn't move, nor would the tears stop streaming down her cheeks. She turned her head away, trying to preserve whatever shred of dignity she had left, but suddenly she felt Garrick's large, warm, and callused hand on her chin. He gently brought her face back to his and kept his eyes on her. Despite the pained look on his face, he forced himself to hold her gaze. It was almost as if he was punishing himself for something, but she didn't know what.

"The horses are ready," Burke said from the door of the barn, carefully eying the two of them.

His words registered somewhere in the back of her mind through the fog of pain. "Horses? We aren't taking the wagon?" she asked.

"Nay, my lady. The wagon will slow us down. We were going to take these horses the rest of the way on our journey home anyway," Burke replied.

She glanced behind Burke and saw that he was leading two enormous stallions, one chestnut and the other bay, out of the barn. Each horse had large saddlebags that were nearly overflowing, and she could make out some strangely shaped items wrapped in cloth sticking out of them. Without thinking, she pointed toward the cloth-wrapped objects protruding from each horse's bags, and asked, "What are those?"

"Those are our tools, lass. Blacksmith's tools," Burke said smoothly, though his face was an expressionless mask. Before she could ask why two unemployed blacksmiths had such fine horses, Burke interjected. "We'd best be on the way if we want to reach Dunbraes before evening."

Garrick reached toward her and wrapped his hands around her waist, lifting her clear out of the wagon. He walked her over to the chestnut horse and swung himself up into the high saddle. Burke led the draft horse and wagon into the barn where their horses had been, and after a quick perusal of the area, swung himself onto the bay's back.

Strange, she thought to herself, that they would leave the good solid draft horse, wagon, and the rest of their supplies here in the middle of the woods. The thought flitted from her mind, though, when Garrick scooped her up so that she sat in front of him atop his enormous stallion.

Though she still wore her thick winter cloak, she could feel his hard body in very precise detail behind her. Her back was pressed against his broad chest, her bottom and hips nestled snugly against his pelvis. His arms came around her to hold the reins. At first he had reached around her arms, but that made it hard for him to grip the reins. She lifted her arms so that his forearms brushed against her waist. Her thighs rested on top of his, and she could feel his legs give the horse a squeeze. The horse leapt forward, and her mind spun as they spirited back south toward Dunbraes.

Chapter Twelve

Garrick swore silently and tore his bleary-eyed gaze away from Jossalyn's backside. They were stopped by a small stream to give the horses and themselves a brief rest after several hours of hard traveling. Jossalyn was bent over, letting the cool stream water pool in her cupped hands before bringing them up to her lips for a drink. He had been staring at her for several minutes, hypnotized by the sight of her heart-shaped rear in the air, her slim hands rising to her mouth, and the extra droplets of water clinging to her rosy lips.

It was just the fatigue, he told himself. Neither him nor Burke had slept a wink the night before, and now, as the sun passed its zenith and approached the angled light of late afternoon, they had already put in several long hours today. Fatigue was making him careless with his attention. He knew somewhere inside that he shouldn't be staring at her like that—like a hungry animal—but he couldn't seem to find the energy to stop.

Their riding arrangement hadn't helped any, either.

He hadn't even considered the possibility of Jossalyn riding with Burke. Even though he knew after they delivered her to Dunbraes he would never see her again, he couldn't resist the opportunity to be so near to her for the few hours they had left together.

But maybe that had been a mistake, for now he felt an ache between his legs that had nothing to do with the long hours on horseback. That firm but deliciously soft bottom on which his eyes were currently locked had been pressing against his cock nonstop as their hips moved in unison with the horse's strides.

And her smell—that unique combination of wildflowers and sunshine—had been hanging around him like a veil since the moment he had pulled her up on Fletch's back and realized that her golden hair was mere inches from his face.

When she had shed the cloak she was wearing a few hours back, draping it across her lap, he had nearly groaned, for it meant he could feel every delicate curve pressed against him all the better.

He couldn't remember the last time a lass had affected him so strongly—but maybe that was because no other lass ever had. Aye, he had enjoyed plenty of willing lasses as a means of escape or release from the horrors of warfare, but he had never let them get to him before. That would endanger his place with the Bruce's rebel force. He always had to be ready for the next mission, which normally meant being gone for weeks on end, working alone, and not getting attached.

This wasn't any different, he reassured himself. Or it wasn't *much* different anyway. He was still following his duty to the Bruce and the rebellion. He was returning the lass to where she belonged, away from him and the dangers he brought with him. He wasn't letting her change him or his plan.

But then again, he wasn't exactly performing at his peak as far as being a cold-blooded mercenary and marksman went. If he had been thinking of nothing but the mission, perhaps he could have left her back in the middle of the woods without an explanation. But every fiber in him rejected such an idea. He only hoped that by doing the right thing and returning her to her village, he wouldn't be risking failing in his duty.

A voice inside his head whispered that it was far from the "right thing" to be forcing the lass to return to her brother, who was not only a bastard for denying her the ability to practice healing, but also a coward and a tyrant for hurting her. The lass was taking charge of her own life, overcoming her oppressor and building a future for herself. Why was he pushing her back into her old life? Her brother was a bastard, but was he any better?

He pushed the thought aside savagely. He couldn't indulge in such philosophizing when lives were at stake. The lass could still escape, just not this time, and not with him. She was strong enough, he knew, to do it again, and to succeed on her own. He just had to be the bastard who denied her the freedom she sought this time.

He could be the villain. He had gotten quite used to the role over the years. He had never been as concerned with justice and doing the right thing as his older brother Robert, and he wasn't an uncompromising leader like his younger brother Daniel, either. And he certainly didn't care to smooth things over and make others comfortable like Burke. Nay, he was the one who was willing to do whatever it took to get a job done.

It took a special kind of person to be able to stake out a mark for days or even weeks, living alone in the woods and trusting nothing but one's own survival skills. And then, when the moment finally arrived, to be willing to shoot and kill an unsuspecting man, in the back as often as in the chest—it wasn't for everyone, not even the most fervent of the bloodthirsty and enraged Scotsmen who had joined the rebellion to fight for Robert the Bruce. Garrick did bad things—he killed without remorse, relied on no one, and cared only for his missions. He could break this one lass's heart and put her back within the grasp of her manipulative and violent brother. It was nothing to him.

"Garrick?"

Jossalyn had turned from the stream and was staring at him with a guarded look. He realized his face was twisted into a scowl and he was glaring at her, his fists clenching and unclenching at his sides. He took a quick breath to try to release the tension that had formed as he stood there thinking. "We should get moving," he said, schooling his features into expressionlessness once again.

Burke was already swinging into the saddle, though he looked just as exhausted as Garrick felt. Jossalyn followed Garrick to Fletch's side and waited for him to mount and pull her up in front of him. She settled herself between his legs as if she were always meant to be there.

He forced the idea from his head. He needed to concentrate on delivering her without issue back to the village at Dunbraes. Then he would have to push her from his mind completely. He wouldn't be able to accomplish what would be required of him in the coming weeks and months if he were distracted.

Even as he thought this, though, her hair, which gleamed in the sunlight, brushed his cheek, and he nearly lost his resolve yet again. Just an hour or two more, he told himself. But if he were honest with himself, he would have to admit that instead of looking forward to being free of Jossalyn's distractions, he was dreading the moment when they would part—for good this time.

Jossalyn knew that this was the last stop even before she spotted the village through the trees. As Garrick and Burked reined in their horses, she could feel the tension radiating from Garrick's body behind her. Before he could help her down, she threw her leg over the large chestnut's neck and slid the considerable distance to the ground. Garrick dismounted too, but she took a step back from him, pretending to adjust her cloak, which she had swung back over her shoulders to avoid having to carry both it and her satchel.

Finally, she found her voice, though it was pinched with emotion. "I'm sorry to have put you in this position. Please forgive me. I wish you a safe journey."

With that, she spun on her heels and half-ran toward the village, too cowardly to meet Garrick's eyes or go through another goodbye with him. She almost expected to feel his big hands pulling her back, spinning her around so that he could apologize, kiss her senseless, and take her back north with him. But his touch never came.

She brushed the tears out of her eyes as she went, forcing herself to keep putting one foot in front of the other, even though it meant growing farther away from Garrick. She told herself this was as it must be, that she would overcome the sorrow, the hollowness inside, that she could still escape Dunbraes and build a new life for herself. None of it eased the crushing weight of sadness that sat like a boulder in her chest.

She stumbled into the village on the outskirts of the square. No one seemed to notice her as they moved about their lives. They all had their struggles and heartbreaks, and she chastised herself for thinking that hers were somehow special or worse.

Wiping away the lingering tears with the sleeve of

her dress, she straightened her spine and turned toward the main road, which ran right through the square from the south and up to the castle above the village.

Just as she took the first step back toward the castle, however, she heard the town crier's clear voice above the mundane sounds of the square.

"Lord Warren returns! The King is dead! Long live the King!"

Jossalyn's heart froze.

King Edward was dead.

Her brother was approaching the castle from the south along the same road on which she now stood.

As she registered each of these pieces of news and what they would mean for her life, she felt all the blood drain from her. With Edward's death, her brother could have potentially angled for a new position—one that could mean more power for him and less for her. It could even mean that they would be leaving the Borderlands. Or perhaps he had already arranged her marriage while he was at the makeshift court in Cumberland for Edward's death.

She had to get away. Now. This could be her last chance at freedom.

But before she could run, she saw the parade of her brother's returning men-at-arms filling the road just to the south of her.

And her brother was at the front of the procession. She saw him squinting toward her for a moment and felt like a deer in the sights of a hunter. There was nowhere to go, nowhere to hide anymore.

He kicked his horse into a gallop straight toward her. Her life was over.

Chapter Thirteen

Garrick had watched her as she had hurried from him, not looking over her shoulder even once. He had willed himself to keep his feet rooted to the ground despite every instinct telling him to give chase, to take her into his arms—but for what? For one more gut-wrenching kiss? For whispered words of affection, or vows that he couldn't keep? Nay, he wouldn't put both of them through it again. She was stronger than he would have been.

When she was far enough away that he trusted himself not to go after her, he walked Fletch to the edge of the forest and watched her as she strode into the village. Burke followed him but didn't say anything, despite the fact that he was likely eager to get going.

Finally, Garrick forced himself to turn his back on her. He faced Fletch and ran a hand down the animal's flank reassuringly. His eye caught on the long object wrapped in cloth sticking out of his saddlebag. His bow. If anything could make him feel more like himself right now, it was his bow, hand-carved and custom-built just for him.

Though they didn't have time to change into their Sinclair kilts at the moment, at least they could resume wearing their weapons, a comfort to any warrior. Burke was already unwrapping his sword, so Garrick did the same with his bow and quiver full of arrows. He too had a sword, which he unwrapped and belted to his waist, but nothing compared to the feel of his bow in his hand once more.

Suddenly he heard a high voice drifting through the village and into the surrounding forest. It was a lad's voice, but it wasn't the sound of horseplay or pranking. He was repeating something over and over. Garrick quirked his ears. When the message finally made sense, his blood ran cold.

"Lord Warren returns! The King is dead! Long live the King!"

His gaze flew to Burke, who stood frozen with wide eyes and a slack jaw. Garrick tried to sort through the tangle in his mind at the news.

Longshanks was dead.

The Hammer of the Scots was *dead*.

While part of his mind rejoiced, the other twisted. He had no idea what this would mean. On one hand, there was likely not another soul on earth who despised the Scots as much as King Edward did. His death could put and end to the wars for Scottish independence once and for all.

On the other hand, the King's son, Edward II, was

now King, and he was an unknown entity. He was said to love the arts and have little of the spirit of war that his father had, but then again, the boy had been raised with a hunger for Scottish blood as if it were his mother's milk.

Then there was Warren's return. Lord Raef Warren was his family's mortal enemy. Garrick had fought alongside his brother Robert and Burke at the battle of Roslin four years earlier. He had seen the coward then, but was more familiar with Robert's description of the man as a snake and warmonger. Warren was responsible for starting that war, which had dealt a heavy blow to the Sinclair clan and its lands. Robert had made it his personal mission to twist the knife in Warren's side at every opportunity, raiding and stealing from him in the Borderlands.

Though Garrick knew Robert's blood still ran hot when it came to Warren, he had calmed somewhat with the arrival of Lady Alwin into his life. Now that she was with child, Robert had entrusted Garrick and Burke to investigate Warren's whereabouts and learn about the movements of the English army.

It had been a relief, when upon their arrival to Dunbraes, they had learned that Warren was away on some court business. It would be hard to avoid him, and Garrick suspected that Warren might recognize one or both of them on sight. But now the pompous arse was marching up the road, perhaps only one hundred yards from where he and Burke stood partly concealed by the thin outskirts of the forest.

All of this crashed through Garrick's mind like a wave. They had to move—now. They couldn't be seen by Warren or his men, and they had to get to the Bruce to deliver this news.

Garrick quickly dug through his saddlebag and retrieved his metal-studded leather vest, throwing it over his English clothes. He hoped to hell he wouldn't need it, but it was better to be safe than sorry. He finished unwrapping his bow and quiver, slinging both over his shoulder. Just before placing his foot in Fletch's stirrup, he let himself take one last look over his shoulder at Jossalyn.

He picked out her gleaming gold hair easily. Her back was still to him, but instead of continuing to walk through the village, she had frozen, and her eyes were locked on none other than Raef Warren. The man was barreling down on her from atop his horse. She held her ground, but even from a distance, Garrick could see that she had hunched her shoulders, pulling herself inward defensively.

What he saw next hit him like a punch to the gut. At the last possible moment, Warren reined in his horse to prevent from trampling her. He then threw himself off his horse's back and closed the remaining distance between himself and Jossalyn, towering over her. She kept her head down as he appeared to shout at her, waving his hands and leaning toward her, despite being in the middle of not only the crowded village square, but also the procession that was escorting him home.

Jossalyn simply stood there, head bowed, shoulders hunched, taking the barrage of shouted insults that Warren threw at her. Her lack of response seemed to infuriate him even more, for he gripped her arms and shook her, hard enough that her head whipped back and forth on her neck several times.

Garrick hadn't realized it, but he had taken several steps toward the scene in front of him. He was now well clear of the forest line, and was nearly halfway to Jossalyn before Burke's hand shook his shoulder.

"What the hell are you doing?" Burke said frantically.

"Jossalyn is in trouble. Warren is hurting—"

Suddenly something clicked into place in his head. The memories of moments that hadn't seemed quite right flooded back to him.

Jossalyn stuttering over both her own last name and her brother's first and last names.

Jossalyn being called "lady" in the village, though she had brushed it off uncomfortably.

Jossalyn being unable to practice her healing art because of her brother's controlling and manipulative ways.

Jossalyn being hurt by her brother.

Jossalyn Williams was actually Jossalyn Warren. Her brother, "Ranald Williams," was Lord Raef Warren.

His mind tried to grasp all the implications of this, but he couldn't seem to get his thoughts in order. He turned back to the scene in front of him, and all thought drained from his mind.

It all seemed to be happening in slow motion. Warren was drawing back one of his hands from Jossalyn's arm. He was raising his palm higher and higher, his hand straight and rigid. Jossalyn tilted her head up, her eyes wide, tear tracks glistening on her cheeks in the slanting sunlight.

Warren was going to hit her. Right across her perfect, innocent face.

Garrick saw red, but at the same time, everything seemed to fade around him and grow quiet. In one fluid movement, he dropped to one knee and drew an arrow from his quiver. His bow was already in his hand somehow, the wood warm and smooth. He nocked the arrow and drew back, his eyes locked on Warren's raised hand. Without thinking, he adjusted for the whisper of evening breeze and calculated how far Warren's hand would travel in the time it took his arrow to reach him.

He exhaled and let his arrow fly. Warren's hand was now descending toward Jossalyn's face. Her eyes were squeezed shut, but she didn't flinch away from him.

Just as Warren's palm was fully exposed in the space between him and Jossalyn, Garrick's arrow found its mark. It sunk all the way through his hand, half of the wooden shaft on either side of his palm. His hand froze in the air, a stunned look on his face. Then slowly, Warren turned to look in the direction from which the arrow had flown. Suddenly, everything seemed to speed up again.

Garrick realized he was sprinting straight for Jossalyn. He threw his bow over his shoulder and drew the sword at his hip as he ran. He faintly registered Burke running just behind him, but he couldn't give the man any of his attention. He was solely focused on Jossalyn, who had also turned in his direction. Now her eyes locked on him and widened in disbelief and he barreled toward her.

Chaos was erupting all around. Warren screamed something, a combination of a pained wail and a command to his men-at-arms marching up the road several dozen yards behind him. A few of the men noticed the arrow protruding from their Lord's hand and broke rank, struggling to draw their swords and face the attack. Even as his men-at-arms advanced, Warren faded backward, scrambling away from the two armed men coming straight at him.

They all seemed to collide right where Jossalyn and Warren had been standing, though Warren had squeezed himself behind his men-at-arms, and Jossalyn had flung herself out of the road.

Garrick brought his sword down on one of Warren's men, landing a fatal blow. He spun just in time to block the swing of a sword aiming to separate his head from his shoulders. The impact of the blow reverberated down his arms, but he held fast to his sword and managed to thrust his enemy's blade away. The man swung again, but this time Garrick was ready for it. He ducked and thrust upward, piercing the soldier through the stomach. The man screamed and fell, his body toppling onto a fellow soldier Burke had just run through.

In a matter of seconds, Garrick and Burke had dispatched half a dozen of Warren's men, but a score more surged toward them. Blessedly, the road on which they fought was creating a bottleneck that allowed only a few soldiers at a time to step up to the deadly swing of the two men's large blades.

But Garrick was more comfortable fighting from a distance with his bow. He realized as he drew his sword across the flesh of an oncoming man that they couldn't hold their position for much longer. The quarters were too close, and there were too many of Warren's men surging toward them. He threw a glance at Burke, who met his eyes quickly before turning back to the soldier he was squaring off against.

"Get the lass! I'll cover you!" Burke panted.

Garrick's eyes flew to the side of the road where Jossalyn had flung herself out of the way. She was pressing herself as flat as she could against a stone wall that lined the road, but she was dangerously close to the sword-wielding men-at-arms who were trying to squeeze their way toward Burke and him.

He hacked through another soldier as he fought against the tide of them pressing down on him. He was almost in reach of her.

"Jossalyn!" he shouted over the near-deafening noise of battle. Her terrified eyes found him, but just as they did, one of the soldiers was shoved by his comrade and went careening toward her, his blade raised in front of him.

Garrick dove forward, putting his body between her and the stumbling soldier. He threw his arms against the wall on either side of her small form, creating a shield with his body. He felt a burning slice on his back, but it barely registered. She was safe.

He turned so that she was at his back and he could face the soldier. With one block and thrust, he had ended another life. He swung his sword with his right hand and used his left to push her along the wall behind him toward where Burke held off three English soldiers at once.

"Go!" Burke shouted as he cut down another man. He took a blow to the leg which sent him staggering backward, but he righted himself and blocked another swing.

"You'd better be behind us!" Garrick shouted back.

Without waiting longer, he wrapped a hand around Jossalyn's wrist and pulled her into a run with him toward the forest where their horses waited. He could feel her stumbling and struggling to keep up behind him, so he turned and lowered his shoulder into her middle, hoisting her over his shoulder like a sack of potatoes. He could hear a whoosh of air from her as he took off running again, but she didn't scream or resist. She was likely too stunned, Garrick thought somewhere in the back of his mind.

When he reached the horses that stood nervously at the edge of the forest, he set her down on her feet again and sheathed his sword. He launched himself onto Fletch's back, then reached down and pulled her up also, but this time behind him. He would need to have unobstructed access to the reins if they were going to make it out of this alive. He leaned over and grabbed Burke's horse's reins and spurred them both back toward the battle. Burke was disengaging himself, backing up rapidly away from the onslaught of soldiers, who were now starting to overpower him.

Garrick whistled as he charged toward Burke, giving him enough warning to take one last swing before bolting toward the forest. Burke only had to take a few hobbling strides before Garrick reached him. He flung himself atop his horse, and Garrick tossed him the reins. They wheeled the animals around hard and sent them flying into the forest once more. Behind them, Garrick could hear Warren's enraged screams.

"To the stables! Every man on a horse! After them!"

Chapter Fourteen

Jossalyn clung for dear life to Garrick's back as they plowed through the dense forest as fast as the horses could take them. She vaguely registered that they were headed northeast, even though Burke and Garrick had traveled northwest the day before to get to their home.

But that was a foolish thought, for these men clearly weren't who they had pretended to be. She had barely recognized him when he had come charging toward her. He moved with the same lightning speed and deadly grace she had noticed in him before, but his face had been twisted in rage and bloodlust, and the way he wielded his sword—she swallowed and tried to push the images out of her mind, for she feared she would be sick if she recalled the blood, the limbs, the blades cutting through flesh like butter.

The forest blurred and spun as it rushed by, and she squeezed her eyes shut. Why was she clinging to this man—this stranger? He was a killer and a liar. Despite all their conversations, their stolen kiss, and the silent glances she thought spoke volumes, she didn't know him at all.

But she realized as she forced her eyes open again, she was trapped now. If she flung herself from his horse's back, she would likely break her neck on landing. And she couldn't command him to stop. He was in complete control of the horse, steering it through trees and bushes with lightning-fast reflexes. There was no chance that she could simply wrest the reins from him.

So she held on, praying she would live to see the sun rise again even as darkness seeped into the forest and night fell.

What must have been hours later, Garrick—if that was even his name—whistled to Burke and reined in his horse. Every bone in Jossalyn's body ached. The riding had been merciless. They had kept up their grueling pace, navigating through the dense forest in the dark without stopping. She felt like her limbs had turned to wood from the tension of holding onto Garrick's back and gripping the horse with her legs.

Garrick threw a leg over the horse's neck and swung down, though he stumbled slightly when his feet hit the ground. He reached up toward her, but she instinctively withdrew, trying not to let this killer's hands grab her. Evasion was impossible, though. He took her by the waist and pulled her down to the ground next to him. Before he could do more, though, she jerked out of his hands.

"Who are you? Where are you taking me?" Her voice came out higher and more frantic than she had intended, but she didn't care. She was not too exhausted to feel a surge of fear spike through her now that they had stopped.

"Christ," he said, his eyes locked on the front of her dress.

She looked down and nearly screamed. She was covered in blood, which was dark against the fabric of her gown in the dim moonlight filtering through the trees.

"Are you hurt, lass?" Garrick's voice was nearly unrecognizable. Instead of the soft Scottish lilt she had picked up on earlier, he spoke with a thick brogue.

Without waiting for her to answer, he began running his hands over her, looking for the source of the blood. His callused fingers brushed her neck, ran down her arms, then skimmed across her chest and waist. She inhaled sharply at the contact, but not in pain.

"I...I don't think I've been cut..." The shock of first seeing Garrick turn from a blacksmith to a warrior, then being whisked away, and now having Garrick's hands all over her was too much. She couldn't straighten out her thoughts or even form words.

Suddenly, a dim memory came back and tugged at the corner of her brain. "Your back..."

"What?"

"Your back. That soldier with his sword..." She took a step past him so that she could look around his shoulder. She inhaled sharply at the sight. A gash ran down the middle of his back, and the fabric of both the leather vest and shirt he wore were cut clean through and covered in dark blood. She had been plastered to his back, clinging on for dear life, and had gotten his blood on her dress.

"I need to treat this." Suddenly, she shifted from scared and confused girl to skilled healer. It didn't matter that Garrick and Burke might very well be her enemies. She had to help.

Just as she reached for his vest to pull it off, she heard a thump and a groan. Several yards away, Burke had reined in and dismounted, but was now crumpled in a pile at his horse's feet.

"Burke! Are you all right?" Brushing past her, Garrick moved to Burke's side and knelt down.

"Ach, just a little stiff is all. This damn cut is bothering me." He was gripping his right leg, and as Jossalyn approached, she saw that his breeches were dark with blood. Burke tried to stand, but winced and groaned again, and would have fallen if it weren't for Garrick's support.

"Burke, you mustn't push yourself. Let me see to your leg." Jossalyn knelt and put her face close to where the blood seemed to be coming from so she could see better in the moonlight. Gently, she prodded the area, which drew a sharp inhale from Burke. She could see a deep gash running down the outside of his thigh, and though it was a clean cut, the wound still bled.

"Do you mind if I…remove the fabric from this area?" she said, looking up at Burke, who still leaned heavily on Garrick.

"I've never said no to a pretty lass asking to take my pants off before," he said with a chuckle, but his voice was tight with pain.

Garrick produced a short dagger from his boot, and she went to work cutting some of the fabric off Burke's breeches. When the blood-soaked material was out of the way, she could see the long, deep cut even clearer. She frowned, but tried to keep the worry from her voice for Burke's sake.

"I need to clean the wound, and then stitch it and wrap it with yarrow to help stop the bleeding. Then you'll need to rest and stay off the leg for several days."

Garrick and Burke exchanged a look, then Garrick said flatly, "That's not going to happen."

She felt her ire rising. "Then you risk continued bleeding, infection, and fever. Burke, you could die if this goes untreated."

"And the three of us are guaranteed to be dead if we stay here much longer," Garrick said coldly.

His eyes were locked on hers, and in the darkness, they looked almost black. She shivered, reminding herself that she didn't know these men in front of her. And she had already witnessed just how dangerous and deadly they could be.

"What could we do quickly, lass? Just for the short-term," Burke said, breaking the tense silence.

Her eyes shifted back to his leg. "We could wrap

the wound tightly and hope that it stops bleeding on its own until I can stitch it and get a proper poultice on it," she replied reluctantly. She hated the idea of being so sloppy in her work, especially if it meant endangering a patient's life.

"Use the material of his breeches," Garrick said, then turned to Burke. "We should have changed earlier outside of Dunbraes anyway. It would have been...entertaining to see Warren's face as he recognized the Sinclair plaid."

This brought a chuckle from Burke and a wry smile from Garrick. At first Jossalyn let the words pass over her head, assuming it was some inside joke meant to lighten Burke's spirits. But something tickled her mind, and as the gears ground together, Jossalyn's mouth fell open.

"Are you saying...How do you know my brother? And what do you mean by 'Sinclair plaid'?"

Garrick sobered and gave her a long look, but then started to turn away. "You'll see soon enough about the plaid, lass. And as for your brother, we can discuss that later." He reached first into Burke's saddlebag and pulled a bundle of cloth from it, then strode to his horse and withdrew a similar-looking dark fabric from his own bag.

Burke, standing with all his weight on his left leg, began undoing the ties to his breeches. Jossalyn spun on her heels, not wanting to see these men disrobe in front of her. Several minutes elapsed, and she felt a blush creep up her neck as she thought about the fact that Garrick might be naked behind her.

"It's all right now, lass."

She jumped at Garrick's voice. He was standing right behind her. As she turned, she was met with the staggering sight that confirmed what she had suspected. Both men were now dressed in kilts. The fabric was the same dark shade of red as the blood on their clothes had appeared in the moonlight.

She shivered unconsciously and took a step back. These weren't English-sympathizing Lowlanders. These men were Highlanders. Suddenly all the pieces fit into place—Garrick's abruptly thickening accent, the enormous swords both men had wielded back at Dunbraes, and now these kilts.

She had met many Scotsmen over the years living in the Borderlands, but they were almost all Lowlanders who were sympathetic enough to the English to at least do business with them.

From what she had always been told by her brother, though, Highlanders were a different sort. He had always said Highlanders were proud, stubborn, and hell-bent on not being controlled. He had called them barbarians, savages, and animals. She could recognize the vehemence and hatred in her brother's voice whenever he spoke of Highlanders, and she normally didn't trust his word or opinion, but without any other information to go on, she had always been apprehensive when it came to the people who lived in the far north of Scotland. And now she found herself alone in the middle of the wilderness with two Highland warriors.

Her face must have clearly shown her unease, for Garrick gave her a wolfish grin that held no mirth, only a raw warning.

She broke their stare, unnerved and unsure of herself. She still needed to see to Burke's leg as best as she could, given the circumstances, so she skirted Garrick's large form and walked toward Burke. When she reached him, he handed her a few strips of what used to be his breeches. Taking them, she knelt next to his right leg once more, and after he shifted his kilt out of the way, wrapped the bandages tightly around the wound. He winced and let a few muffled curses slip but didn't complain. When she was done, she turned and found Garrick watching her closely.

"I should tend to your back as well," she said carefully.

"I'll be fine. We need to keep moving."

As if his words concluded the discussion, he went to Burke's side and helped him into his saddle, then turned to his own horse. Unsure of what to do, Jossalyn simply stood there. She certainly didn't want to be left in the middle of the woods, hours of riding away from anything, but she also couldn't just go north with these men—these Highland killers—willingly.

Apparently reading the war on her face, Garrick reined his horse around so he loomed over her in the darkness. But instead of threatening her or simply throwing her over his saddle and tearing off into the night, he spoke in a low voice, quiet enough for only her to hear.

"Burke needs you, lass."

His words shook her to the core. He was asking her to help them, to use her healing skills. He believed in her ability to help Burke, and in her sense of duty to aid someone who needed her.

Yet, she still didn't truly know these men. They had lied to her and deceived her. They were clearly dangerous, and they presumably meant to wage war against the English, based on what she had seen back at Dunbraes. And now they were fugitives, fleeing from her brother and the English army in the dead of night. Would they harm her? Would they use her against her brother and the English? Or could she trust this kilted Highland warrior, who had kissed her with so much tenderness and heat that she blushed at the mere memory?

He extended his hand toward her. Reluctantly, she placed her hand inside his, and he swung her up onto the saddle in front of him. He spurred his horse, and they were charging north once again.

Chapter Fifteen

The hours of darkness and tense maneuvering through the woods blurred together. Jossalyn felt her hold on alertness slipping as the exhaustion from a night in a bumpy cart, another day on horseback riding back to Dunbraes, the battle there, and now a long and frantic night of riding caught up to her.

By the time the sky started to lighten with the first signs of dawn, she felt like she was holding herself together by mere threads. Neither of her companions made a sound or an indication that they, too, were exhausted, and injured as well, but then again, they were hardened Highland warriors.

She had only made her exhaustion worse by chewing on that fact for hours as they rode. Why had they lied to her and deceived everyone back at Dunbraes village? How did they know her brother? And perhaps most bewildering of all, why had they taken her with them?

The sound of a soft whistle from Garrick snapped her out of her tangled thoughts. He and Burke both pulled their horses to a halt, and Garrick dismounted behind her. Burke stayed in his saddle, though, and even in the bluish light of pre-dawn, Jossalyn could make out a grimace on his normally smooth and congenial face.

Garrick went to his side, and as Burke began to let himself slide from the saddle, Garrick caught him and supported his weight. Burke got his good leg under him, and was able to stand upright as long as he put all of his weight on his left leg. Even still, the wound must have been throbbing and aching terribly; it needed to be properly tended to, and he was risking infection every minute that the wound was open.

Without realizing it, Jossalyn had slid from Garrick's towering horse and was now in front of the two men, her eyes tugging toward Burke's leg. It was plain to see that blood had already soaked through the makeshift bandages she had wrapped around the wound. She pressed her lips together.

"This cannot wait. I need to see to Burke's leg," she said softly, turning to Garrick.

He only nodded. He didn't even argue or insist that they had to keep going, which worried her. It meant he could see as clearly as she could that Burke was in trouble.

"We can rest here for a few hours," he said simply.

Jossalyn glanced around the dimly lit forest. It looked the same to her eyes as the rest of the endless woods through which they had been traveling for the last several hours, but Garrick seemed to have chosen this place to stop. As if reading her thoughts, he said, "There is a shelter just over there, and a large creek runs a little way past it."

He propped his shoulder underneath Burke's arm and turned toward a large rock outcropping tucked in among the trees and underbrush. Jossalyn took the two horses' reins and followed.

For some reason, she was expecting to find a house or at least a shed, but she all she saw was more untouched forest even as they halted in front of the rocky protrusion. She shot Garrick a questioning look, but then she noticed he had stopped right next to the towering exposure of rock. Several dead trees had fallen against the rock, and ferns and other small plants had sprung up on top of the logs, creating a small covered crawl space between the rock and the leaning tree trunks.

She felt her eyes grow wide as Garrick helped Burke to the ground and got him scooted into the covered nook. She had never had to work in such conditions before. But then again, she thought, trying to shake away her shock, she had never been whisked away by Highland warriors before either. She would just have to make do.

She approached the little shelter and knelt down next to Garrick at the opening. There appeared to be just enough room for her to scoot inside and work on Burke's leg under the cover of the dead logs and regrowth over them, which was good, because even though the sky was clear to the east where the sun was near rising, dark clouds were moving in from the west.

Setting these thoughts aside, Jossalyn let herself become totally engrossed in the task at hand: Burke's leg. She unwrapped the cloth that covered the wound and forced herself to suppress a gasp. The gash was deeper and longer than she had thought when she assessed it in the dark earlier. Garrick didn't bother covering up a low curse.

"That bad, eh?" Burke said, trying to lighten the mood, though he spoke through slightly clenched teeth.

"I've given myself worse with my fletching dagger," Garrick said wryly for Burke's benefit.

Ignoring them both, Jossalyn pulled her satchel from across her body and began digging in it.

"Fetch me some fresh water," she said to Garrick, still rooting in her bag for her sewing kit and the yarrow she would need when she rewrapped the wound.

By the time Garrick returned with a full waterskin, Jossalyn had already laid out what she needed. She poured water over the wound, washing it of blood so she could see it clearly. At least it had been made by a sharp sword, she thought grimly. The cut was clean, so the skin had a better chance of healing. She threaded her needle and took a deep breath, steadying herself.

"Hold him still, please," she said to Garrick.

He leaned into their shelter as much as he could and placed one large hand on Burke's chest and his other arm across his legs.

Blessedly, the sun had just cracked over the horizon, and a beam of light somehow managed to filter through the trees into the opening of the shelter, illuminating the interior. Without hesitating and risking losing the light, Jossalyn bent forward and began stitching the wound closed.

At the first tug of the needle, Burke jerked and groaned, but Garrick kept him almost completely immobile, saving Jossalyn from misplacing a stitch. She worked quickly to save Burke from more pain but kept the stitches tight and in line. She had done this enough times to trust in the steadiness of her hand.

When the last stitch was in, she tied off the thread and turned to the cloth bandages and yarrow she had laid out. Normally, she would have boiled the yarrow and soaked the bandages in it to help stop the bleeding and heal the wound, but there was neither the time nor a fire to do that, so she settled with crushing the yarrow and spreading some of its paste and juices on the inside of the bandages. Garrick helped her lift Burke's leg so she could wrap the bandage around his thigh several times.

She had felt his eyes on her the entire time she worked, but it wasn't until the bandage was securely tied that she allowed herself to register his stare. She worried she would find him glaring at her, or looking at her suspiciously, as if she might hurt Burke, but when she met his gray eyes, they penetrated into her with a dark intensity. She wasn't sure how to read them—they certainly weren't shooting anger or suspicion at her. But why was he looking at her like...like he had right before he kissed her?

She broke their gaze and turned to look down at Burke. "How do you feel?" she asked, trying to shake the feeling of Garrick's eyes still on her intently.

"A bit poked and prodded but better," Burke said.

"You'll need to rest and stay off the leg if you want it to heal properly," she said firmly, but Burke and Garrick exchanged a look that made it clear that they wouldn't be following her instructions.

"We'll rest and let the horses catch their breath for a few hours at most," Garrick said flatly.

He pinned her with those intense eyes again, and she found that even though annoyance bubbled up at his refusal to listen to her, she couldn't seem to find her tongue.

Garrick withdrew from the shelter and turned to see to the horses. When his back was to her, she suddenly remembered his wound, which also needed to be tended.

"Your back!" she called to him as she scooted out of the lean-to and stood. "I can stitch it as well."

He half-turned back to her. "Nay, lass, I'm fine. It was only a scratch."

She crossed her arms over her chest in exasperation. Why did men so often insist that they were invincible? "At least let me look at it."

He quirked an eyebrow, likely at her tart tone, but she wasn't going to back down. Finally, he took a step toward her.

Suddenly she felt like he was a hunter and she was in his sights. He moved slowly, deliberately, but with deadly grace. She had to will herself to keep her feet rooted in place rather than take a step back from his powerful frame as he drew closer. When he was standing directly in front of her, he slowly turned on his heels so that his back was facing her.

Now that he wasn't bearing down on her like some perfectly honed warrior-god from a nightmare—or a dream, she thought fleetingly—she let out a breath she didn't realize she was holding. She prodded around the slit in his leather vest and shirt, but there was too much dried blood to be able to see the extent of the cut.

"I can't see it very well. Perhaps I could wash some of the blood away."

He looked at her over his shoulder for a moment. "I was going to take a dip in the creek anyway. You can look at my back there if you'd like."

Though his words were innocent, something in his tone held a dark invitation—and a promise. She felt her cheeks grow hot and her stomach flutter. He would be naked, bathing in a woodland creek, and he wanted her to come along so it would be just the two of them?

"N-no, I'll stay here and watch over Burke," she said in a rush, her voice shaky.

He raised a dark eyebrow but shrugged, not commenting on her uneven voice or the blush she was sure currently reddened her face.

"As you wish, lass. But you know where to find me." With that, he strode away in the direction she assumed the creek was in, leaving her to stare after him, red-cheeked and longing for something, but she didn't know what.

Chapter Sixteen

Garrick needed a cold dunk, and fast. And it wasn't just because the smell of horseflesh and battle clung to him, or because he wanted to wash away the blood that had dried on his back.

It had started with having Jossalyn seated in front of him in the saddle as they rode through the night. Hell, if he was honest with himself, it had started the moment he had laid eyes on her outside of Dunbraes, but it had gotten much worse over the last several hours.

Just like on their ride from the safe house back to Dunbraes, he had felt her slim shoulders and back pressing into his chest, her soft bottom wedged against his groin, their hips moving in unison. It had felt good—too good, considering he needed to be on high alert, making sure they weren't being followed and guiding them northeast through the tangled forest. The importance of the task at hand, plus his worry over Burke, had forced him to keep his mind on task and away from the feel of her pressed against him.

Then as he had watched her work on Burke's leg,

he had been caught off-guard again. Her golden head had been bent over, her brow furrowed in concentration, but her hands had been steady and swift. He had never seen a lass operate so calmly under pressure—or operate at all, for that matter. In all the time he had spent in Robert the Bruce's war camp, they had never had a real healer, someone trained and tested under pressure. Mostly, the men just saw to themselves and each other. Witnessing Jossalyn work made him realize just how valuable real healing skills were. He had stared at her in fascination, amazed at her calm coolheadedness.

But his real undoing had been when she had offered to help him, and he had thought about taking off his shirt in front of her again and having her slim hands skimming over his skin exploratorily, as she had done back at the smithy. Despite his exhaustion, that thought had made his cock jerk under his kilt.

Then she had crossed her arms in annoyance at him, which caused her breasts to be pushed together and up, and he thought he might have to adjust his kilt to hide his overeager manhood. When he had approached her, he watched as she let her eyes run all over his body. He doubted she knew what she was doing, but he caught the light of hunger that flickered in her eyes, and noticed that her lips had parted slightly, her breathing just a touch more shallow than normal.

He knew he shouldn't have, but he had let his

words about bathing be an invitation. It was neither the time nor the place, and even if it were, she was an English lass—and Raef Warren's sister. He couldn't just dally with her for a few hours and enjoy some shared pleasure, then move on like he normally did with the lasses. He had a mission to complete and a rebellion to return to.

And what the hell had he been thinking when he had rescued her? Even thinking the word "rescue" brought on an internal grimace.

He was no hero, and it was ridiculous to indulge in the idea that he was. Aye, he had gone mad with rage at the sight of Warren about to hit her, and he never tolerated any man raising a hand against a woman, but what did he hope to accomplish by taking her with them? He had been right when he told the lass that Burke needed her. The wound was bad, and left untreated, Burke could die from it. He still wasn't even out of the woods yet. They had several days of hard travel ahead of them, and infection could set in at any time.

So he had hacked his way through a dozen English soldiers and thrown her onto Fletch's back because Burke needed her healing skills?

That wasn't the real reason, he admitted to himself as he reached the bank of the wide, slow-moving creek. He felt protective of her. And possessive of her. He couldn't stomach the idea of her brother beating her into submission like a dog. It had been gut-wrenching to decide to return her to Dunbraes despite her begging to go north with them, and it was only made harder in light of his knowledge that her brother controlled and abused her. But now that he knew that her brother was Raef Warren, he would never put her in his grasp again.

As if his own experience fighting against Warren in the battle of Roslin four years earlier wasn't enough, Garrick had heard from his brother how Warren had attempted to first abduct and then murder Robert's new wife Alwin. Warren was a base and cowardly bastard.

Not that Garrick was in a position to dole out judgment. He had done despicable things in his life, but he would never involve women or children in his violent duty to the Scottish rebellion. Aye, he had killed, and done it in cold blood too, not just in the heat of battle. That was what it took, and he would do the jobs that no one else could or would do. He would hunt and watch commanders of the invading English army until he had the perfect shot. He would track and kill Scottish power players who had secretly aligned with the English and who were spying and selling their knowledge to the enemy. He had done it before, and once he could figure out what to do with Jossalyn and get back to the Bruce's side again, he would do it again. But he hoped that he would never be as lowly and dishonorable as Warren.

Garrick shed his leather vest and shirt, then unbelted his kilt and let the material slide from him. He tugged off his boots, and then took a moment to let the early-morning air cool his flesh and his mind. He would have some serious sorting to do regarding this mess he had put himself in, not only in terms of dragging Jossalyn with them, but also with the way the sight of her, the feel of her, the smell of her fired his blood, making him want to forget everything and sink into her.

Pushing the thought away, he stepped into the creek, which was almost more of a river considering how wide, deep, and slow-moving it was. Despite the fact that it was the heart of summer, the water was surprisingly cold and refreshing around his legs.

He waded further in, then crouched and dunked himself so that he was completely submerged. He let the water block out all the noise in his head about Jossalyn, Warren, Burke, the Bruce, and his mission.

He vaguely registered that the water stung the cut on his back slightly, but he wasn't worried. He could tell it had already closed itself and wasn't serious. Not like Burke's injury. No matter how long he stayed underwater, he realized, he couldn't escape or fully block out everything that was going on. Reluctantly, he reemerged. He blinked his eyes open, but cursed at the sight before him.

Jossalyn stood frozen on the bank, her eyes locked on him and her lips parted in surprise.

She hadn't meant to see him bathing. That's what she kept telling herself as her eyes devoured the sight of his water-slick, muscular torso. It was just that a moment after he had walked toward the creek, she had realized that she would need to gather more yarrow, since Burke would likely need several more bandages with fresh yarrow crushed into them in the coming days. And yarrow grew near water.

So she had carefully made her way toward the creek, but kept her head down, both so she could keep an eye out for the distinctive feathery leaves and white flowers, and also, she had admitted, so she wouldn't see Garrick changing or getting into the water. She spotted the plant and plucked it, tucking it into her bag, then saw another a little farther ahead, then more of them clumped together, and she knew she must be close to the creek.

Just as she had knelt to pluck another one of the plants, she had glanced up and spotted a pile of red fabric along the creek bank. She blushed and averted her eyes immediately, but then she realized that she didn't see or hear Garrick at all. She stood and glanced around quickly, but still didn't see a sign of him. Uneasiness crept through her. Where could he have disappeared to so quickly? Could he be hurt somewhere? Was the wound in his back worse than she had thought?

She took a few steps toward the creek, but suddenly the surface of the water exploded and Garrick emerged. Naked.

She assumed he was naked, anyway, since his lower half was still submerged in the creek. Her eyes traveled down to where the water lapped just below his hip bones. She gasped at her own brashness, and quickly spun on her heels so that she was facing away from him.

"I—I'm sorry. I was just collecting more yarrow, and then I didn't see you…"

"Did you want to see me, lass?" His voice was closer than where he had been standing a moment ago. He was coming toward her. And he was naked. Her stomach seemed to flip over.

"No, well, yes, I mean, I…I saw your clothes but you weren't anywhere, and I was worried about the cut on your back, and…" She was babbling like fool. She took a deep breath and attempted to gather her wits—and tried to force her mind to stop picturing the water dripping from his dark hair onto his shoulders, his chest, his stomach…

"Would you mind handing me my kilt? Unless you don't mind if I get it?"

She looked down at her feet and realized that she was nearly standing on his pile of clothing. "I'll get it!" she said frantically, grabbing the red plaid so that he wouldn't reach around in front of her to fetch it himself. She held the fabric out behind her and felt him take it out of her hand. So now he was within arm's reach of her. Still naked. She squeezed her eyes shut and willed herself to stop blushing like a fool, but it didn't work. Her face was hot.

Actually, her whole body was hot, despite the cool morning air. She told herself she was being more than a fool—she was being a blind, naïve fool, for, she reminded herself, she didn't even know this man behind her. Yes, they had talked and interacted and even kissed, but this was a different Garrick than the one who pretended to be a Lowland blacksmith. This Garrick was a mysterious Highlander who had killed people in front of her.

That thought cooled her blood somewhat, and she opened her eyes again. Looking down, she realized the rest of his clothes were gone from her feet, though she hadn't heard him move or felt him brush past her. Then she heard water splashing and turned around to face the creek. Garrick knelt at the water's edge, his kilt fastened around his waist by his belt, but his torso still bare. He had his bloodied shirt in his hands and was dunking it into the creek.

Her eyes locked on the red slice running down the middle of his back, and she stepped forward to view it more closely. As she looked at it, she had to admit he was right—it wasn't much more than a cut. It was only about six inches long and not very deep. She absently ran her fingers around it to make sure the surrounding skin wasn't swollen or becoming infected. He jerked and stiffened at her touch.

"I doubt this needs stitches after all. I should check

on it tomorrow to make sure it is still healing properly, though," she said, still absorbed in assessing the injury through her healer's eyes.

Then she realized she was touching his exposed skin, which was warm under her fingertips. She had also just said that she would check on him tomorrow without considering the larger question of where he would be tomorrow—and more importantly, if she would be with him.

She withdrew her fingers from his back, and an awkward and laden silence stretched. Finally, he wrung out his shirt and stood, turning to face her. His steely eyes locked onto her, and he said what she had wanted to say and yet feared to broach.

"We have some things to discuss."

Chapter Seventeen

He searched her large green eyes, looking for a hint of her state of mind.

Normally, he could read people as if they were open books. He had become skilled at analyzing people's movements and unspoken thoughts out of necessity, since he normally worked alone and at a distance. He had learned how to figure out what a mark was thinking, and then anticipate his next move in order to adjust his aim accordingly. But as he let his eyes drink Jossalyn in, he couldn't figure out what she was thinking. He saw a mixture of dread, anticipation, uncertainty, and—was he just fooling himself, or did he see a flicker of desire in the emerald depths of her eyes?

He pushed the thought aside. Aye, he hungered for the lass, and they had clearly had a connection earlier, back when she thought he was a simple blacksmith and he thought she was a pretty English lass. But nothing could come of it. Now he knew that she was the sister of his enemy and an English noblewoman. And now that the truth of who he was had been revealed—or at least part of it—he would be a fool if he thought she could still desire him for the Highland killer that he was. She would probably be even more horrified to learn that he was an elite member of Robert the Bruce's army, and the best archer-assassin in the Scottish fight for independence. But it was time to tell her—or maybe just explain a few things.

He took a breath to steel himself, preparing for the inevitable: her horror, disgust, shock, and fear of him.

"As I'm sure you've figured out by now, Burke and I are not blacksmiths."

She nodded, keeping her eyes locked on his.

"We are from the Highlands and are part of the Sinclair clan." He waited, but her eyes didn't register anything at the name of his clan.

So, Warren had kept her in the dark about his affairs and activities against the Scots, and the Sinclair clan in particular, he thought. He would have to tread very carefully, then. He wanted to explain things to her but didn't want to give her too much information. It was safer for her if she didn't know too much, he thought grimly. He didn't know how long she would be with them, but at some point, he would have to figure out some place safe for her to go—away from both him and her brother. It wasn't wise for her to be with either of them. He hated to have to admit that he had something in common with Warren, but when it came to Jossalyn, they were both dangerous to her, albeit for different reasons.

"Why did you lie? Why did you say you and Burke

were from the Lowlands and that you were blacksmiths?" she asked, a hint of hurt creeping into her voice.

Her pain stung him, but he couldn't let himself focus on it.

"We were...gathering information on the English army's movements." He paused, weighing how much he could say, but then added, "For the Scottish cause for independence."

"You're a freedom fighter?"

Her words caught him off-guard. It wasn't often that the English called what the Scots were doing "freedom fighting." Rebelling, yes. Acting like savage barbarians with their raiding and slaughtering, yes, according to those who opposed them. But "freedom"?

The only other time he had heard words that sounded even vaguely sympathetic to the Scottish cause coming from an English mouth was when he had met his brother's wife. He had been instantly suspicious about her loyalty to Scotland given her nationality, but love seemed to be strong enough to overcome Robert and Alwin's differences.

Someday you'll understand. His brother's words floated, unbidden, to his mind, but he pushed them away, not wanting to consider why they lingered in his thoughts.

"Aye, we fight with the Bruce for our independence."

Her eyes widened, but instead of fear or horror, he

saw interest and curiosity. He felt himself harden inside with suspicion. Years of isolation and subterfuge had made him distrustful of people, but it had also kept him alive. Why would she be interested in the fact that he was part of the Scottish rebellion, rather than frightened or disgusted? Could she be part of some scheme? She was English, after all, and Warren's sister to boot.

He must have been glowering at her, for she blinked and took a step back. As if understanding his silent suspicion, she said "I have always felt an affinity toward the Scottish people. Ever since my brother and I moved up to the Borderlands, I have…understood the desire for freedom." She trailed off at the end, lowering her eyes to the ground between them.

"Is that why you tried to escape with us earlier into Scotland rather than back to England?" he said, some of his suspicion dissipating.

She nodded then met his eyes again, but this time her brow was furrowed. "How do you know my brother?"

He ran a hand through his dripping hair. Explaining this to her was necessary, but also dangerous. If Warren ever did manage to get his hands on his sister again, he would pump her for information on her "kidnappers," and she would have to tell him that the members of the Sinclair clan, at the order of Robert the Bruce, were spying on him and readying themselves for a war.

"Have you heard of the battle at Roslin?"

Her furrow deepened, and she shook her head

slowly. "It sounds vaguely familiar, but I'm not sure."

"It happened four years ago in Scotland—on Sinclair land. Your brother instigated the attack, but we were victorious." He watched her closely for her reaction. She was letting her eyes wander, and he guessed that she was scanning her mind for information.

Finally, she spoke. "I remember my brother returning from a battle about four years ago. He never let me be privy to information on the war, but that wasn't long after our parents died and we moved to Dunbraes. He was…strange after that."

"What do you mean, strange?"

She struggled for words for a moment, biting her lower lip. Despite telling himself to stay alert and keep his mind on task, his eyes kept tugging to her mouth, where that plump lower lip was caught between her teeth. Thankfully, she spoke.

"He didn't take our parents' death well. He blamed the healer who had tried to help them, and when she couldn't save them, he became obsessed with being in control and maintaining order. I think…" She hesitated, choosing her words carefully. "I think he began to see Scotland as some sort of disease that England had to defeat, and that the Scots' way of life was dangerously wild and needed to be controlled and stamped out before it could spread."

Her words struck him. He had always thought Warren was an evil warmonger, but his hatred of Scotland and the fact that he was leading the English charge against them took on a new twist in light of Jossalyn's insights. Then something else clicked into place.

"And he hates you just as he hates all Scots and Scotland, because you are a healer. You deal with disease and injury, but even you cannot overcome nature. You cannot save everyone, and you can't control nature's course, so he loathes you, as he loathes himself."

Her eyes widened, but she nodded slowly, and Garrick felt a pinch of something in his chest. He understood her, or at least understood some of her suffering.

A tiny part of him selfishly wished she could understand and know him too. But he pushed the thought away harshly. He had no right to ask her to see his true nature and accept him. He was beyond this innocent lass's redemption.

He forced his mind back to the issue at hand. "Your brother has caused much pain and suffering in Scotland, and for the Sinclairs in particular. I was sent to gather information on the English army's movements. Your brother is at the forefront of the conflict, not only in terms of being the northernmost English holding in the Borderlands, but also in terms of his…fervor for battle. So we infiltrated Dunbraes village to investigate."

He was expecting her to recoil despite his careful wording—he hadn't quite said it, but he was telling her that he was a spy, and had lied and deceived freely. He had even used her for information. But her next question surprised him.

"What did you learn?"

His suspicion crept up again, but he paused to consider her question before his distrust shuttered him to further conversation. This lass was more than an English noblewoman. She had endured a harder life than some pampered lady at court. She had been living in the Borderlands among a combination of her war-hungry and abusive brother, Borderlanders who feared war and had to keep their alliances fluid, and likely, some Scots with thinly-veiled hatred for their new overlord—and his English sister.

Despite all that, she had managed to ingratiate herself to the entire Dunbraes village from what he had seen, likely because she offered her healing skills freely and earnestly, helping anyone who needed it. And she had suffered her brother's control and abuse, all the while longing for her own freedom.

He hesitated for a long time as he chewed on all of this, eying her warily. When he continued not to answer her, her face finally contorted into the expression he had been expecting this whole time—frustration, hurt, and withdrawal.

"You don't trust me, do you?"

"Do you trust *me*?" He took a predatory step toward her. "Because you shouldn't, lass."

Finally the inevitable was happening. She took a

step back warily, but he took another forward. She would see who he really was, even without him having to tell her all of it, and she would flee him, or at least turn away from him.

He couldn't have her stay with him—for too many reasons. The most obvious was that he had a mission. He had to tell the Bruce about Longshanks's death and give him time to plan their next step. Then his work in the Bruce's army would continue. There were always more marks. He couldn't simply walk away from his work and into the arms of a waiting Jossalyn. The thought was like a punch to the stomach, both the achingly honeyed idea of being with her and the bitter truth that he never could, not long-term anyway.

But another reason besides his duty to the Bruce and his mission whispered in the back of his mind. She would never be able to care for him, to understand what he had done over the long years of warfare and battles. It was better that she know the truth now before either one of them let their attraction go any farther. He wasn't the hero. He did what had to be done, including pushing her away—or rather, giving her a glimpse of his life and letting her turn away from him in revulsion.

"I'm not the man you met back in Dunbraes. I am a warrior, a killer, not some innocent blacksmith. You shouldn't be out here alone with me."

She began to take another step back, but then halted, lifting her chin. "If you are so dangerous, then why am I still alive?"

"Like I told you before, Burke needs you, and I need Burke to complete my mission. Don't think it means you're safe."

Part of him hated trying to scare her like this, but the other, louder part reminded himself that it was true—he wasn't a safe person to be around. Danger followed him—nay, he sought it out. He couldn't just bring her along with him to the Highlands and into Robert the Bruce's war camp. He still had no idea what he was going to do about all this, but he had to put some distance between them. She couldn't think of him as some sort of champion, and he couldn't let himself indulge in the pleasure of her nearness. He had to be bigger than his desire for her.

Just then, her eyes flicked from his face down over his torso, which was still bare. He watched as a flutter of heat seeped into her eyes, and he felt himself snap. He could crush down his own craving for her, but her desire for him was his breaking point.

In one stride, he closed the distance between them, and his body slammed into hers.

Chapter Eighteen

A war raged inside Jossalyn. Garrick's words of warning registered, for she too had been unsure of whether or not she should fear him. What he said was true—he had lied. He was actually a Highland warrior, and clearly, a very skilled one. But for some reason, his threat about being dangerous to her rang hollow. She couldn't explain it, but she simply didn't believe him.

For one thing, the more she thought on it, the more she realized he hadn't snatched her away with him—he had saved her, first from her brother's impending strike, and then from the battle that had boiled all around her back at Dunbraes village.

Moreover, she had seen for herself how protective he was of her, both when he had first seen the bruises her brother had left, and again when her brother had been about to hit her. He may have deceived her before, but she didn't think he could fake the visceral, instinctive protectiveness he had shown her.

But all of this was hard to wrestle from her mind, for her eyes kept tugging down to drink in the sight of his incredible physique. He had donned his kilt but still wore nothing on his upper half. Every plane and muscle seemed to work in hypnotic coordination when he moved. She remembered the feel of both his warm skin and hard muscles when they had kissed back in the smithy—vividly. He was so strong and large, and yet he could be so gentle with her.

He was attempting to intimidate her by taking a step forward, trying to prove his claim that he wasn't a safe person to be around.

It was true, she didn't feel safe around him, but not because she feared he would hurt her or mistreat her somehow. Instead, she feared her own reaction to him. She had felt the fluttering of girlish affection before, but this completely eclipsed her youthful attachments. She was drawn to him as a woman is drawn to a man, not as a girl daydreams over a lad. He made her feel something she had never felt before—or rather, he awakened something inside her that she had never known had been there all along: desire. Raw, hungry, bodily desire.

She couldn't resist it anymore. She didn't want to. She let her gaze slip down from his steel-sharp eyes to the corded muscles of his shoulders and arms, the broad expanse of his chest, and the narrower, chiseled planes of his trim waist.

In a flash, the perfected physique she had just been gazing at was pressed against her, his lips burning into hers. She gasped in surprise at the sudden contact, and he took the opportunity to invade her mouth with his tongue. He stroked and caressed her, but there was an edge of urgency and insistence in his kiss, which she felt rising inside herself as well. She wouldn't have been able to articulate it before, but this was what she wanted—to feel him against her, to let their mouths meld together, to feed the hunger she had for him.

One of his hands was wrapped around her waist, holding her close to his body. The other drifted lower to settle on her hip, pulling her against him even tighter. Her arms had risen of their own volition and were now wrapped around his neck. Her fingers entwined in his dark hair, which was still dripping from his dunk in the creek. His clean, masculine scent invaded her senses. He smelled of warm skin, leather, and the outdoors.

He started moving forward, which forced her to step back, but he held them together so that they moved as one, never breaking their kiss. A moment later, she felt the bark of a large pine tree pressing into her back. She was pinned between the tree's unyielding trunk and Garrick's rock-hard body—and one hard part in particular was pressing into her. Heat shot through her at the sensation, firing her limbs. It gathered especially in her mouth, her breasts, and between her legs.

The hand on her waist began to move upward, and though she had never been touched there before, she suddenly longed for him to let his hands settle on her breasts, which were achy and needy for something, like an itch but…deeper. And more pleasurable.

She arched her back slightly in anticipation of his touch, and he made a noise in the back of his throat that was somewhere between appreciation and pain. He kept his movement slow, though, his hand inching up to brush against the outside curve of her breast. Then he let his thumb move over so that it skimmed against the swell of her breast.

Even through the material of her dress and chemise, the touch sent a jolt of sensation through her, and she gasped again. The urgent achiness hitched higher, both in her breasts and between her legs, where she felt warm and damp. She pressed her hips into his even harder, longing for both relief from the sensation and more of it.

The hand on her hip suddenly clutched the material of her skirts and pulled it up by about a foot. Then abruptly, the cool morning air slammed into her, replacing his warmth. Her eyes fluttered open, and she saw him before her, panting, clenching and unclenching his fists.

"Christ," he breathed.

She brought a shaky hand up to her lips, trying to feel herself to make sure she was still real and that this wasn't some heady dream.

He dragged a hand through his hair, which was disheveled from her fingers. "We can't do this."

As if she weren't reeling enough from the intensity of their kiss and the longing coursing through her, his words spun through her head and she struggled to make sense of them.

"Why?" That was the best she could manage. She had a dozen more articulate and important questions about what had just happened, but she couldn't seem to sort them out.

"Because..." He took a breath and rolled his shoulders, trying to relieve the tense knots of muscles that were visibly clenched. "Because you are Raef Warren's sister, and I am a Sinclair. Because you are English and I am Scottish. Because you are a healer and I am a killer. Because it's wrong."

It hadn't felt wrong. In fact, it had felt more right than anything she had ever experienced. She had been completely entwined with him, communicating without words, sharing in a free and untamed passion she didn't know she was capable of. She couldn't explain it, but she felt drawn to him like a moth to a flame.

"What does my brother have to do with this, or my country of birth, or my healing skills?" She couldn't quite manage to say the part about being drawn to him like no other, embarrassed at the thought of sounding girlish or naïve. But she wouldn't just accept his reasoning—not when she longed so badly to be back in his embrace again.

"I don't think you fully understand the gravity of this situation, lass, or the mess I am already in just by having you here."

His tone was like a splash of cold water, waking her

from the dizzy dream of desire in which she had been floating. "Then why don't you explain it to me, since you were the one who brought me here."

Garrick struggled for a moment, longing to soothe the clear frustration and injury he was inflicting on Jossalyn by pushing her away, and yet also wanting to solidify the distance he had just wedged between them.

"I can't tell you any more. We are all already endangered by how much you know," he said through clenched teeth.

He had told her that he was a Highlander and part of the rebellion, and that he had been spying on her brother and Dunbraes. That was enough to have them all hanged, but at least she wasn't completely in the dark anymore. He would be crazy to explain further—about how he was Robert the Bruce's go-to marksman, that they were heading toward his secret camp near Inverness, that the Bruce was developing a new strategy to attack the English using stealth rather than meeting them on the battlefield, and that Garrick was central to this plan. She would just have to accept staying in the dark while he figured out what to do with her.

"We should discuss where you'll be headed once Burke is well again," he said carefully, wanting to change the subject, but finding just as many thorns in this new line of conversation.

She drew her brows together and crossed her arms

over her chest, understanding his meaning. He was trying to offload her once her usefulness to his mission was over. He suppressed a wince at the harshness of it, but it was true. He shouldn't try to soften it or ease the rejection for her. She couldn't stay with him, no matter how much he wished things were different. And he did.

"I'm sure I can take care of myself," she said flatly. "Just drop me off in a village, and I'll be fine."

"You still plan to stay in Scotland?" For some reason, this surprised him, though it shouldn't, now that he thought about it. She had already tried to escape to Scotland once, and he doubted there was anything for her to return to in England—least of all her brother's keep.

"Yes. So you see, just as you are using me to heal Burke, I am using you to gain my freedom and start a new life in Scotland," she said, lifting her chin slightly.

He wanted to argue with her, to tell her it wasn't safe and that he couldn't just leave her in some random village. But then he realized she was only making the best of the situation he had put her in.

He cursed himself yet again for acting so rashly. He should never have let it go this far. He should have kept his nose out of it and left her to deal with Warren. But his whole being rejected the thought immediately. He could never have sat idly by and watched Warren harm her, or leave her to fend for herself in the middle of a battle that his actions had instigated. Christ, this was a mess.

"Very well, lass, we will use each other. But we should not...touch each other that way again. It will only make things more complicated."

He didn't try to explain how or why things would get complicated if they continued to let their attraction rule them, because for every reason he came up with against it—she was a maiden, she was English, she was Warren's sister—his body came up with a counter—her soft pink lips, those firm, full breasts, her innocent yet heated response to his touch. He had nearly taken her right there and then against the tree. If he hadn't reined himself in instead of hitching her skirts up higher, he might have done something irreversible.

She didn't respond, and instead, searched him with her gaze, trying to read him. He dropped a veil of flatness over his demeanor, suddenly afraid that if she looked too closely, she might see that his reasons for keeping his distance were paper-thin and could be torn away with the slightest brushing touch from her.

"I'll go check on Burke," he said brusquely. "You should see to your dress. There is still blood on it."

She looked down and registered the blood—his blood—that had stained the front of her dress the night before. The sight chilled him, reinforcing what he needed to do. If he didn't follow through with his mission and keep her at a distance, one or both of them would be hurt. He was used to closing himself off, to doing what needed to be done, even if no one else was willing to do it. This was just another mission, he repeated to himself over and over, forcing his feet to turn away from her and walk back toward the shelter.

Chapter Nineteen

Jossalyn didn't bother to take off her dress. Instead, she knelt next to the creek, cupped water in her hands, and splashed it down her front. She ended up damper than she would have liked, but the thought of peeling off the dress and standing in the open air in nothing but her chemise—with Garrick only a short distance away—was too much. So her entire front was soaked, but at least most of the blood had washed away.

She made her way back to their makeshift camp slowly, trying to give herself time to chew on everything that had passed between her and Garrick. It hadn't come as a complete shock that he was a Highland rebel—she had gathered nearly as much with the combination of witnessing him fight, hearing his thick accent, and seeing him in a kilt.

But she had had no idea her brother was such a well-known and hated figure in these battles for Scotland's independence. He very rarely told her anything about his trips to the north or the movements of the English soldiers who frequently passed through Dunbraes, but she had known he was some sort of player in all this—just not quite so central a player.

The real shock had been her kiss with Garrick—their second kiss, which had somehow managed to be even more intense than the first. But her mind swirled at his harsh words of warning and the way he was distancing himself from her. His body and his words were telling two different stories, and she wasn't sure which one to believe.

She was uncomfortably aware of the fact that she was inexperienced, and he…well, he wasn't. But she trusted her sense that his attraction to her was real. Could a man simply fake the kind of bodily reaction he had had with her?

The memory of his hard manhood pressed against her stomach flooded back to her, and despite the fact that she was alone with her thoughts, she blushed. She didn't think he could fake that.

And she didn't believe he was faking his protectiveness of her either. From what she had seen, he had a strong sense of honor, of right and wrong.

So then why did he keep warning her about how dangerous he was? Why did he make it clear that he didn't trust her, and that she shouldn't trust him? There was more he wasn't telling her, she was sure of it. He wouldn't tell her why, but he was convinced that he was some sort of dangerous villain, which simply didn't fit with what she had seen of him, even after he had transformed from country blacksmith to Highland warrior.

Her thoughts were interrupted by the sound of a groan up ahead of her. She quickened her pace toward the shelter, worry itching at her. As the shelter came into view, she broke into a run.

"Stop! Put him down!" she shouted at Garrick in shock. He had pulled Burke out from inside the lean-to shelter and was supporting his weight under his arm. Burke was leaning precariously against Garrick, his face white and glistening with sweat, despite the cool morning air.

"He can't be moved yet! He needs more time to rest!" she panted in frustration as she came to a halt in front of the two men.

"There isn't time to rest anymore. We have to move," Garrick responded coolly. He had donned his shirt and leather vest again and looked prepared to ride already. His tone was authoritative, brokering no argument, but Jossalyn paid it no heed.

"You said you wanted me to help Burke, but I can't very well do so if you are dragging him all over the forest, can I?" she said acerbically.

He raised an eyebrow at her tone, but didn't bother answering. Instead, he guided Burke around her toward their horses. Burke had all his weight on his good leg, but even just moving was bringing grunts of pain from him. When they reached his horse, Garrick paused for a moment, letting Burke catch his breath and steel himself.

Through clenched teeth, Burke said over his shoulder, "Garrick is right, we have to keep moving. I'll be fine, lass."

Garrick boosted Burke into the saddle, but the motion of swinging his wounded leg over his horse brought a string of muffled curses from Burke. Garrick was grim-faced but didn't say anything. He turned to his own horse, preparing to mount, but Jossalyn strode to Burke's side and took the reins firmly into her hands.

"I cannot condone this. You are endangering Burke by forcing him to ride."

Garrick brought his horse on the other side of Burke's, so that he was towering over her and pinning her between the two horses. "And we are all in danger if we stay here. No doubt your brother and his English army are barreling down on us as we speak. Our only hope is to take advantage of the fact that we are fewer in number and know the landscape better. We have to outride them."

Jossalyn felt a surge of helplessness and frustration wash over her. It went against every instinct as a healer to put one of her patients in danger by ignoring his wound and risking infection.

On the other hand, she had no desire for her brother to catch up with them. She felt her stomach twist at the idea of another confrontation between her brother's army and Garrick and Burke. The images of the blood, death, and maiming she had witnessed at Dunbraes flooded over her, and she had to swallow to force her stomach back down her throat. But this time, Burke wouldn't be able to fight, so Garrick would be on his own against who knew how many soldiers. The thought of him dying beneath her brother's blade brought a stab of fear and nausea to her.

She locked eyes with Garrick, trying to communicate her struggle to him. His steely gaze cut into her, determined, but she thought she saw a flicker of his own fear for a moment as well.

Just then, Burke groaned again, but this time he began slumping forward over his horse's neck limply. Garrick flung himself from his horse and darted to her side just as Burke began to topple sideways out of the saddle. He caught Burke just before he would have fallen unconscious, either onto the ground several feet below his horse's back, or right onto her, which would have likely crushed her.

"Take him back to the shelter," Jossalyn said as she locked her eyes on Burke's leg. It was bleeding again, and the fresh bandages she had put on no more than an hour or two ago were already soaked through.

Garrick half-dragged Burke's large frame back toward the lean-to. When Burke was settled inside the shelter on his back, Jossalyn crawled in and placed a hand against his damp forehead. He was burning with fever. She muttered in frustration, something between a curse and a prayer, then unwrapped the bandage on his leg. He had reopened the wound, likely trying to stand and mount his horse. But more concerning was the fact that the flesh around the cut was now red and puffy.

"What is it?" Garrick said softly from the opening of the lean-to. He was watching her closely, his eyes hard and grim.

"Infection," she said as her mind raced for a solution. "We'll need a fire after all."

He grimaced and opened his mouth to argue, but she held up a hand to silence him.

"Garrick, listen to me. Burke will die if this goes untreated. And even if I had every herb, tincture, and tool a healer needs at my disposal, I'm not sure whether or not I can save him. I have to try everything I can, even if it means risking discovery." She held his gaze and watched a war rage across his face.

Finally, he cursed and raked a hand through his hair. "What can I do?"

She turned her attention back to Burke, relieved that she had won the battle. "We need a fire and boiling water. The best we can do out here is to soak the bandages in yarrow water and force some tea down Burke's throat."

It was a long shot, but the yarrow would absorb into the wound better if it were boiled and soaked into the bandages. Yarrow was their best bet to get the bleeding stopped and hopefully stave off the infection. She would have to re-stitch the wound, too.

Garrick set about building a fire a few feet away from the shelter. Jossalyn dug in her bag again, hoping to find anything that might help, but she had taken very little with her when she left Dunbraes to stow away with Garrick and Burke. The memory of packing for her grand escape seemed to have been formed ages ago, although only a few days had elapsed. She had had no idea when she was packing what kind of tangled calamity she would find herself in just days later. A man's life was in her hands—and all of their lives hung in the balance.

A fire now crackled cheerily in front of the shelter, a stark contrast to her mood. Garrick had pulled a small tin pot from his saddlebag and had filled it with water from his waterskin, then placed the pot over the fire to get a boil started. Jossalyn crawled out of the lean-to and toward the fire, a clump of yarrow plants in her hand. She pulled off the soil-covered roots but pushed the rest of the plants—feathery leaves, white flowers, and all—into the pot.

Reminding herself that a watched pot never boils, she crawled back into the shelter alongside Burke and went about preparing to re-stitch his wound. This time, since he was unconscious, she wouldn't need Garrick to hold him down. As she threaded her needle, she glanced out at the fire in front of the shelter, but Garrick was gone.

She tugged her attention back to the task at hand, pushing away her thoughts about him. She could gaze at his strikingly handsome face and body or chew on his enigmatic words and behavior some other time, she told herself firmly.

After she had re-stitched the wound in Burke's leg, she went to the fire to check on the yarrow water. The plants had turned pulpy and withered, and the water was nearly boiling already. She looked around and noticed that the horses were gone, but their saddlebags sat on the ground a few feet away. Garrick had likely seen to them. She felt a wave of gratitude at his small action. It meant she was no longer going to have to fight him on whether or not they could move Burke and resume their travels. It was a small act, but she was glad to have one less thing to worry about.

She rummaged in one of the saddlebags until she found a small tin cup. She dipped the cup into the pot, ladling out some of the yarrow water, then brought it to Burke's side within the shelter. She lifted up his head and poured some of the warm brew down his throat, pleased when she saw that he swallowed several gulps of the tea. Laying down his head as gently as she could, she scooted out of the lean-to and refilled the cup at the fire.

She managed to get one more cup of the yarrow tea into him, which boosted her spirits slightly. Yarrow was a powerful anti-inflammatory, antiseptic, and anti-fever medicine. She thanked her lucky stars that she had left some of the plant in her bag when she had packed, and that there was more growing in the area.

This time as she crawled out of the shelter, she brought all the bandages she could rummage with her.

She would only be able to soak one at a time since the pot was so small, but it was better than nothing. Just as she was pushing one of the strips of cloth down into the pot with the waterlogged plants, she caught a glimpse of Garrick's red plaid through the trees.

She watched as he approached, but when she could finally see him fully unobstructed by the trees, her breath caught in her throat. His arms were overflowing with yarrow. He strode to the fire where she knelt and dumped the armload of plants on the ground, making an enormous pile of them.

"Is this the kind of plant you need?" he said, his eyes on her.

She didn't know if it was the lack of sleep or the razor-sharp anxiety of the past few days that brought it on, but all at once tears blurred her vision. She nodded, not trusting her voice.

Suddenly, he was kneeling next to her. "What is it, lass? Is everything all right? Is it Burke?" Fear pinched his voice, so she shook her head quickly.

"No, Burke is resting. It's just...You found all this yarrow, and..." She took a shaky breath and tried to pull herself together. "Thank you," she eventually managed.

She was so struck by his kindness and eagerness to do something useful that she nearly lost her hold on the tears again. This was a man of action, a warrior used to being able to do something with his hands to change things. He was no healer, as she was sure he would vehemently insist, but he clearly cared enough about his friend to act like one. She wouldn't let herself indulge in the thought that he wanted to be of help to her too, that he wanted to protect and care for her in the only way he could think of. That was just sentimental wishful thinking, she told herself firmly.

"The horses?" she said, trying to get her mind back on reality.

"They've been fed and watered. I found a shallow cave on the other side of this rock formation that is mostly covered over with shrubs. It's not perfect, but it will have to do."

She nodded, again grateful for the fact that he had taken care of things. "I managed to get some tea into Burke, which will hopefully help cut the fever, and if we are lucky, stop the infection." Using a stick, she drew out the strip of cloth that had been soaking in the yarrow water. She let it cool in the air for a moment as she pushed another piece of cloth into the pot in its place. Then she took the soaked cloth into the shelter and began wrapping it around the wound. Garrick followed her silently, helping her lift Burke's leg again.

When the task was done, they returned to the small fire. "How often does the bandage need changing?" Garrick asked quietly as they both stared into the flames.

"About once an hour." She registered that her voice was flat with exhaustion, but she was too tired to care.

"And when should I give him more tea?"

"When should *you*?" Though she felt foggy with fatigue, she didn't miss what he had said.

"Aye, lass. I can tend to Burke. You need to rest."

"What about you?" He hadn't slept since the night she had stowed away in their wagon—two days ago.

He scrubbed his hand over his face but didn't try to deny his own exhaustion. "Why don't we take turns?" he said finally.

"Very well. You'll go first," she said firmly. He started to argue, but she interrupted him. "I slept a bit in the wagon. And besides, I need to prepare some of this yarrow and make a fresh batch of this brew before I can rest."

He still looked like he wanted to object, so she placed a hand on his shoulder to still him. Despite their exhaustion, both of them seemed to grow alert at her touch.

"Sleep," she said softly, then gave his shoulder a little push to get him to lie down.

He mumbled something about stubborn lasses, but he let himself be tilted over to the ground. She watched him settle his arm underneath his head and close his eyes, not bothering to find a more comfortable position. Within a minute, she could hear a change in his breathing as he slipped into sleep.

She let herself gaze down at him for a moment, drinking in the sight of him. He still looked fierce, even in sleep. His dark hair was disheveled, and several days' worth of stubble covered his jaw and cheeks. Though he was relaxed in sleep, his muscles were still corded and well-defined. His large chest rose and fell rhythmically with his breathing, and even lying down he looked like a giant.

But there was also something incredibly intimate about being so close to him as he slept. He was completely vulnerable. Jossalyn doubted very many people ever saw him like this. Based on what she had observed, he was normally guarded and cautious, but here he was, stretched out a mere foot away from her on the ground in a deep sleep. She suddenly had to fight the urge to lean into him, inhale his scent, and run her fingers along his hard jawline to feel the bristly stubble there.

She shook herself, forcing her eyes back onto the pot on the fire. She went about adding more water and stuffing more yarrow in along with the strip of cloth, all the while telling herself not to think about Garrick—not think about him sleeping next to her, not think about being pressed against him again, not think about what their next kiss would feel like.

Despite her best efforts, the dark and inexplicable desire had taken root in her, and there was no going back.

Chapter Twenty

Garrick woke to the sound of thunder. He jerked upright, reaching instinctively for the fletching dagger he always kept in his boot. Suddenly, his eyes locked on Jossalyn, who was frozen in surprise in front of him, her eyes wide and startled.

"Sorry," he said, easing his hand away from his dagger. "Habit."

She let out a breath and nodded, relaxing somewhat. She had been working over the fire, stirring the mixture of plants, water, and cloth inside the pot. Despite her diligent attention to the task at hand, she looked haggard and exhausted. Her golden hair was mussed and coming out of its braid, her shoulders slumped forward, and he had noticed dark smudges under her eyes a moment ago when she had been staring at him.

"How is Burke?"

"About the same," she said, her brow furrowed. "But he took more tea, which is good."

He stood and went to her side. "You need to rest, lass."

"But you only slept for a few hours," she responded, but there wasn't much fight in her voice.

He actually felt surprisingly refreshed. He was used to sleeping outdoors and working long hours. He doubted that she was, though.

He glanced up at the sound of another roll of thunder and noticed the storm that had been brewing to the west earlier in the morning had now arrived. As if to prove his observation, he felt a large raindrop hit his shoulder.

"You shouldn't be out in this storm anyway. I can watch over the fire. You go check on Burke and get some sleep."

She only nodded, confirming for him just how tired she was. She disappeared inside the shelter for a moment, but then reemerged.

"He's still asleep, but there's not enough room in there for both of us," she said wearily.

Garrick glanced around for a spot that would work as a second makeshift shelter during the storm. Several more drops of rain had fallen, and the sky was growing increasingly dark despite the fact that it was midday. Not far from where Burke lay underneath the overgrown leaning logs, there was a slight inward curvature to the rock face. If he could gather enough fallen trunks and branches, he could create a second lean-to that wouldn't look out of place.

He set about dragging several tree limbs from the forest floor to the rock outcropping, propping them against the rock to create a little space underneath them for Jossalyn. Once the structure was in place, he covered the logs with freshly fallen branches that still had leaves or pine needles on them to provide more protection and make the lean-to blend in more. When he was satisfied, he peeked inside. Even as the rain started to come down in earnest, the inside of the little structure was staying dry.

He turned away from the shelter, only to find Jossalyn staring at him, an unreadable look on her face, but a softness in her eyes. Feeling uncomfortable under her scrutiny, and not wanting to think about why her soft look made his chest pinch, he cleared his throat and said gruffly, "That should do."

"Thank you." She kept her large green eyes locked on him as she approached, only breaking their gaze so she could duck her head down and crawl into the shelter. One more idea occurred to him to make her sleep more comfortable. He went to his saddlebag, which was still next to the fire, and retrieved an extra length of plaid, then went back to the new shelter and knelt in front of it.

"Here," he said, extending the plaid toward her. He realized suddenly that perhaps he was fussing too much over her. He berated himself silently, reminding himself that he was supposed to be keeping his distance from her. Why should he overexert himself just to make her comfortable?

A voice in his head whispered that he wasn't exactly living up to his self-appointed title of villain very well. But just because he was an assassin in Robert the Bruce's army didn't mean he was a cold-hearted bastard. What was so bad about trying to make the lass comfortable, especially when it was his own blockheaded and moon-eyed "rescue" of her that had put her in this situation?

She took the proffered plaid but was gazing up at him with that look in her eyes again—a combination of tenderness and desire. He had to get out of here before he did something stupid again.

"I'll be back," he said tersely, standing.

"Wait! Where are you going?" A thin edge of concern cut through the surprise in her voice.

"Hunting." They could use some fresh food, but the real reason was because he needed to calm his mind and straighten out his thoughts, and nothing did that better than having his bow in his hand.

"Oh."

Just as he was turning away again, she called after him once more.

"I was wondering…why does your bow look so strange?"

He couldn't help the smile that quirked up one side of his mouth. So she had noticed. As far as he knew, he was the only Scot with a recurve bow from the Holy Land, and likely the only one in all the British Isles.

"It's called a recurve bow. You've seen normal longbows?"

She nodded.

"Then you'll know that they are long and almost straight, and can be as tall as their shooter. They are made out of yew, which makes sense in these parts since it's fairly common and sturdy wood. They are also easy to make, which is important in wartime, like now, because it doesn't take as much time or skill to produce them. What did you notice was different about my bow?"

She thought for a moment. "It was curved or warped somehow, and was a bit shorter than the bows I've seen. The two ends seemed to be going the wrong way."

He nodded. "That makes it far harder to make, but more accurate and precise. Most English armies line up in long rows and shoot a swarm of arrows at their opponent, hoping some of them reach a mark, but relying more on sheer numbers rather than accuracy. My bow is designed to be shot from horseback or among tree cover, so it is more maneuverable and precise."

He surprised himself at his own loquaciousness, but he felt a twinge of pride, not only for his bow, but also for the fact that she had noticed it.

She tilted her head to the side a little. "Where did you get it?"

"The Holy Land. I was on a mission." He almost added that he had been hunting a target for the Bruce, but decided to withhold that information. For some reason he didn't like the thought of her picturing him hunting down and killing someone on the order of the King of the Scottish rebels. He shouldn't care what she thought of him, but he did.

Her eyes widened in amazement, and he reminded himself that most people never traveled more than a day or so away from their homes. In her case, she had moved from England to the Borderlands, and was now in Lowland Scotland, but her circumstances were rare and unique. He had seen more of the world than most people could dream of. Working for the Bruce had taken him to Ireland, France, and even the Holy Land.

Though he believed in the importance of his work and was honored to call the Bruce his King and commander, the reminder about how different his life was from hers sat like a stone in his stomach. Yet another piece of evidence that the two of them could never be together.

That thought startled him, for he didn't realize that some small part of him was still looking for a plan that would allow him and Jossalyn to be together. He shouldn't need to collect evidence for why it wouldn't work. He should already have moved on from his little fantasy.

"I won't be long," he said, turning to go again, "but you should sleep." He had to get his head on straight before he forgot all his reasons and logic and duty. Because if he didn't start thinking clearly, he would join her in the shelter and do something that no amount of reason or logic or duty would undo.

The rain was finally unleashing its full might, just in time for him to be trying to keep their little fire alive. Upon his return from his hunt, he had stowed their saddlebags inside Burke's shelter to protect them from the mounting downpour. Then he had skinned, cleaned, and skewered the rabbit he had shot. Now he was trying to roast it over the meager flames, but the rain seemed to have other plans.

Both Jossalyn and Burke were still sleeping, Jossalyn peacefully inside her dry little shelter, and Burke somewhat fitfully. Garrick had forced more tea down his throat and had changed the dressing on his leg a few more times, but Burke's fever still burned, and the wound looked angry and enflamed.

He had thought of rousing Jossalyn, first to have her check on Burke to see if anything else could be done, and then to share the rabbit with him, which would have been done cooking by now if the skies hadn't decided to open up and nearly completely douse his fire. It was already sometime between late afternoon and early evening if Garrick could judge correctly through the heavy cloud cover. She had been asleep for several hours, but he was glad he hadn't roused her. She needed it, and who knew when they would get a place and time to rest again?

Unfortunately, his bow had offered him little in the way of solace or clarity as he had hunted. He still had no idea what to do about Jossalyn. He knew that he couldn't keep her with him, at least not after Burke healed—God willing. He still wouldn't let himself wonder what would happen if his cousin, his brother's right-hand man, and, he grudgingly admitted, someone who had become a companion and friend to him over the last few weeks, somehow didn't pull through. He had to believe Burke would make it, and that they would still be able to complete their mission together.

When—not if—Burke was well enough to ride, they would need to continue heading north, and fast. But Garrick had to get to the Bruce, whereas Burke needed to report back to Garrick's brother Robert. Although Robert was still Garrick's Laird and leader of the Sinclair clan, the Bruce's position as the King of Scotland trumped his brother's authority over him. Burke could report back to Robert on what they had learned in the Borderlands about Warren's movements, and Garrick would deliver the news of Longshanks's death and the crowning of Edward II to the Bruce.

But where did that leave Jossalyn in all of this?

He still didn't like the idea of leaving her in some random village in the middle of Scotland. He hated to admit it, but he felt too protective of her to do that. Though her healing skills would be welcomed anywhere she went, the farther into Scotland they traveled, the less amenable people would be to having an English lass in their midst. Some would likely distrust her, while others might even be openly hostile toward her. Plus, word of a bonnie English lass in the middle of nowhere in Scotland would likely draw attention. Her brother might be able to find her, or maybe someone looking to kidnap and ransom her would be drawn in. Either way, her presence would stand out and draw unwanted notice.

But he couldn't very well take her with him—could he? Though he longed to cling to any thread of an idea that would mean he could stay in her presence longer, he couldn't think desperately or let his desire for the lass cloud his judgment. He couldn't involve her further in the rebellion—it wasn't safe for her to be in the middle of a war. And besides, he doubted that the Bruce or the others in the army would appreciate him bringing an English lass—and Raef Warren's sister no less—into their secret camp.

His mind continued to churn, still unable to find a solution.

Just as he was about to give up on the rabbit ever getting cooked, he heard the distant whinny of a horse and froze.

He strained to hear through the patter of rain in the trees, praying he had been mistaken. But then he heard it again—another whinny, a bit to the left of where the first had come from.

He bolted upright, and in a flash, had kicked dirt over the fire, rabbit and all. Luckily, the ground was soft and damp enough that the fire was quickly smothered, and the ground looked relatively undisturbed. He grabbed his bow and quiver, which he had wisely kept with him after his hunt instead of returning them to where the horses were stowed. His mind tried to picture how well the animals were hidden, and he prayed they were resting quietly behind the thick screen of shrubbery that blocked the entrance to their little cave.

A cursory glance around their makeshift camp didn't reveal any obvious signs of their presence. Then again, someone was about to stumble upon them, and Garrick would bet his bow that it was Warren and a small English army. But the ground hadn't held their footprints, and the two shelters looked to be naturally-occurring.

He quickly ducked his head into Burke's shelter, but his cousin was still sleeping relatively soundly, so he covered the entry with a few extra branches and went to Jossalyn's lean-to. She was curled in a ball on her side, her blonde hair splayed across his plaid, which she was using as a pillow. At any other moment, he would have lingered to drink in the sight of her, but as it was, there was no time to indulge himself. He eased his way inside the shelter, though the quarters were tight, and pulled another few needled branches behind him to cover the entry as best as he could.

Just then, he heard the snap of a branch, closer than the whinnies had been. Someone—or a group of people on horseback—was nearly on top of them.

Chapter Twenty-One

The heavy weight of a callused hand clamped over Jossalyn's mouth. Her eyes sprung open, panic stabbing through her.

"Don't make a sound," came the low voice right next to her ear. She tried to thrash away from the man behind her who was holding his hand over her mouth, but his arm pinned her upper body, and he threw a large leg over her kicking legs.

"It's me, lass. It's Garrick." His breath tickled her cheek and neck, and despite the fact that he spoke right into her ear, she could barely hear him, he spoke so quietly.

He eased his hand back slightly from her mouth, trying to make sure she wouldn't scream or thrash again. She turned her head slightly so she could lock eyes with him. He shook his head in a warning, and then jerked it toward the entrance to her shelter, indicating something outside.

She froze and felt her eyes grow wide. *Burke?* she mouthed silently. He jutted his head backward to where Burke was apparently still lying inside his own shelter. Then he leaned in and his lips brushed her ear, sending shivers through her.

"Men on horseback," he whispered. He lifted his arm and leg off her and twisted toward the entrance of the lean-to, which was covered with a few branches to obscure the view of them inside. She sat up next to him and peered out into the woods, which were darkened with the bluish-gray light of evening. The clouds were still thick overhead, further dimming the light, and rain fell heavily.

Through the trees and underbrush, she began to see shadowy figures emerge. She felt her stomach tighten and twist. As the group moved closer, she guessed there were over a dozen of them, their armor dull in the low light. She could tell just by their armor that they were her brother's men, but instead of riding in two tight rows side by side like she had seen them do on their way in and out of Dunbraes, they were fanned out and moving slowly across the forest.

They were hunting them.

She couldn't quite suppress a shudder of terror. What would her brother and his men do when they found them? She suddenly pictured a sword sinking into Garrick, his blood seeping out of him as he crumpled to the forest floor. She squeezed her eyes shut, trying to not only will the image away, but also push her brother and his men in a different direction.

But they kept moving closer. When they were only fifty yards away, she unexpectedly caught sight of her brother. He still wore the same fine clothes he had been clad in when he had arrived at Dunbraes from Cumberland with word of the King's death, though they were wet and rumpled now. There was a bandage wrapped carelessly around his right hand, where Garrick had shot him. The bandage, white except for a dark smear of blood, glowed bluish in the dim light. He and his men must have been pursuing them just as hard as they had been fleeing, though this group traveled slower since there were more of them, plus they had to pick out the signs of their trail.

Her brother spurred his horse forward and ahead of the arc of soldiers sweeping the forest, more tense and alert all of a sudden. She watched as he turned his head this way and that, scanning the woods. He sniffed the air suspiciously and turned his horse in a slow circle.

Jossalyn held her breath, praying they would move on but fearing the worst. She felt a movement at her side and glanced at Garrick. Ever so gradually, he was nocking an arrow into his curved bow, which he had raised in front of him. He slowly pushed the tip of the arrow through a small gap in the branches covering the opening of the shelter and drew back the bowstring.

Panic sliced through her. If he fired, their hidden position would be revealed, and it would be Garrick against more than a dozen armed soldiers. And he would have her and Burke to worry about also. But her fear was suddenly eclipsed when she looked down the shaft of the arrow and saw who he was aiming at.

Garrick was pointing the arrow right at her brother's heart, and he was about to fire.

Garrick slowed his breathing, focusing on the sound of his heartbeat as he locked his eyes on his target. Warren continued to look around suspiciously. The second Warren spotted them, he would let his arrow find its mark deep within the man's chest. He had nine arrows in his quiver, ten if he counted the one that was currently aimed at Warren, plus his fletching dagger in his boot.

He had left Burke's and his swords with the horses, which he regretted now, but if all of his arrows flew true, he would be able to take out most of the men before they could reach him or Jossalyn. Once the arrows were spent, he would have to count on his skill and a lot of luck to be able to take out the remaining men, who all had armor, swords, and horses. It was a long shot, but if they were spotted, he had no alternative.

He let all this slide through his mind like sand through his fingers as he homed in on his target. He always found this sanctuary of calm right before he let one of his arrows fly. He was totally in the present, letting sensations and thoughts wash over him as he became completely focused.

Just as he reached this internal refuge, Jossalyn wrapped her hand around the arrow and pulled it out of line with his target.

"No," she breathed, her voice breaking through the silence in his head.

The arrow's jerk sent a slight ruffle of movement through the branches of pine needles blocking the shelter's entrance. Warren's head whipped around, either sensing the movement of the branches or hearing Jossalyn's whispered plea.

In a flash, Garrick released his bow and pulled her back against his chest. He wrapped one large hand around both of Jossalyn's wrists, clamping the other over her mouth. It was probably too late, but he held her still, trying to quiet even their breathing. He could feel her breath hitch and knew that she, too, was staring at her brother, whose eyes scanned their area.

Time stretched. It felt like Warren was looking right at them, his eyes boring into their shelter. Garrick again visualized taking on all these men, but this time without the element of surprise. Warren would give the signal at any moment, and all those armored soldiers would come crashing down on them. He might be able to get a few shots off, but it would come down to his six-inch fletching dagger. It would be a lost cause. He and Burke would be killed quickly, and the Bruce would never get his information in time. And Jossalyn would either be killed or dragged back with her brother, probably to be locked away, never to see the light of day or use her healing skills again.

He tried to savor this moment, since it would likely be his last pleasant experience on earth. Jossalyn's hair was brushing his nose, and he inhaled her scent—wildflowers, as if she had rolled in a field of them. He closed his eyes for a second and let himself drink in the image of tumbling with her through a springtime meadow in the Highlands, the sun warm on their skin and the sweet new grass cushioning them.

He released his hold on her wrists and slowly reached for the dagger in his boot. She stayed motionless, her slim back pressed into his chest. If he had to die, at least he had known a sliver of happiness in Jossalyn's presence. She was like a balm to his black soul, making him feel like he was a good man, or at least that he was better than he thought himself to be. He had put her in the middle of this chaos, though. He could only pray she would be safe after he was gone.

"Lord Warren!"

Garrick snapped his eyes toward the voice. One of the soldiers had broken rank and was riding toward Warren. Reluctantly, Warren broke off his searching gaze and turned toward the soldier who had called him.

"What?" he hissed irritably.

"The men must rest, my lord," the soldier said in a low voice. "We cannot search every inch of the forests of Scotland, at least not without getting some sleep and giving the horses a break."

"How dare you question my orders?" Warren wheeled his horse around so that his back was to the shelter and he was facing the soldier. "You *can* and *will* keep searching." Then he turned to some of the men in the fanned arc and said, "You there, on the end! Quit lagging! I said a northwesterly angle!"

The soldier at Warren's side looked tense. "This is a fool's errand, my lord. This rain is washing away any tracks, and there is no way we will catch up to them if we keep zig-zagging like this."

Warren clumsily drew his sword with his bandaged hand, and then swung it at the soldier's neck, halting just inches before making contact. "Are you calling me a fool, Samuel?"

The soldier, whose eyes were wide as he tried to look sideways at the blade at his neck, said, "No, my lord."

Warren let the blade rest near the soldier's neck for another moment, and then sheathed it with a hissed curse of pain for his hand. "If I knew exactly which angle at which they were riding, we wouldn't have to keep cutting back and forth across this damned wilderness, Samuel," he said, attempting coolness. "I won't just plow north like an idiot. It's what those bastard Scots would want me to do, so they could lay a trap and double back on us."

"And you're sure they were Scots, my lord?" Samuel said carefully.

Warren sighed exasperatedly like he was explaining something to a child. "They fought with the large broadswords of the Scots. They headed north. And they took my whore of a sister with them. She has always been overly sympathetic to the barbarians and their rebellion, and she likely aided them in their attack."

Garrick felt Jossalyn jerk uncontrollably at her brother's words, but she didn't make a sound. Christ, the bastard was cold-hearted. Warren's words were more than insulting, though. If Warren believed that Jossalyn was sympathetic to the cause for Scottish independence, or worse, that she had something to do with his and Burke's attack and flight, she was in more trouble than he had originally thought. She wouldn't just be locked away at Dunbraes—she could be hanged for treason.

"Is that clear enough for you?" Warren went on. Not waiting for an answer, he shouted to the others, "Keep moving!" He rode back to the front of the arc of soldiers, apparently letting his initial suspicion about the area drop.

The soldiers continued their slow and weary march heading northwest. Garrick still wouldn't let himself move a hair until they were long gone and he could no longer hear them in the distance.

What seemed like ages later, he eased his dagger back into his boot and released Jossalyn from his hold. She scooted around to stare at him wide-eyed, her features hard to read in the growing darkness. He was sure that she was still reeling from all that her brother had said, but he suddenly felt his anger rising, and something else—betrayal.

"You damn near got us killed," he said in a low but heated voice.

She inhaled sharply, caught off-guard by his anger. But she recovered and retorted, "You were about to kill my brother!"

"Yes, I would have killed your bastard brother if he had spotted us. Would you have preferred for me to wait for him and his men to be on top of us with their swords drawn first?"

"No, but—"

"Why would you protect him at all? He hurts you, denies you the ability to practice healing, and has publicly proclaimed you a traitor!" he interjected. His blood was about to boil over, and he realized this was why he was so heated—because she had chosen her brother over him. Some small voice of reason in his head screamed that he was being ridiculous, that she hadn't "chosen" her brother *or* him, that she likely hadn't wanted *anyone* to get hurt, but he quashed the voice ruthlessly.

"He's my brother!" she shot back, her voice rising. "I hate him, but he is still my brother!"

In the back of his mind, something clicked into place. Through the fog of anger, he could understand her reasoning. He loved his brothers and would protect them with his life, but even if he hated them, they were the only family he had. They were his blood, no matter what. But the haze of fury still clung to him, and no amount of reason or logic would cut through it.

"You are too naïve to understand. Just because he is your brother doesn't mean he shouldn't pay for his evildoing."

"And just because I am not a cold-blooded killer like you doesn't mean I'm too naïve!"

He recoiled as if she had slapped him. Her shot had found its mark, and he guessed from her heavy breathing and hurt-filled eyes that his had too. He had in effect called her foolish and blinded by compassion, and she had called him what he feared to be most—just a killing machine. He had no heart, no happiness. His whole life could be summed up by his kills. Perhaps they were both right. He had been a fool to hope to be anything better. Even worse, he had been a moon-eyed idealist to think that she could care for him as he was.

She, too, seemed to sense that they had both crossed a line, brushing too close to the truth, or at least too close to each of their feared flaws. She pressed her lips together and averted her eyes, despite the fact that there was barely anything else to look at but him in the cramped quarters inside the shelter. Finally, she broke the tense silence.

"I need to check on Burke."

"I'll get a fire started again and prepare some bandages. The English likely won't cut back eastward for several hours, if not a day, and they'll miss us to the north anyway," he said gruffly.

She nodded and crawled out of the shelter. He followed her out, but forced himself not to watch her as she went to Burke's lean-to. The rain had finally let up, and the deeper darkness of night was settling in on them. At least it wouldn't be raining on him as he slept out in the open on the sodden ground, he thought grimly.

He got a small fire going just as Jossalyn reemerged from Burke's shelter.

"I think his fever has gone down a bit," she said woodenly when she reached the meager flames.

"And the infection?"

"About the same, though the fact that it's not getting worse is a good sign."

"We'll stay here for the night, then," he said as he positioned his hands near the flames, trying to soak in some of their warmth and cheer. It didn't help the dead coldness he felt since he and Jossalyn had closed themselves off to each other, though.

Without speaking, she turned and retreated back to her small shelter, leaving him to watch the fire as it sputtered out, unable to take hold on the soggy wood. It would be a long, cold night indeed.

Chapter Twenty-Two

Despite the dry, soft floor of her shelter, Jossalyn lay awake, chewing on the clash she and Garrick had had earlier. As she rolled over yet again, trying to find the peace of sleep, she guiltily remembered the way Garrick had built this shelter for her when the rain had started. He hadn't even bothered trying to make one for himself, or to make this one big enough for both of them to share. He wouldn't push himself on her, or even hint that he would want to share the shelter with her, despite the fact that neither one of them was trying to hide their attraction.

She knew he was right when he had said back at the creek that they couldn't touch or kiss anymore—it would only make things more complicated and painful for both of them when she parted company with him and got herself established on her own.

Even after everything that had happened, Jossalyn still believed she could start a new life in Scotland as a healer. She would have to lie low to avoid drawing the notice of her brother, whom she now knew would throw her to the wolves for disobeying him. Maybe, though, he would consider her lost to Scotland and give up looking for her and Garrick and Burke.

She was just as naïve as Garrick said she was, she thought bitterly. She knew her brother too well to believe he would simply give up when he imagined his pride, his control, and his crushing grip on power were affronted. He would continue to hunt them, even though he thought so little of her.

But another thought whispered in the back of her mind. What if her brother's accusation about her aiding the Scottish rebellion were true? Would that be so bad?

For as long as she could remember, she had wanted to help people. She had learned the skills of a healer so she could aid the injured, the sick, and those who needed another chance at life. And since she had moved north to Dunbraes after her parents died and her brother was assigned to hold the castle, she had known somewhere inside that she felt more at home there, among the overpowering beauty and wildness of nature and the earnest, but harried, people of the north.

Though she could heal their bodies—or at least ease their discomfort—she couldn't heal the deeper wounds they suffered under the late King and his hungry armies. What they needed, she couldn't give them: freedom from oppression, invasion, and domination. But she at least understood them, for she longed for the same thing.

She had already decided that she wanted to stay in Scotland and offer her skills to its people, probably in some remote village to avoid attention. But what if there were more that she could do to help Scotland and its people overcome their English attackers? What if she could help more directly?

She discarded the nascent idea even as she felt excitement bubbling inside her. She would never be able to find Robert the Bruce and his army in the first place. He and his supporters were famously elusive—not only were the English hunting him, but if the rumors she heard were true, some Scots who sided with the English were looking for him too, but to no avail. She had overheard one of her brother's messengers say that every once in a while the Bruce and his rebels would appear, strike the English, and vanish just as quickly. One English girl—*woman*, she told herself firmly—wasn't just going to locate his base of operations and march in, demanding to help.

But, the voice whispered back, she wouldn't just be searching blind. She had a connection: Garrick.

He had said that he was working for the Bruce and the rebels, though he had been evasive about saying more. Perhaps he could help her reach the rebellion's secret location, maybe even introduce her to someone who could help her within the movement. At least he could point her in the right direction.

Based on Garrick's reticence, though, she doubted he would be eager or even willing to help her. She would just have to convince him that not only was she in earnest about helping Scotland secure its freedom, but that she was strong and capable enough to continue on without him to the rebel headquarters.

She would also have to wait for the right time and phrasing. After their sharp words to each other, she very much doubted Garrick would want to help someone whom he thought was not only naïve but also still protecting her cruel English brother.

The first step to her new plan would be to apologize to him.

She gave up all hope of finding sleep and sat up inside the shelter. She felt the same surge of energy she had experienced when she had decided to escape from Dunbraes to Scotland several days ago. She was taking charge of her life, making her own decisions, and forging her own path. Her brother's determined search for her and her two companions wouldn't stop her, nor would Garrick's willingness—or unwillingness—to help her.

She peered out through the branches that served as a makeshift door to her shelter. The clouds had blown away, and the silvery light of the half-moon illuminated their small camp. No fire glowed in the fire pit several feet from the entrance of her lean-to, but she saw a shadowy lump huddled in front of it. As her eyes adjusted, she thought she could make out the color and pattern of the Sinclair plaid covering the form on the ground.

Just then, the form rolled over, and she could see Garrick's profile as he lay on his back. She could tell his eyes were open, for the moonlight danced in them. Even still, they were dark pools, appearing nearly black in the low light.

She moved the branches aside, crawled out of the shelter, and stood, brushing off her skirt. He turned his head and watched her draw nearer as if he had sensed long ago that she was awake and about to approach. She wouldn't put it past his knowledge, she thought as she stopped in front of him. He had an uncanny ability to anticipate things just before they happened, and his senses seemed honed to a razor-sharpness.

She knelt down at his side, but he remained silent, his dark eyes following her.

"I wanted to…apologize," she began somewhat awkwardly. She had felt so confident and sure of herself a moment ago, but something about his eyes, unreadable in the low light, made her feel unnerved, and her stomach fluttered. The memory of their last kiss flew unbidden into her mind, and the flutter turned into a full flip. She took a breath and forced her insides to calm down, chastising herself for her unruly thoughts.

"I shouldn't have said you were a cold-blooded killer. You have shown me nothing but kindness and gentleness through this whole…ordeal. And though I was upset at the thought that you would kill my brother—my only living family left—I understand your reasons."

There. That hadn't been so hard, she told herself, though her voice had been tight as she spoke. It was only because the thought of Garrick killing her brother did indeed still frighten her. It had nothing to do with his steely-black eyes pinning her as he sat up, closing some of the distance between them. And even though it was part of her larger plan to enlist his aid, she surprised herself by meaning what she had said about understanding why he would have shot her brother.

The silence stretched, and she began to fidget, but finally he spoke. "I apologize as well. I shouldn't have called you naïve. Although your brother has kept you away from much of the world, you clearly know more than I do about trust and honor."

The words came out haltingly, as if he weren't used to apologizing or having to explain himself. For some reason, that made his words all the more meaningful. A wave of relief flooded through her. She hadn't realized it before, but his silent anger, and her own angry words hanging in the air between them, had been nearly unbearable.

She cared a great deal about what he thought of her, she realized, and also wanted to see the best in him. It wasn't just his strikingly handsome visage that made her twist longingly inside; it was also the desire for him to respect and like her. For she couldn't deny it in herself any longer—she cared for him.

A pang of something like pain shot through her.

She had already told herself back in Dunbraes that she couldn't grow attached to this man, no matter how much the mere sight of him—let alone his touch or kiss—made her heart race and her breath hitch. Yet here she was, another heady and intense kiss later, and she was coming to care for him.

But what could come of all this? She didn't know when they would part company, since Burke remained in a dangerous stage of infection and her brother and his men still scoured the forest for them. Sooner or later, though, Garrick would continue with his missions for Robert the Bruce, and she would journey on in search of the headquarters of the rebellion to offer her healing skills. They would never get to know each other more, or share more kisses, or—she wasn't even sure what would come after that, but the dark promise of their passion lingered in her mind, making her think of possibilities that would normally cause her to blush.

Her mind began spinning a new option, though. If they would indeed part ways soon and never see each other again, what was the harm in one more kiss? Her eyes dropped to his lips, which suddenly parted as he breathed a curse. Startled, she jerked her eyes back to his. She was met with the sight of a dark storm of passion just before he closed the remaining distance between them, his lips coming down on hers.

Chapter Twenty-Three

Garrick had watched as a sea of change washed over Jossalyn's delicate features, which were illuminated in the moonlight. Her skin looked like porcelain, and her normally golden hair looked icy blonde in the silvery light. Her eyes were depthless, and he felt like he could drown in those emerald pools a happy man.

He had been listening to her tossing and turning several feet away inside the shelter, and had heard her little sighs, which, despite her distance, made the hairs on the back of his neck stand up in anticipation—of what, he wouldn't allow himself to contemplate.

When she had knelt before him, her mouth had been tight with tension, but after they had spoken their apologies, those berry-red lips had parted unconsciously. He watched as she had gone from content but distant to unsure and then finally, a hungry look had transformed her features. Her eyes had drifted to his mouth.

He couldn't withstand this kind of torture. He knew he shouldn't want her this badly, and even more importantly, that he shouldn't act on his desire. But she so clearly desired him, too. How was he supposed to resist this beautiful lass, who had surprised him with her iron will and healing gift, her compassion, and her strength?

He couldn't fight it anymore—couldn't fight himself, or her desire.

The first taste of her lips sent a bolt of pleasure through him. Her softness and scent enveloped him instantly as he pulled her to him, pressing their bodies together as he tasted her lips. But it wasn't enough. He deepened their kiss, his tongue caressing hers, her warm mouth shooting sensation all the way to his cock. He felt her arms snake around his neck, pulling him into their kiss, which only fired his blood more. She wanted him too. She knew at least part of who he was and what he did, and she still wanted him.

He let one hand tangle in her hair, holding her mouth in place, while the other rose to one of her breasts. He nearly groaned aloud at the feel of her firm, soft breast, which fit perfectly into his hand. He imagined what they would look like if he ever got to see her naked. Her flesh would be velvety smooth and the color of fresh cream, and each perfect mound would be tipped in pink, the same color as her lips.

Before he let himself be completely washed away by the torrent of passion coursing between them, he tore his mouth from hers, leaving both of them panting.

"We can't do this, lass," he breathed huskily.

She blinked at him, the haze of desire clouding her eyes. "Why not?"

Christ, that wasn't a question he was prepared to answer at the moment. He forced himself to speak, though. "Because you are innocent, and as much as you may want this now, you will look back and regret it."

The words pained him to say, but he had to be an honorable man, at least for once in his life. He had accepted the fact that he was a lone wolf, hunting and killing his prey, but Jossalyn wasn't just another mark. He could never live with himself if he used her knowing full well they would part ways, probably in a matter of days, and never see each other again. He had to be the one to tell her that she deserved better. A woman of her standing, a lady, couldn't just give her innocence to a mercenary assassin in the Scottish rebellion.

"Why would I regret being with you, Garrick?" she said as she pulled back a little, more of the fog clearing from her eyes.

"Do you know what you're saying, lass? You're a virgin. You'll never be a virgin again if we keep going."

She faltered for a moment, her eyes shifting away from his. "I just...I just want..."

He saw the struggle play out on her moonlit features, and understood exactly how she felt. He, too, wanted something that he shouldn't or couldn't have.

But then she took a steadying breath and went on, more firmly this time. "All my life, I have been told what to do. First, my parents taught me how to act like a lady, telling me I couldn't run or ride horses too much or look for plants in the forest. Then, my brother took over my life and tried to force me to stop being a healer. He kept me inside whenever he could and was working on a marriage arrangement just before I left that would benefit *his* position, but would mean all but the end of my life."

Garrick's hands, which had fallen away from Jossalyn as she spoke, clenched in frustration on her behalf.

She sighed, collecting her thoughts for a moment, then went on. "I'm so tired of everyone telling me what's best for me or trying to control me. I left Dunbraes with you the first time because I wanted to make my own choices, to start my own life. And I'm glad you took me away the second time, during the attack."

She shuddered slightly. He guessed that she was remembering the scene of the battle. His stomach sank, her reaction reminding him that a healer could never be with a warrior, a killer. But then her words surprised him.

"I'm glad because I have another chance at freedom, at being in control of my own life. I want to stay in Scotland and be a healer." She paused and bit her lower lip, seeming to hold something back.

He almost pushed her to tell him what else was

lurking behind her deep green eyes, but she spoke before he could.

"And I want to be here with you, and...kiss you again."

Her words sent a jolt through him. He suddenly felt humbled that this lass wanted him in this moment. Who was he to tell her what to do or what she should want—or not want? But he still feared she didn't know what would come after kissing if they were to give over to their desire. She was innocent, and though she had surely been drilled from the time she could crawl to guard her virginity with her life, she didn't seem to know what it would mean to let it go—both between them, and after, when she would find some other man to love and marry.

The thought of another man being the recipient of Jossalyn's love and passion sent a spike of pain and rage through him. *He* wanted to be that man. But he never would be, at least not in the long term.

Yet a voice whispered in the back of his mind that he was here now, and she had made it clear that she wanted him. Even if it couldn't last, he could have a taste of paradise for a moment. He would be able to hold on to the memory for the rest of his life.

He wouldn't take her innocence, however. Though rusty from disuse, his sense of honor was still intact enough to know that he would be responsible if he used her and then left her to deal with the consequences.

"You know I want you too," he said. It felt foreign to lay himself bare like that, but for some reason, he was able to speak his heart to her. "There are...things we can do that will still leave you intact," he said, a strange mix of awkwardness at his words and anticipation of what they meant coursing through him.

Her eyes widened slightly. "More than kissing?"

He felt the corner of his mouth twitch up. "Aye, lass, if that's what you want. More than kissing, but I won't take your innocence."

Even in the dim moonlight, he could see the blush creeping up to her cheeks. "I didn't know...that is, I didn't realize that there were things...in-between..."

He let his fingertips brush against her heated cheeks. His eyes locked on hers, and he moved in slowly, deliberately, for another kiss. Her lips unconsciously parted as he drew closer, hitching his desire higher. This time, he tried to communicate to her through his kiss all the longing he had for her just below the surface, and the dark promise of what they would share.

Her arms snaked back around his neck, which was all the indication he needed. He scooped her into his arms and stood, catching the plaid he had been using as a blanket as it slid from him. He strode away from their makeshift camp to give them more privacy from Burke's presence and approached the slow-moving creek several dozen yards ahead through the trees. When he reached a little open area right next to the creek, he set her on her feet but held her close for another promise-laden kiss.

He broke their contact just long enough to spread his plaid out on the soft ground, and then pulled her down on it next to him. He could hear that her breaths were fast and shallow in anticipation. He kissed her again, this time deeper. Part of him kept thinking she would turn away from him or push him back, changing her mind about wanting to be with him. But instead, she pulled him closer, her hands weaving into his hair, which had come loose from its normally tidy queue at the nape of his neck.

He leaned toward her so that she reclined down onto his plaid. He pulled his mouth from hers so he could drink in the sight of her. Her pale blonde hair was splayed out across the dark reds of his clan colors, and her lips were swollen and red in the moonlight.

"God, you're beautiful," he said on an exhale. There was no way he deserved to be here with her now, but he didn't want to question it. Instead, he rested his weight on one elbow and let his hand skim across the narrow part of her waist and brush over the rise of one of her breasts. She shuddered and inhaled at his touch, and his already hard cock pressed even more firmly into her hip.

He lowered his mouth to hers yet again and let his tongue caress and tease her while his thumb brushed over the peak of her breast. She arched into his hand, so he made the contact firmer. Through the material of her dress and chemise, he could feel her nipple harden under his touch. He let one of his legs settle between her thighs, and she raised one of her knees, hugging him closer and pressing his thigh into the crux between her legs. She made a little noise that was half-sigh, half-moan against his mouth. He couldn't believe how much passion she contained within her, how eager and hungry she was for his touch.

He made a trail of kisses from her mouth, across her cheek, and to her ear. He nibbled the lobe for a moment, his blood firing at her gasp of surprise. Then he drew his lips down the smooth, slim column of her neck. He could feel her rapid pulse beating hard there.

He moved to her collar bone, and lower still to the slight swell of her breasts at the neckline of her dress. She twisted and clenched her leg around his thigh harder as his lips brushed over the sensitive flesh while his thumb still swirled over the peak of her breast. Her hands clutched his shoulders, her fingers digging into his flesh, which only made him more ravenous.

Suddenly impatient to increase both of their pleasure, he pressed his hips into hers, letting his cock rub just above the junction between her legs. They both breathed heavily at the contact, and he realized he had to stop himself before he did exactly what he said he wouldn't.

He rolled back off her slightly but let his hand trail from her breast across her waist, over her hip, and down her bent leg. His fingertips brushed the hem of her dress, and his hand found her ankle. He wrapped his fingers around it easily, enjoying the feel of her delicate bones, and then slid his hand farther up to her calf, which was stocking-free due to the warmth of summer.

Her breath hitched even more as his hand continued to rise up her leg. His fingers lingered on the back of her knee, causing her to gasp and jerk a little. As he inched one hand higher, he let his other hand slip under her back while still keeping his elbow under him to support his weight. He fumbled for a moment but eventually found the ties running down the back of her dress and tugged them loose.

He moved his mouth back onto hers even as he continued to loosen the ties of her dress, while his other hand continued to travel up the smooth flesh of her thigh. He had to have more of her skin exposed to his eyes and mouth.

Finally, he had her dress loosened enough so he could sit up part way and tug gently at the material on her shoulders. She shimmied her shoulders, helping him pull down her dress. Her white chemise glowed in the moonlight as he got her dress past her breasts. Then he went to work on the ties of her chemise, but kept his other hand on her soft thigh. But he was losing patience. He didn't bother loosening her chemise very much, and instead, pulled it down over first one of her creamy shoulders and then the other.

He was rewarded with a gasp from her as the cool,

fresh night air hit her heated skin. He tried but failed to suppress a growl at the sight that met his hungry eyes. Her skin was nearly as pale and silky white as the material of her chemise. He let his eyes devour the swells of her pert breasts, each one tipped with a pink, hard nipple.

She writhed under him, reminding him that she still wanted more. He longed to give her everything she desired, but he also wanted her to be near mad with wanting, just as he was. He let his hand inch farther up her thigh, and her bent knee fell open slightly. He trailed his fingertips along the inside of her leg, leaning his head closer to her breasts. When he blew his hot breath against one of her nipples, she shuddered and arched, a moan slipping from her lips. He moved torturously slow, his own cock throbbing with need, but forced himself to let the pleasure build even higher in both of them.

Right as his fingertips brushed the damp crux of her legs, he brought his mouth down to capture one of her nipples. She inhales sharply, jerking and twisting under both his hand and his mouth. He let his tongue swirl and tease her nipple, just as he had with their kiss. Meanwhile, he drew one finger over her damp folds, then slipped it inside to glide and press against that button of a woman's pleasure. What he wouldn't give to taste and caress her there with his tongue, just as he was doing now to her nipple, then sink his aching cock all the way into her.

Just as he was about to come undone at the thought, he felt her hand brush against the front of his kilt, where his cock was pressed against her. He jerked his head up and locked eyes with her. She was panting through parted lips, her eyes half-lidded and hazy with pleasure as his finger continued to caress her.

"Do you feel it too?" she said breathily, gliding her hand gently over the swell in his kilt.

"Aye, lass," he managed through gritted teeth. If he had been about to come undone just at the feel of her wetness and the thought of sinking into her, he surely wasn't going to last under her tentative but curious touch.

He brought his hand out from under her skirts and took her wrist, gently guiding it underneath his kilt. He let her take her time brushing her fingers over his upper legs, but he jerked uncontrollably when she came into contact with his bollocks. Then her fingertips were exploring his shaft, and he nearly cursed.

When he couldn't take any more of her feathery touches, he took her hand in his and wrapped it around his length, moving both their hands up and down. In a moment, she caught on to the motion, and he let go of her hand, seeking her warm wetness once again.

They groaned in unison as they each stroked and teased the other. He lowered his head to her breast once more, capturing a nipple in his mouth and laving it before switching to the other to give it the same treatment. He could hear her breath coming even faster now, and he hitched up the rhythm of his stroke against her clitoris. She seemed to unconsciously do the same, pumping her hand faster around his cock. He was ready to explode, but he wanted her to join him.

He let one finger slip inside her opening while his thumb resumed the caress of that pleasurable spot just above. This must have sent her into another plane of sensation, for she called out his name and arched against his mouth.

Suddenly, she shuddered and cried out again, and he could feel her convulsing against his hand. It only took one more pulse of her hand around his cock to send him over the edge after her. He groaned and thrust into her hand, making the contact deeper as he spilled his seed.

He forced his eyes open despite the fact that he was spiraling down from his own ecstasy, wanting to drink in the sight of her. Her skin and hair were luminous in the moonlight, her breasts and cheeks faintly flushed from his kisses and her release. He could feel her bent leg quivering as he eased his hand from her and out from under her skirts.

Her eyes fluttered open and met his gaze. "That was…" She gave up searching for words and instead withdrew her hand from under his kilt, but quickly threw both arms around his neck, dragging him down to lie next to her on his plaid. She tossed a leg over one of his languidly, all traces of tension and shyness gone.

For some reason, though, her relaxation sent a

thread of apprehension through him. He tried to push away the voice that shouted admonishments inside his head, but he couldn't quite silence it. What was the harm in their sharing some pleasure while they could? It wasn't as if he had taken her virginity. They had merely scratched the itch that they clearly both had. But the voice wouldn't be silenced, for even though they hadn't done anything physically irreversible or permanent, he couldn't say the same for his growing and undeniable feelings for her.

Yes, he had come to care for the lass. It had started innocently enough when he thought her a simple but suspiciously evasive healer back at Dunbraes. But now that he saw her true character—her strength in the face of the hell she must have endured with a brother like Raef Warren, her genuine kindheartedness, and the ocean of passion within her just below the surface—he was becoming too attached.

Nothing could come of this, he told himself as she nestled her head against his shoulder, her hair smelling of sunshine and wildflowers.

Nothing.

Chapter Twenty-Four

Jossalyn felt the pull of sleep but resisted for a few seconds. She wanted to savor this moment—it might be the only one like it with Garrick. She still needed to tell him that she wanted not only to stay in Scotland, but also wanted to become directly involved in their fight for freedom. She hoped that after everything they had shared, he would understand and be willing to help her. But even if he wasn't, she wouldn't be deterred.

She would have to cross that bridge when she came to it, but for now, she wanted to soak in this moment, her head nestled against his shoulder, her body still humming from his touch. She'd had no idea what she had just experienced was possible—the aching need, the building pressure, and the flood of ecstasy that left her weak and limp like a milk-drunk kitten.

She let a smile creep to her lips at the thought that she had given the same experience to Garrick, both of them striving for and finding that tidal wave of pleasure with each other. She had always been told by her nursemaids and instructors on a lady's behavior that being intimate with a man—with her husband, only ever her husband—was her duty. They had always made it seem like it was something to be endured, that men would want it from her, but that she herself would never desire or enjoy it.

How wrong they were.

Was it always like this? She doubted very much that whichever old widower her brother would have selected for her could make her feel the way she did in Garrick's embrace. And she didn't want to find out. She would never again let someone else make decisions for her, especially when it came to finding a mate for life. She knew she shouldn't let herself indulge in girlish fantasies, but after all she and Garrick had shared, she suddenly saw the dim promise of a new path ahead of her. Though hazy, she could imagine a future filled with the kind of passion she had just discovered in herself—and maybe more.

Was it foolish of her to think she could share a love with someone who accepted her for who she was? Perhaps. But she had also once believed the kind of sensual fire she had just experienced didn't exist.

And was it foolish of her to think Garrick could be part of that future? She had tried before to push down her feelings for him, to not let herself grow too attached to him, and that was before she knew he was a Scottish freedom fighter and a deadly shot with a bow. She shouldn't let herself indulge in such sentimental wishing when she now knew he was a warrior, not likely to be tied down to one place—or one woman, for that matter.

But the truth was, she *did* wish, in her heart of hearts, that she would never have to say goodbye to Garrick again, that they could talk and touch and perhaps even laugh together—forever.

He would say it was too dangerous, that he was a warrior and she a healer, a masochistic match if there ever was one.

He would say he had his missions, that she would be at risk if she knew anything more.

But his words and his reasons rang hollow to her, and she had seen the look in his eyes as they brought each other pleasure. He was possessive of her, and protective. He hungered for her just as much as she hungered for him, but it was more than that.

The memory of his rage at the sight of the bruises her brother had inflicted, his words that her healing gift was valuable and special, his trust in her to heal Burke—he cared for her. And she couldn't deny that she cared for him too. Now she would just have to come up with a plan so that she could not only offer her healing skills to the Scottish rebellion, but also stay near Garrick—at least long enough for them to explore whatever was growing between them.

With this thought swirling through her mind, she finally succumbed to the pull of sleep within the warm embrace of Garrick's strong arms.

The cool morning air was tickling her neck, so Jossalyn

hunkered down deeper into the warmth of the plaid covering her and the heat of Garrick's skin. She jerked a little as she realized she was plastered against the wickedly handsome man with whom she had shared her body and her passion last night. One of her legs was thrown over his, and her head and arm rested on his chest. A powerful arm was wrapped around her, his hand absently stroking the curve of her waist.

"You're awake," he said into her hair.

She craned her neck so she could catch a glimpse of his face, but it was unreadable. "Have you been up long?"

"I didn't sleep much," he responded, more flatly than she had hoped after their night together.

"We have much to discuss," he went on.

"Yes, I have some things I wish to say," she said, trying to steel herself against both his apparent distance and the task of telling him her plan.

"We'd better get back to camp in case Burke needs you," he said, sitting up a little and forcing her to move her head.

She watched him closely as he stood and straightened his kilt. His mouth was in a firm line, the edges slightly downturned. He also seemed to be focusing on anything but her.

She sat up and reached behind her, trying to refasten the ties at the back of her dress. Sometime in the night, she must have pulled the fabric back over her shoulders for warmth, but the ties were now tangled and loose.

He must have noticed her struggling, for he knelt down behind her and silently helped her retie the ties. Once the task was done, he turned to the creek and splashed water over his hands and face, his back to her.

She stood and straightened out her dress as best as she could, trying not to let his distance get to her. Just as she had let her mind tumble through her thoughts and had come up with a plan that suited her, he had likely been chewing on what their intimate encounter meant and what to do about their uncertain future. She would just have to convince him that her plan would work—assuming that he, too, wanted to stay in her presence for at least a little while longer.

When he turned back to her, she opened her mouth, about to let all of her jumbled thoughts spill out, but he avoided making eye contact, and instead, snatched up the plaid, which they had used both to lie on and cover themselves. He shook it out without a word and turned to walk back toward their makeshift camp. She was left standing there for a moment, mouth still open, before hurrying after him.

He may be confused and worried, she thought, her temper flaring, but he didn't have to be rude. Just as she was about to cut into him with an accusation of ignoring her and their shared intimacy, he halted, and she nearly bumped into his back. She peered around his shoulder to see what had caused him to stop so abruptly.

Burke was standing in the middle of their camp, and looking right at them with a quizzical expression on his face.

"Burke! You're up! I mean, you're awake, and standing!" Even as she rushed to his side, she felt a flush of heat in her cheeks. Could he somehow tell what they had been doing last night? She felt so different in her own skin now that surely it was written plainly on her face.

"How long was I asleep?" he asked, letting her guide him to a nearby rock to sit.

"Two days," Garrick said flatly.

Burke's eyes widened at that. "What happened?"

"You passed out on your horse, so we had to stop here for a while. That wound was infected, and you had a fever. You shouldn't be up and about." She placed a hand on his forehead, but his skin was a normal, healthy warm.

She turned her attention to his leg and began unwrapping the bandage that covered the wound.

"Warren and his men came through the area while you were out," Garrick said grimly.

Suddenly, Burke was alert and focused on Garrick despite her handling of his bandages.

"They were looking for us, but they moved on without spotting us," Garrick went on. "They are cutting an arc back and forth across this entire area, moving northward."

Burke nodded, and then winced as the last covering

of bandage fell away and fresh air hit his leg.

Jossalyn gasped at the sight of the wound.

"What is it? Is it bad?" Suddenly Garrick was kneeling at her side, a crease between his brows.

"No, no, it's fine. It's better than fine," she replied in a rush. "The infection is gone, and the skin is healing nicely. All the stitches are intact, despite Burke standing on it." She shot a glare up at him, silently admonishing his behavior.

He smiled back widely. "We Sinclair men are harder to kill than that, lass."

"Sinclair or no, you still need to rest so the wound doesn't become infected again or you reopen it," she said sternly.

Burke and Garrick exchanged a dark look that told her they had other plans.

"If we cut due east, we should be able to get out of Warren's search path," Garrick said to Burke.

"That will slow us down," Burke replied.

"Only by a day, two at most. It's better than running into Warren and more than a dozen of his mounted, armored soldiers."

Burke nodded, his eyes focusing on the distance as he thought. "If we head due east, then cut north, you and I will both be pointed toward our destinations."

Both men seemed to remember Jossalyn all of a sudden, who was kneeling between them, looking back and forth as they spoke. They turned their eyes on her, both frowning in thought, and she suddenly felt distinctly like a problem that needed fixing.

"Have you told her about your brother or the Br—"

"Nay," Garrick interjected quickly.

"Actually," Jossalyn jumped in, shooting a look at Garrick before turning to Burke, "I know you two work for the Scottish rebellion and that you are on some mission that is likely connected to Robert the Bruce. Also, I know that you two are working in secret against my brother."

Burke raised an eyebrow at Garrick. "And how do you know all that, lass?"

"Garrick told me some of it, and it wasn't hard after seeing you two don kilts and wield weapons against the English. Garrick seems to be holding something back, though, because he says it's too dangerous for me to know everything."

Garrick gave a slight shake of his head in response to Burke's questioning look. They seemed to understand their unspoken communication.

Burke turned back to Jossalyn. "And what do you make of all this, my lady healer?"

She chewed her lip for a moment, unsure of how much of her plan she wanted to reveal. She had hoped to explain everything to Garrick in private, since it partially involved their—whatever it was between them. She had also hoped to explain things when he was receptive and open to what she had to say. At the moment, he was alternating between shooting his scowl at Burke and her, his eyes hard and sharp.

She took a breath and dove in. "I know you two are working for Robert the Bruce, but you apparently have different destinations. Based on what Garrick has told me, I'm guessing one of you is going back to the secret headquarters of the rebellion." She lifted her chin slightly. "And I'm going with you."

Both men were suddenly speaking at once, denying her claims and telling her there was no way she was going with them.

"No way in hell," Garrick said forcefully.

She let them carry on for another moment, and then held up her hand and waited for them to fall silent.

"I'm not asking, I'm telling you what I'm going to do. I decided a long time ago"—it was only a matter of days, but they didn't need to know that—"that I would escape my brother and live a life of my choosing in Scotland. At first, I thought I could live anonymously in some quiet village, working as a healer and making decisions for myself."

She sighed, forcing herself to let go of that path. "After overhearing Raef's words yesterday, though, I realize now that his hatred, his disdain, both for me and for all of Scotland and its people, goes deeper than I ever knew. I will never go back to him, but I can't be entirely sure that I would be safe from him or someone who would report back to him, even in the most remote of villages."

Garrick nodded grudgingly at her words. Good. At

least he agreed with her on this last point. She went on.

"So, as I'm sure you have both realized, I'm stuck. I can't go back to the Borderlands or England. I have no family other than my brother, and I doubt I would go unnoticed for long among so many of my brother's allies. And I can't simply plop myself down in the middle of Scotland, going about my life, as if a young English healer wouldn't eventually draw notice."

"You'll forgive us, lass, but that pretty much sums up our problem with you," Burke said apologetically. "I believe you've saved my life, and we—along with all those who are depending on us—are grateful to you for that. But we can't very well take you with us any farther. Garrick is right. You are in danger by being in our presence. We are both needed elsewhere, in places an English lass shouldn't know about, let alone go."

"But that's just it," she said, her voice straining with excitement. "What better or safer place is there for me than hidden away at the secret headquarters of the Scottish rebellion?"

Both men quirked an eyebrow at her, and she could suddenly see their blood relation in their skeptical look.

"Hear me out," she began. "The rumors have been swirling around Dunbraes for years now about some sort of moving camp out of which the Bruce and his rebels fight. But despite the English army's efforts—not to mention my brother's searching and raiding—it has never been found. I wouldn't be surrounded by curious and potentially talkative villagers. I'd be hidden among Scottish rebels who would have no interest in spreading word of my presence, especially not if it meant helping my brother in any way. I know he is well-known and reviled in many parts of Scotland."

Garrick began to argue with her, but Burke held up a hand, cocking his head to the side to indicate she should go on.

"Most importantly, though, the Bruce's camp is the place where my skills would be needed the most," she said firmly.

"But why would you want to help the Scottish rebellion?" Garrick said sharply. He took a breath and went on in a slightly gentler tone. "I know your brother was cruel to you and didn't allow you to practice your healing art, so I understand why you wouldn't want to go back to living under his control. But you are English."

She caught the implication behind his words and lowered her eyes, hurt that he would question her motives simply because of her nationality.

"The country of one's birth doesn't always align with one's true home," she said quietly. "As I've told you before, ever since we moved to the Borderlands, I have felt an...affinity with Scotland and its people. I understand the desire for freedom, and I think everyone should have a chance to live as they choose without being crushed under a more powerful force."

She willed herself to meet his gaze again. His gray

eyes were stormy, but she didn't drop her gaze, trying to show him that she wouldn't be deterred.

"I want to help with the cause for independence, and the best way I know how to do that is by healing those who are sick or injured. What better place to help the ill and wounded than within an army?"

"She makes an excellent point, Garrick," Burke said cautiously.

Garrick cursed quietly and ran a hand through his hair, searching the sky for answers. But Jossalyn didn't want to give him a chance to formulate another objection. She had one more arrow in her quiver.

"You said before that I saved your life, Burke. Well, you both saved *my* life. I doubt I could have survived much longer under my brother's rule. Consider us even—a life for a life. Now I am going to go find Robert the Bruce's secret camp and offer my healing skills to him and his army. You can either help me find him, or at least take me farther north, or you can go on without me and I'll travel northward alone."

Burke and Garrick exchanged a laden look. They seemed to be communicating silently with each other again, so she waited, folding her hands in her lap. She was proud of herself for saying her piece and not backing down, even in the face of Garrick's fierce glare.

Finally, Garrick spoke, though he sounded weary. "As I said before, we will head due east for a day's worth of travel before heading north." He turned and began to walk toward where he had hidden the horses, apparently ending the conversation.

"Does that mean I'm going with you?" Jossalyn said, glancing back and forth between the two men.

"Aye, lass, it does," Burke said, a tired smile on his face.

"But we can't leave right now," she said, suddenly alarmed.

"Why not?" Garrick said irritably, turning on his heels back toward her.

"Burke needs more time to rest and regain his strength," she said firmly. "You can't expect him to simply jump on a horse again after two days of battling a fever and infection."

Though Burke began to protest that he was fine, she crossed her arms over her chest resolutely.

Garrick sighed, and then surprised her by saying "The lass is right. We could all use a bit more rest. Besides, we haven't had more than dried meat and hardtack for days." He glanced up at the sky, gauging the position of the morning sun. "We can rest for the day, then travel at night. I'd guess Warren and his men are well to the northwest of us now, but we stand a better chance of going unseen at night anyway."

Though he had just said they should rest, Jossalyn felt a surge of excitement and energy course through her. "I'll prepare you another bandage and some tea, Burke," she said, jumping to her feet.

Burke's eyes suddenly locked on her hair, and he stood up next to her, still keeping most of his weight on his good leg. "Is that a leaf in your hair, lass?" he said, drawing away a green leaf from her tresses, which had completely come undone from her braid last night as she and Garrick had been—

She could feel Burke's eyes boring into her, though she kept her gaze on her feet, afraid her face would give something away. Nevertheless, she could feel the heat rising to her cheeks under his scrutiny.

"Why were you both down at the creek when I awoke?" he said carefully, shifting his gaze to Garrick.

Garrick coughed but managed to answer. "We were fetching some water. For tea. For you," he said haltingly.

Burke glanced around their small camp, then said pointedly back to Garrick, "Funny. I don't see any water."

"We forgot the waterskin. I'll go get it now," Garrick answered quickly, turning away so he wouldn't have to answer any more of Burke's suspicious questions.

Jossalyn, unfortunately, didn't have any such errand to escape Burke's gaze. He turned back to her, one eyebrow raised. "Be careful, lass," he said quietly. "Garrick is dangerous, and I don't just mean with a bow. He cares about his work above all else, and he fancies himself a villain because of it. He may need more healing than even you could manage."

She opened her mouth, fumbling for words to deny Burke's implied assumption about Garrick and her relationship, or to argue against Garrick's self-imposed label as a bad man, but she couldn't manage to formulate anything that didn't smack of defensiveness or outright blindness. Finally, she closed her mouth and only nodded.

Chapter Twenty-Five

The three of them passed the day in near silence. Garrick returned with water, and as he built a fire, Jossalyn went about preparing fresh bandages and tea for Burke. Though insistent that he was fine, Burke stayed seated as much as possible and looked more tired than usual. At one point, Garrick disappeared for about an hour, but when he returned he had a rabbit and several wild carrots and onions in his hands, his bow and quiver slung over one shoulder. They made a simple stew over the fire, and the food seemed to revitalize Burke somewhat. Eventually, though, he crawled back into his shelter and slept a few more hours in the afternoon.

"You should do the same," Garrick said, nodding toward Burke's prone form inside his shelter.

This was the first time they had been alone and able to talk since they had woken in each other's arms. The memory caused Jossalyn to blush, but she didn't want to launch into a discussion of all that had passed between them right now. She had said the most important part of her goal already—to join the Scottish rebellion. She felt weary at the prospect of another battle with Garrick, especially if it would be a battle in which they were on opposite sides of the issue of their feelings for each other.

So instead of talking more, she only nodded and headed toward her shelter. She still had one of Garrick's plaids, which she had been using as a pillow. Once she had laid her head down on it and closed her eyes, though, his masculine scent, faint but lingering, invaded her senses. Strangely, she found it comforting. She let the scent envelope her as she drifted off to sleep for a few short hours before their journey would continue.

Garrick knew he needed sleep too. They were going to travel through the night, and he had been restless the night before. But he had even more to chew on now than he had last night.

On top of the impossible bind he found himself in—both wanting Jossalyn more than anything and knowing that he couldn't have her—now he was going to take her with him to the Bruce's camp.

This was exactly what he had been trying to avoid. It put her in too much danger to be so close to the wars and battles in the middle of which he always found himself. She had made a compelling case, but it didn't stop him from doubting the sanity of bringing an English lady—and Raef Warren's sister, no less—right into the middle of the Bruce's resistance operation.

For one thing, he still had lingering doubts about her allegiance. He hated himself for being so suspicious and untrusting, but thinking the worst of people—nay, thinking realistically—had saved his life more than once. He believed she identified with Scotland's struggle for freedom, and that she wanted to be in a place where her healing gift would help the most number of people. But the memory of her grabbing his arrow just as he was about to shoot Warren still chaffed. If push came to shove, would she side with her brother, or with the Scots?

Even assuming she would be loyal to his people, there was the problem of the Bruce's men themselves. Garrick doubted they would trust her, especially if they knew who she was related to. If they didn't accept her into the camp, she would be in more danger than she was now. They could turn on her, or simply let it be known that an English healer lass was in their presence. Word would get back to Warren eventually, Garrick was sure of it.

The one glimmer of hope he allowed himself to indulge in was the thought of her being in the Bruce's camp with him. It meant that instead of days, they might have weeks together—until the Bruce sent him on another secret mission.

But would having more time in each other's presence only make things harder on both of them? A small part of him had hoped that by sating their lust for each other last night, the razor-sharp passion between them would be dulled. He would have scratched an itch that was long overdue, given the fact that he hadn't been in the company of a lass in a long while. And she would have gotten to explore her newfound sexual desires with someone who wouldn't take her virginity. That could have been it.

But he knew such a possibility was a long-shot to begin with. He hadn't been terribly surprised when his desire for her hadn't been blunted at all by their encounter.

What he hadn't anticipated was that his longing for her, body and mind, would redouble in force. He wanted her more than ever before, the memory of her body writhing in pleasure, his name on her lips, her hand touching his—Christ, he had to keep his mind on track.

That was precisely the problem. With Jossalyn around the Bruce's camp, Garrick didn't fully trust himself to be able to think clearly, let alone act as one of the Bruce's top advisors and warriors. And what would happen once he was sent off on another mission? He would be forced to leave Jossalyn, the most beautiful, tantalizing, enthralling woman he had ever met, in the middle of a camp filled with randy and virile Scottish warriors. He forced himself to release his jaw, which had clenched at the mere thought.

He should just be grateful that he had gotten to spend any time with her at all. He was a lucky and undeserving bastard. Perhaps instead of worrying about the future, he should just enjoy what he had while he had it.

With that thought, he hunkered down on the ground in front of the dying fire. The sun was already sloping toward afternoon. He had a few hours left to rest before they would start the next leg of their journey northward. He might as well enjoy the dreams of Jossalyn that were sure to lace his sleep.

Jossalyn woke to a little shake of her shoulder. She tried to ignore it and reenter her dream, which had involved Garrick's hands, lips, and tongue, but the soft shake came again. She muttered and turned away from the hand on her shoulder, only to hear a faint chuckle behind her. Garrick's husky laugh sent a thrill through her, blending her sensual dream with an image of his smiling face in her foggy, half-awake brain.

"You are fussier than an old cat, lass."

She jerked upright, fully awake now.

"I've let you sleep as long as I can, but the sun has set, and Burke and the horses are ready. It's time to head out."

The teasing lingered in his voice at first, but then he turned into the serious warrior she was becoming familiar with. He was leaning into her shelter, the warmth of his body invading the small space.

Despite her excitement to be headed toward Robert the Bruce's secret camp, she felt obligated to say, "I still think it is too soon for Burke to travel."

"I think he and I will both go stir-crazy if we are pinned down like a fox in its den with your brother and his men sweeping the area," he said with a raised eyebrow.

She nodded and picked up his plaid, which she had been sleeping on, and extended it toward him.

"Nay, keep it, lass," he said quietly. "You can use it tonight as we ride if you need to. The nights have been cool."

She averted her eyes, remembering how warm the previous night had been when she was pressed against him and tucked snugly under his plaid. He retreated out of the shelter, and she followed, hoping her cheeks weren't as bright red as the Sinclair colors in her hand.

Just as Garrick had said, everything was ready for their departure. The air was the pale blue of early twilight, but she could make out Burke standing next to his horse, leaning his weight on one leg. Garrick helped boost him into the saddle, and Burke managed to swing his leg over his horse, grunting slightly. Then Garrick mounted his own horse and guided the animal over to where she stood.

He extended a hand to her, which she took, and was immediately lifted into the air. Garrick pulled her in front of him so that she was straddling his horse, her back and bottom plastered to his front. The position was familiar to her now, but it nevertheless sent a shiver of heat through her.

As he nudged his horse forward, reining it eastward, she took a quick look back over her shoulder at their temporary camp. No trace of their presence remained. It was odd, she thought, because she would never forget this spot for as long as she lived.

It was where she had decided to join the Scottish rebellion.

It was where she had shared her body with Garrick, their pleasure intertwining next to that slow-moving creek.

It was where she had come alive.

She turned her head forward again, ready to meet her future.

Chapter Twenty-Six

Despite his best efforts to remind himself of all the reasons why he didn't deserve the lass riding in front of him on Fletch's back—why he didn't deserve happiness at all—Garrick felt joy seeping into his limbs.

Jossalyn's hair kept brushing his face, and the combination of her scent and her soft, slim body pressed against him was becoming familiar yet thrillingly tantalizing. Burke had come through the fever, and his leg, though still healing, would eventually be fine. And he was headed back toward Robert the Bruce's camp—once they turned northward anyway—where he would be able to deliver the news of Longshanks's death and complete this mission. With Jossalyn at his side.

Though the fears and worries still bubbled up through his growing happiness, it felt as though the decision were already made, and since Jossalyn was coming with him to the Bruce's camp, he might as well enjoy their connection. Despite all the odds, despite his dark deeds as part of the Scottish resistance, and his attempts to resist what now seemed inevitable, they were together for this journey, and they sought the same destination—the Bruce's headquarters.

They even both sought the same work, in a way. They both wanted to help the Bruce and the other Scottish rebels achieve their freedom. He still didn't dare let himself get carried away in his imagination, but a seed of hope was beginning to take root in his mind. Perhaps there was a chance they could have a future together. He knew he should just be grateful for the time he had with her now, but he was greedy. He wanted more of her.

He let himself indulge in the pleasurable ache for her throughout the long night as they cut eastward across the Lowlands. He savored the moment when she leaned back against his chest about halfway through the night, her head tucked under his chin and her body warm and limp in his arms. He let her wildflower scent wrap around him. He even gave over the lead to Burke, allowing himself to simply follow his cousin instead of cut the path himself as he relished the feel of her against him. She slept like that for a few hours, but all too soon the sky began to lighten with the first traces of dawn, and she slowly came awake.

"I'm sorry," she said softly, turning her head slightly over her shoulder. "I didn't mean to fall—"

"Rest all you like, lass. I don't mind." And he meant it. He wasn't thinking about the fastest path back to the Bruce and his camp at the moment. He was here with her now.

Suddenly, Burke reined in his horse and cursed.

Garrick tore his eyes away from Jossalyn's upturned face and followed Burke's gaze. They had come upon a clearing in the woods, and the pre-dawn light revealed a small cottage along with a barn and shed nearby.

But something was wrong.

Instead of a trail of smoke winding out of the cottage's chimney, there was smoke rising from one of the corners of the thatched roof. Or what was left of the thatched roof. The charred remains of the thatch appeared black in the bluish light, and though one corner still smoked, it looked like the fire had been out for several hours.

The glen was dead quiet.

Instinctively, Garrick reached for his bow, which was sticking partway out of one of his saddlebags. Burke's hand was already on the sword at his waist. Garrick clutched the bow, but there was nothing to shoot at, and besides, Jossalyn's position in front of him would prevent him from firing an accurate shot anyway. She suddenly tensed, seeing the cabin and apparently sensing the men's alertness.

He swung down from the saddle but didn't reach up to pull her to the ground after him. Instead, he placed the reins in her hand.

"Stay on Fletch's back, lass," he said in a low voice. "If anything happens, I want you to kick him as hard as you can and guide him toward the north." He indicated the direction with the curved end of his bow, and then locked eyes with her, making sure she understood.

She swallowed and nodded, her eyes wide and dark green in the dim light. He pulled his quiver out of his saddlebag and slung it over his shoulder, keeping his bow firmly gripped in his hand. Burke had already dismounted and had drawn his sword all the way. The two men made eye contact, each giving the other a little nod. Then they slowly approached the cottage, both sweeping their half of the glen with their eyes, weapons at the ready. Nothing moved except for the grass around each man's feet, and the glen was silent and still.

When they were about halfway to the cottage, Garrick thought he made out a dark lump in the high grass, but he wasn't sure. He slowly stepped closer.

Jossalyn's scream cut through the silence like a knife.

He spun around, an arrow already nocked and his bowstring drawn back to his cheek. Jossalyn still sat atop Fletch at the edge of the forest, but her eyes were locked on something on the ground off to her right. Garrick shot Burke a quick glance, and after Burke's nod to him, Garrick sprinted back toward Jossalyn, the tip of his arrow lowered but the bow still half-draw and at the ready.

As he drew nearer, he could make out the look of horror that was transforming Jossalyn's delicate features. Once at her side, he let his eyes follow the line of her gaze. Several feet away in the forest's undergrowth, he saw a small shoe. His eyes trailed farther still, and when he saw what had caused Jossalyn to scream, he swallowed hard.

A child lay motionless in the underbrush, face-up and open-eyed.

His throat was slit.

Garrick unnocked the arrow and slipped it back into his quiver, then quickly slung his bow over his shoulder and turned to Jossalyn. Her eyes were wide and horror-stricken, her mouth open, but no scream came out.

"Jossalyn, sweeting, look at me," he said quietly at Fletch's side. "Look at me, Jossalyn," he said more firmly when she remained frozen.

She didn't respond or seem to have heard him, so he wrapped his hands around her waist and pulled her down from Fletch's back. Fletch was now between her and the child's lifeless body, and she was forced to tear her eyes away from the scene. He took her chin in his hands and leaned into her face, locking his eyes on hers.

"Jossalyn, listen to me. No matter what, that boy was innocent. Do you hear me? No matter what happened, that boy is in heaven now. Jossalyn, he is in heaven now, and nothing can hurt him."

She blinked. His words may have penetrated to the recesses of her mind, but she didn't show it. She stared blankly at him for a moment, and then furrowed her brow.

"Where is the rest of his family? He is too young to be playing in the woods by himself. Where is his family?" She spoke in a detached tone that frightened him. She began walking toward the cabin, muttering, "Where is his family?" under her breath. She sounded like she would chastise the boy's parents for letting the child into the forest by himself, as if he hadn't been murdered and left there to rot.

He tried to grip her arm to stop her from going farther into the glen, but she shook him off and walked faster.

"Jossalyn, don't!" Burke shouted from the cottage's doorway. He had sheathed his sword and poked his head inside, but his face was hard and tight from whatever he had seen within.

But it was too late. She had made it halfway across the glen, Garrick hurrying behind her, when she halted dead in her tracks. She had reached the dark lump in the grass that had been indiscernible to Garrick earlier in the pre-dawn dimness.

Now he saw that it was another body.

A woman's body. She lay face-down in the tall grass of the glen, but her skirts were pulled up and twisted around her waist. Suddenly, Jossalyn turned away and retched into the grass.

Garrick hardened himself to the sight before him on the ground. He had seen the likes before. He hated himself for turning off inside, but it was the only way he knew how to cope with the sight of the violation and slaughter of women and children. He knelt briefly by the woman's side, tugging her skirts down so that at least she had some dignity in death. He whispered a prayer for her as Burke came to his side, limping slightly. His cousin was grim-faced and ashen, even in the warming light of the pre-dawn sky.

Garrick indicated toward the woods and said quietly, "A child."

Burke nodded and swallowed, then jutted his chin toward the cabin. "It's burned out in there, but there was another…a girl…"

He couldn't go on, but he didn't have to. Garrick could picture perfectly another murdered child, but because she was a girl, she had likely been raped like her mother. Garrick turned his back on the entire scene, fearing that like Jossalyn, he would become sick. She had finished retching in the grass and was slowly pulling herself upright as she dragged a shaky hand over her mouth. He strode to her side, then took her by the arm and walked her to the opposite edge of the forest, so that her back was to the glen.

On the other side of the glen, she suddenly seemed to come to pieces. A moan escaped her, and she leaned limply toward him. He wrapped his arms around her, steadying her as sobs racked her body. He felt useless and hollow but tried to give her every last shred of himself as she cried into his shoulder. He stroked her hair, whispering every endearment he could think of. When his English ran out, he switched to Gaelic, murmuring all the sweet words his nursemaid used to say whenever he or his brothers were sick.

The sky grew lighter, and then the sun cracked over the horizon and through the trees at the edge of the forest where they stood. Garrick was vaguely aware that Burke had moved slowly around the glen, finishing their sweep of the area and gathering their horses, and was now approaching. Jossalyn's crying was slowing and quieting, and eventually, she placed a hand on his chest, pushing back a bit so she was standing upright on her own two feet. He kept his hands on her upper arms to steady her, though. She wiped both hands across her face, drying the tears with the sleeves of her dress. She took a few deep breaths, trying to regain some composure.

"What happened here?" she said finally. Her voice was cracked and dry from her sobs.

Garrick exchanged a look with Burke, weighing how much to tell her.

"The English," he finally said simply.

A look of shock and horror briefly returned to her face. "What do you mean? You think the English did this?"

Garrick nodded. It chilled him, but he knew it was the truth. He only wished she hadn't had to face the horrible reality that was his world. Death. Rape. Razed villages. Murdered children. This was his life. He had immersed himself in it, lived with it, and returned kill for kill. He knew he still had a shred of honor—he had never violated women or killed children—but he doled out death to the English, just as they doled it out to the Scottish. Now she would finally see him for what he was. Now his beautiful, foolish dream of a future with Jossalyn would be over. He steeled himself, closing himself off to the pain just as he did at the sight of death.

He turned and took Fletch's reins, preparing to mount.

"That's it? How do you know this was done by the English? You are just leaving?" Her voice rose in anger as he swung into his saddle.

"I can explain more later, but I don't plan on lingering here any longer," he said, a bit more curtly than he had intended.

"But what about the b—the bodies?"

He couldn't quite suppress a flinch. It was despicable, but they would have to leave them as they were. "If whoever did this comes back through the area, they will know someone else was here and may still be nearby. Avoiding detection is our best chance to get to the north in one piece."

"He's right, lass," Burke said, far more gently than Garrick would ever be able to manage.

For some reason, he hated his cousin for a moment. He was always able to find the right words, to be kind and understanding, while Garrick was rough and curt. Of course, Burke's ability to think and act smoothly on his feet had saved them more than once, but some small part of him was jealous that compared to Burke, he was a walking, talking sledge hammer.

Jossalyn suddenly looked exhausted. There were dark smudges under her red-rimmed eyes, and her shoulders slumped forward like it was an effort just to stay upright. She didn't say anything, but walked over to Fletch and extended her hand to be pulled up into the saddle, though she didn't make eye contact with Garrick. Once she and Burke were both settled, he spurred Fletch due north. The time for dallying was long gone.

Chapter Twenty-Seven

By the time they stopped a few hours later, Jossalyn was numb inside. She didn't speak as Garrick helped her down, or as he forced some dried biscuits and meat, along with his waterskin, into her hands. She took a few bites, but the food tasted like sand in her mouth. The water helped rinse away the taste of sickness that lingered in the back of her throat, but she only managed to take a few sips.

Yet even as she retreated into herself, struggling to comprehend what she had seen back at the glen, several questions whispered in the recesses of her mind. She had let them wash over her as they had ridden hard toward the north, but now they were ready to bubble over.

"You never answered me," she said finally, startling both Garrick and Burke, who had sunken into the silence and were leaning over a small fire that Burke had built. "How do you know that it was the English?" For some reason, her mind rejected the idea that her countrymen—former countrymen, she reminded herself—could do such things to innocent people.

Garrick recovered from his surprise first, but his gray eyes turned hard and flat. "Why do you doubt that it was?" he asked quietly.

He didn't say it, but she caught his implication. She claimed to be sympathetic to the Scots, but when it came down to it, she was still English—and always would be.

She faltered for a moment, unsure of herself. Why did she resist the idea that Englishmen could do such horrible things? She had heard whispered stories of atrocities on both sides, but seeing for herself was different than hearing rumors. "I just...I don't know how you can be so sure. I have heard before that the Scots raid each other's lands and even have blood feuds—"

Garrick spat into the fire, startling her. "Lass, feuding clans steal sheep from each other. They don't rape and murder women and children," he said vehemently.

She jumped and leaned back from him slightly at his tone and words.

"Easy, cousin," Burke said lowly, putting a hand on Garrick's arm.

He shrugged it off and stood. "If you want the truth, lass, that was in all likelihood the work of your brother and his soldiers." The words came out cold, but Garrick's eyes flamed with gray fire.

She was so shocked at his words that she jerked upright from her seat next to the fire and took several steps backward.

"Garrick." Burke's voice was laden with warning.

"She wanted the truth, didn't she?" Garrick said, turning his anger on Burke. "She should be able to face the realities of war—of England's tyranny over Scotland—before she joins the war effort. Perhaps now that she knows what happens to Scotswomen under English invasion, she'll no longer want to adopt the Scottish cause. Maybe she'll finally want to go home to her brother."

She closed the distance between them in two strides. Before she knew what she was doing, she raised her hand and slapped him across the face as hard as she could.

He saw the slap coming but stood still. He deserved it. He was spewing out all his anger toward the English at her, like her nationality was her fault, or that she had caused not only the scene back at the glen but the countless others like it he had seen over the years.

But it went deeper than that. She had to know the truth—about the war, about the English, and about himself.

He hadn't liked the idea of her joining the war effort from the beginning. Though she was a gifted healer and her skills would surely be valuable to the rebellion, the thought of her having to face the realities of their battles against the English disturbed him. She obviously already knew how cruel her brother was. But he had assumed that since she sympathized with the Scots, she understood the low tactics English soldiers and their commanders stooped to in order to control and oppress the Scots.

But perhaps it was worse than simple naiveté on her part. Maybe she still felt the need to defend the English for their behavior. The thought chilled him, for he didn't want to doubt her, but twice now she had hesitated when it came to recognizing the cruelties of her brother and the English, and he had to remind himself that blood ties and birth origins couldn't just be sloughed off with a change of location.

Even if his doubts about her loyalty were misplaced, the fact remained that she was deeply averse to war and its results—as she should be. Most people didn't live as close to the violence and death as he did. He was proud to aid the Bruce and the Scottish rebellion in the best way he could—with his bow—but he could no longer deceive himself that the tenderness and strength of one lass could save him from all he had seen and done. He was past redemption.

It sickened him to push her away like this, to make her see the fact that he wasn't some knight in shining armor, but he had indulged his fantasy too long.

He kept his hands clenched at his sides, feeling the sting in his cheek slowly fade. She stood in front of him, panting, her hands balled at her sides as well.

"Are we done now, lass?" he said lowly. Surely now she would be through with arguing, but more, she would be through with *him* and the nightmare into which he had dragged her.

She inhaled sharply through her nose, and then intentionally unclenched her hands. "No, we are not done. We need to talk about all of this further."

He had been bracing himself for her rejection, for her to turn her back on him and leave his life forever, with only the faint memory of brief happiness to hold onto during the long, cold nights alone on some mission. That kind of pain would have been sharp, and he was ready for it, but he wasn't prepared for her to say that they needed to talk things through. Suddenly, he felt the anger and tension leave his body, to be replaced by confusion and uncertainty.

Burke coughed surreptitiously, breaking the silence that stretched as Garrick and Jossalyn stared at each other. "I think I'll scout the area. I'll be gone at least two hours." With that, he quietly slipped away into the surrounding forest and left them alone.

"What do you mean, we need to talk?" Despite his surprise at her words, Garrick still spoke in a guarded tone.

She sighed and wrapped her arms around herself. "I'm sorry I slapped you," she said, not addressing his question.

"I deserved it."

"Why do you think my brother and his men were responsible for…for what happened back in that clearing?" She sounded weary rather than angry this time.

He scrubbed a hand over his face, feeling exhausted

himself. "They were coming from the east when they passed our camp. They could have come across the cottage as they cut northwest in one of their sweeps."

She swallowed, and tears shimmered in her eyes again.

"It could have been some other band of Englishmen looking to cause trouble and send a message to the Scots," he said gently, trying to ease her pain. "But..."

"What? Tell me."

"Raef Warren is known to have done similar things elsewhere in Scotland," Garrick said reluctantly. She didn't need to picture her brother doing such terrible things to more innocent people, but Garrick had been on Sinclair lands when the English swept through four years ago. They had waged war not just on the Scottish warriors, but also on the small villages and crofts filled with women and children.

She sat down hard on the ground all of a sudden. "I know he is capable of such things," she said, her voice pinched with emotion.

He knelt next to her, struggling to think of something to say or do to ease her suffering. Tears had begun streaming down her cheeks, but she swallowed her sobs, visibly trying to maintain some of her composure.

"Jossalyn, you don't have to be a part of this." To his ears, his own voice was low but slightly strained. "You can still leave. Go back to England and make a new life for yourself in some small village. Or stay in Scotland but don't join the war effort." Saying these words was hard, but it was the right thing to do. He couldn't be selfish. He had to let her go.

Her face transformed from pained control to shock. "But don't you see? This is exactly why I want to join the fight for Scottish freedom!"

He furrowed his brow. He didn't see.

Perceiving his confusion, she went on. "I can't stand the thought of living in a world where such terrible things happen, where the strongest and meanest get their way at any cost. Maybe I am foolish to think the world could be any different than that, but I at least want to try to make it better."

He was stunned for a moment by her conviction and strength. She had explained her reasons for wanting to help the Scottish cause before, but perhaps he hadn't truly listened to her. He had likely immediately started to calculate all the reasons why it was too dangerous for a lass—for a lass he cared so much about—to involve herself, rather than actually listen to her commitment to do what she thought was right. Aye, he would still worry about her, but who was he to try to control her or take away her ability to pursue her sense of duty and justice?

"I owe you an apology, lass," he said, lowering his head. "I should have listened to you before when you made your mission clear. I won't doubt you again."

She seized his hands in hers, bringing his eyes back

up. Her tears were drying now, and her eyes were wide and bright with surprise. "Do you mean it?"

"Of course. I was harsh with my words before, but I hope you can forgive me for worrying about you. I just...don't want any harm to come to you," he said haltingly.

Suddenly, she was in his arms. She flung her arms around his neck and slammed into his chest, pressing her face into his shoulder. He nearly toppled backward out of his crouched position but managed to stay upright.

"And I won't question your loyalty again, either," he said into her golden hair. "You've more than proved yourself. You saved Burke's life, and you could have alerted your brother to our location back inside that shelter, but you didn't. I think I've been suspicious of people too long and couldn't see what was right in front of me."

She pulled back a little and looked up into his face with those wide emerald eyes. "And what was in front of you?"

His chest squeezed in a strange but not entirely painful way. Now was the time to speak the truth of his feelings. He had first tried to deny and downplay them, then ignore them, and finally prayed they wouldn't leave him a broken man when he thought that he and Jossalyn would be forced to part ways.

"You are the bravest, strongest, most beautiful lass I have ever known." He let his hand brush against her strawberries-and-cream cheek, soaking in its velvety softness.

She closed her eyes for a moment at his touch, and he couldn't read her for a fraction of a second. A flicker of fear stabbed him. What if she didn't feel the same way?

But then her eyes opened again, and he was drowning in their green depths. They shone with emotion, but instead of pain, they radiated deep joy. Then, suddenly, a shy smile crept to her lips.

"Garrick, I have tried for a while now to…not think about you—about us—but I can't seem to help it," she said, lowering her eyes as she struggled to find her words.

"I have been having the same problem, lass," he said, capturing her chin in his hand and raising it so her eyes met his again.

"And have you come to any solutions?" she said with a slightly arched eyebrow.

He felt the corners of his mouth quirk. "Aye, I have, but they all involve things that are not polite to talk about in front of a lady."

Her eyes widened, and a rosy bloom appeared on each of her cheeks. He couldn't help it. A chuckle rumbled in his chest at how enjoyable it was to get a rise out of her. But he sobered quickly, returning to the problem both of them seemed to be struggling with.

"I have also thought myself in circles about what might lay ahead for us."

She furrowed her brow. "I...enjoy your company greatly. But I also want to go to Robert the Bruce's camp and work as a healer."

For some reason, her words conjured an image of her tucked safely behind some castle's fortified walls, running a keep and busying herself with needlework or some other occupation for ladies. It was all wrong. She would wither like a plucked wildflower if she were kept inside or forced to abandon her healing practice.

He suddenly realized that she was warning him. She wouldn't be happy as a lady-wife inside some fortified castle. He had never let himself go so far as to fantasize that they could be together for life, but now that the thought had entered his mind, he knew that they would never have a traditional union.

Instead of frightening him, though, he felt a wave of hope at the realization. One of his fears had been that he could never have a wife or family because of his work with the Bruce. But with Jossalyn joining him at the Bruce's camp...

"Do we have to choose, lass?"

"What do you mean?"

"I'm going to the Bruce's camp also. And I greatly enjoy your company as well." He emphasized his words by letting his thumb brush across her lower lip. She shuddered involuntarily.

When she could speak, she said, "Are you saying...are we saying that...?"

"You captivate me, lass. I can't lie to myself or you

any longer. I care about you, and I want to…enjoy your company more." He let all his shades of meaning come through in his voice with those last words.

It was clear she understood him, for another blush washed over her face.

"I want that too."

Her words struck him, causing his chest to squeeze again. He couldn't believe he had been able to speak what had been growing inside of him the entire time he had known her. Even more astonishing, she felt the same way about him.

Her lips parted again, but he was done talking. He needed to feel her, taste her, communicate to her how much he longed for her in a way that didn't involve words. Without waiting, he brought his mouth down on hers in a searing kiss.

Chapter Twenty-Eight

If Jossalyn had thought that Garrick's words would undo her with the flood of emotion they caused, nothing could prepare her for his kiss. It branded her, seared her to her core with its passion and intensity. She let herself be washed away in the torrent of sensation and emotion.

His hands were everywhere at once—in her hair, on her waist, running up and down her back. She registered vaguely that her hands, too, seemed to have a mind of their own. They gripped his shoulders, circled his neck, tangled in his hair as she pulled herself closer to him. Even pressed fully against his chest, with their mouths locked, she wanted more. She wanted to be completely intertwined with him.

She had tried to deny how much she longed to be with him, and then tried to live with the thought of only having a short amount of time left to be in his presence. But now that they had spoken honestly with each other about their feelings, she was overwhelmed by the strength of her desire. She was tired of denying her true feelings and tired of forcing herself to settle for what little she could have with him. Now she wanted it all.

She moaned a little against his mouth, impatiently tugging at the ties at the neck of his shirt. She didn't know how to voice her longing, so she tried to communicate it to him with her body. He seemed to understand completely, for he deepened their kiss, caressing her tongue with his in a sensual rhythm that sent heat shooting through her limbs.

Suddenly, though, he broke off their kiss. The air flooding against her damp lips startled her, and she searched his face for an explanation. He seemed to be struggling with something, for his eyes were stormy with passion but his brow was furrowed.

"Lass, there's still something…"

Worry crept in at the edges of her passion-hazed mind. He had said that he accepted her goal of helping the Scottish rebellion with her healing skills, and he had proclaimed that he cared and longed for her, just as she did for him. What else could there be?

"I'm not some courtly knight," he said with difficulty. "I have done things that may be hard for you to understand, things you may not be able to accept."

She felt like a cold bucket of water had just been dumped over her head. He had alluded to his work as part of the Scottish rebellion several times, and she already knew that he was a warrior. Was there some horrible secret he was keeping?

"What do you mean?" she said cautiously.

He scraped a hand through his loose, dark hair. "I mean that I am a killer and you are a healer, lass. I long for you so badly, but I fear my black soul will sully you." He sat back on his heels, as he spoke, putting space between them.

"Have you done things like we saw back at that cottage?" Her stomach twisted at the thought, but she tried to keep her voice level. She could indeed never accept such acts, and if he was saying that he was truly as bad as whoever did those things, she would have been sorely mistaken in her impression of him.

"Nay!" he said quickly. "I would never stoop so low."

Relief washed through her. She could trust her intuition about him. But then why was he trying to put distance between them yet again? They had struggled enough just to be able to voice their mutual feelings. What did he think he was saving her from?

"But I am not so different from the English, or any other soldier. I have killed mercilessly. I've shot men in the back, I've hunted them like animals, and I've done so without regret." His voice was tight and low, and his face had taken on a hard, defensive look.

Suddenly, she realized what he was doing. "So you are punishing yourself for the things you've done by trying to convince me that you are evil?"

He struggled for a moment before speaking again. "I don't think of myself as evil. I believe in the Bruce's cause, and I would fight to the death for freedom. But

I'm not a hero either. And you deserve a hero."

"I thought you said you wouldn't doubt me again."

This brought his head up sharply. His gray eyes bore into her, his expression unreadable. "What do you mean, lass?"

"You said you wouldn't doubt me, and yet here you are, questioning my feelings for you and my judgment of your character."

"What are you saying?"

"Have you ever murdered innocent women and children as part of your missions for the Bruce?"

"Nay, and I never will," he said vehemently. The look of disgust twisting his face at the thought confirmed his words.

"And you have never…used force against a woman?"

"Nay."

"Have you sought out innocent farmers or laymen on your missions?"

"Nay…usually leaders in the English army, the ones making strategic decisions. But also soldiers sometimes." The anger and shame were fading from his voice, to be replaced by cautious curiosity at her line of questioning.

"Have you tortured men, drawn out their suffering, or maimed them intentionally?"

"Nay."

She leaned forward and placed a hand on his forearm. "My brother has done all of those things, and probably more that I don't know about." The words were hard to say, for the thought of her only living family member being so horrendous and cruel twisted her stomach, but she had to make him understand. "I have known bad men, Garrick, and you aren't one of them."

He inhaled sharply, his eyes suddenly flooding with pain. "You mean...you don't care that I've killed, and that I'll keep killing for the Bruce?"

She paused, choosing her words carefully. "What I truly wish for is peace," she said finally. "I hope that some day you no longer have to fight for Scotland's freedom, that you no longer have to carry the burden of taking lives for the cause."

He sank his head into his hands, and she couldn't read his expression for a moment. But then he raised his head again, his eyes searing her with their intensity and depth of emotion. "How is it that you understand me so well, that you accept me and my flaws, and at the same time make me better?"

His words shattered her. "You deserve forgiveness, Garrick. And happiness."

"I don't think I deserve *you* at all, lass. But you're right," he said ruefully, "I said I wouldn't doubt your judgment."

"And I want to be with you," she said, emotion tightening her voice. "I am choosing freely, and I choose you." She had already given him her heart. Now she wanted to share her body and her pleasure with him.

He seemed to read her mind. "Are you sure? There would be no going back, and nothing is certain about our future. The war could go on, or something could happen…"

He didn't have to say it, but he was warning her that he could be hurt or even killed. But she had worked as a healer long enough to know that nothing was ever certain about the future. She had seen healthy, strong men fall ill and die in a matter of days, and she had seen the weak and sickly recover and lead long lives. The only thing she could do was seize happiness when it came. And she was happy with Garrick, despite everything they had been through together.

"I'm sure."

He rose slowly and extended a hand to her to help her off the ground. His eyes were locked on her, their intensity burning into her. Just as he pulled her closer to him, a thought popped into her head.

"What about Burke? What if he comes back?"

A little smile played at the corners of his lips. "He does have impeccably bad timing," he said.

She didn't quite manage to suppress a nervous giggle. Everything they had said, everything that had passed between them, and the thought of what was about to happen, were all swirling inside her, creating a heady maelstrom of anticipation.

He bent and grabbed a stick from the ground, then quickly scrawled out several words in the dirt.

"*Nemo me impune lacessit*...that's Latin for 'no one attacks me with impunity' isn't it?" she said, reading over his shoulder.

"Aye. It's a phrase that's been floating around the Bruce's camp, and has lately spread to some of the other clans getting involved in the rebellion. It's a motto of sorts, a reminder that Scotland is like a thistle—you can't grab us without at least getting a handful of thorns." He smiled wolfishly at her, and she had to suppress another giggle.

"If Burke comes back before we do, he'll know that all is well when he sees this," Garrick said.

Suddenly, he seemed to forget all about Burke and his message, for he dropped the stick and turned the full power of his gaze on her. His eyes were hungry, and she abruptly felt like she was his mark, that he was homing in on his target. It thrilled her to be so desired by this hard yet good-hearted man. Reading the heated look she was sending back at him, he took her by the hand and started walking off into the woods.

"Where are we going?"

"To find some privacy," he said. "I want to do this right."

Another shiver of anticipation went through her. They were going to make love, to fully sate their desire for each other—if it could be sated. All of their previous kisses and that passionate night by the creek had only increased her hunger for connection with him.

She tried to ignore the tiny stone of fear sitting in

the bottom of her stomach. She had been told she would bleed, at least the first time, and that it would be painful and unpleasant every time. But she reminded herself that no one had ever told her there might also be longing and pleasure involved, only that she shouldn't want to do it, and that there would be consequences if she did. She was beginning to realize, though, that her nursemaids had hidden much from her. She wished suddenly that her mother were still alive, or at least that she had a close friend to confide in. After her parents' death, however, her brother had kept her isolated and ignorant. But he was no longer in control of her. She was making her own choices now, and her heart told her that it would be right with Garrick.

He wove through the forest quickly, and she hurried behind him, her hand in his. His ability to move swiftly and smoothly still caught her off guard, but at the moment, she was grateful for his confidence and speed in traversing the forest. The woods changed slightly as they traveled farther away from the Borderlands. Now the forest surrounding her was comprised more of pine trees rather than oak and yew. The ground had also become rockier and more hilly, reminding her that they were headed toward the more rugged northern regions of Scotland.

He halted next to a large rock outcropping surrounded by trees. She didn't see anything particularly noteworthy about this specific rock face, but then he pushed his hand through a clump of shrubs, parting the leafy branches with his arms, and a hollow cavity appeared in the rock. He held back the shrubbery, and she squeezed past him into the cave. He followed her in, and when he let the branches go, they snapped back into place, concealing the opening of the cave.

It was dim inside despite the bright midday sunlight on the other side of the shrubbery. The temperature was cool, and the smell of stone and dried leaves hung in the air. The top of the cave was high enough for her to stand upright, but Garrick had to stoop slightly, even at the mouth where the ceiling was highest. The little hollow space in the rock only extended a dozen feet or so, narrowing as it went back.

She turned from her perusal of the cave and nearly bumped into him. He had silently moved in closer to her. Her heart was suddenly pounding in her chest, and her skin felt flushed and itchy despite the cool air of the cave.

Slowly, he reached for her hair, undoing the ribbon at the tail of her braid. Most of her hair had already come loose, but his hands wove through the remains of her braid, pulling her tresses free and sending them cascading wildly across her back and shoulders.

"So beautiful," he murmured to himself, letting the strands slip through his fingers.

Then, he turned his gaze on her face, and the rapt hunger in his eyes nearly made her gasp. Before she could, his mouth descended on hers in a penetrating kiss.

She tried to match his caresses and teases, but he overpowered her, taking control of her lips and tongue. She surrendered to both of their passion, thrilling in the feel of his strength and powerful desire. He slipped a hand around the back of her head, holding her in place and tangling his fingers in her loose hair. He squeezed his hand slightly, tugging on her hair, and she gasped at the tingling sensation that shot from her scalp to the spot between her legs, which was already aching in anticipation.

He pulled her closer, his other hand reaching behind her to the ties running down the back of her dress. Her breasts felt tight and needy, and their contact against his chest was only making it worse—or better.

He tugged distractedly at the ties as she rubbed her chest against his with a little moan. That seemed to drive him even wilder, for he ripped his lips from hers so he could grip the material of her dress at the shoulders and tug it down. Her dress passed her breasts, then her hips, and was soon in a puddle on the floor of the cave.

The combination of her heated skin and the cool air brushing against her thin chemise sent a shiver through her. But it didn't last long, because he pulled her to him again, and she was enveloped in his warmth and his masculine scent. She could feel the heat of his hands through the material of her chemise as he moved over her waist, back, and eventually to her bottom. He gripped her, pulling her against him, and she could feel his hard length pressing into her stomach.

He moved his kiss from her mouth to her neck, where he nibbled and teased her sensitive skin. Her breath was coming more quickly now, and her body was taking over. She wasn't thinking anymore, only feeling and responding. She let her fingers sink into his shoulders, twisting in the material of his shirt.

Suddenly impatient to feel more of his skin, she tugged up on his shirt. He helped her pull it the rest of the way over his head, and she was rewarded with the sight of every chiseled plane and honed line of his muscular torso.

Mesmerized by the sight of his perfect physique, she let her fingers gently trail over his shoulders and down his broad chest, then lower still to his trim, yet muscular, waist. She dragged a fingernail along the top of his kilt where the fabric met his skin. He shuddered under her touch, letting her explore him.

But soon, he, too, grew impatient, for he growled lowly. Then his hands flew to the ties on her chemise. In a matter of seconds, the ties were loose, and the fabric was slipping from her shoulders. It whispered past her hips, and then joined her dress at her feet.

For a moment, she felt exposed standing naked before him, but then she noticed the way he was staring at her. His eyes devoured her like she was the most delicious thing he had ever seen. She watched him as his gaze moved over her naked body, his eyes lingering on her breasts, her waist, the flair of her hips, and her legs—especially where they met.

Garrick jerked slightly as if waking from a dream. He reached his hands toward her slowly, as if to make sure that she was real. When he touched her, it was feather-soft, and she shivered at the contact. He skimmed his hands over her exposed skin, seeming to try to memorize every contour of her body just by touch. Finally, he seemed to be assured that she wasn't going anywhere. He let his hands drop from her, but only to unfasten the belt holding his pleated kilt up.

In one smooth motion, he undid his belt and caught the material of his kilt even as it began to unpleat and slide down his hips. She couldn't help staring at the sight that was revealed to her. The hard lines of his torso continued down his hips and muscular legs. But what really drew her attention was his large manhood standing up from his body.

She felt her lips part slightly of their own volition. She had felt him with her hand before, and had begun to get to know the smooth hardness of his manhood, but seeing it was different. She hadn't realized it was so—big. She knew the basics of what would happen next, but she was suddenly unsure if it would work.

He spread his plaid out on the floor of the cave and brought her down to sit next to him on it. "Don't worry, lass," he said, seeming to read her mind. "It can be even better that it was by the creek."

"Better?" she breathed, the memory of the aching buildup and soaring release causing more heat to flood her body.

"Aye," he said huskily.

He pulled her down further onto the plaid so that she lay on her back with him leaning on one elbow over her. He bent his head toward her, but instead of kissing her, he captured one of her nipples in his mouth. She gasped and immediately arched, all traces of doubt fleeing as another wave of sensation crashed over her. One of his hands trailed down between her legs, and as he had before, he brushed across her most sensitive place with his fingertips. She instinctively opened her legs slightly, giving him more access.

"That's it, lass," he whispered against her breast.

Just as he had before, he teased the damp curls and folds, then found that electric spot that shot instant pleasure through her. The aching was building inside her, but she longed for more contact, more sensation.

As if knowing exactly what she wanted even if she couldn't have articulated it, he let one of his fingers slip inside her. She gasped and moaned at the added sensation. She suddenly felt a deeper ache, one that would not be relieved by the feathery touches he had given her earlier.

He withdrew his finger slowly, and the needy emptiness grew, but then he slid back in, and the motion sent her even closer to the paradise she now knew waited ahead. He set an achingly slow pace, sliding his finger in and out as he swirled his tongue around her nipple. She was sure that at any moment she would come completely undone.

Suddenly, he cursed and removed both his hand and his mouth from her body. Her eyes flew open in surprise, and she realized he was positioning himself between her legs. His jaw was clenched and his face was taut with pained concentration, and it dawned on her that even though she had barely touched him, he was wound tight with desire.

"I have to have you. Now," he breathed.

His manhood nudged at her entrance, and she realized that the moment had finally come. She would no longer be a maiden. She would be a woman, and one who had chosen the most enthralling man she had ever known as her lover.

He eased into her slowly, and at first, the sensation was not painful, just foreign. But as he continued to move into her, the tightness increased. He was so large that she felt stretched to her limit. The pleasure slipped toward discomfort, then he pushed all the way in, and pain stabbed through her. She cried out, and he cursed but held himself inside her.

He was all the way on top of her now, but he had his weight propped on one elbow so that he wasn't crushing her. With his free hand, he began circling one of her nipples with the pad of his thumb. The pain still tore through her, but it began mixing with some of the old pleasure. He withdrew partway from her, which eased the pain, but then he sank in again. When he was all the way inside, the tightness and pain pinched again, but this time slightly less that before.

He kept up this slow rhythm, and each time he pushed into her, the pain mingled with her building pleasure. When she was panting and moaning once more in anticipation of the flood of pleasure ahead, he let the hand on her breast drop to grip one of her thighs, pushing her bent leg up higher. He sank even deeper into her now, and his thrusts increased in pace.

She hitched even higher, sensation tearing through her. She kept climbing and climbing, reaching for release. He pulled back and sank inside her again, and it was the final straw. She felt herself shattering into a thousand shards of pure pleasure. Molten heat suffused her, and she cried out in ecstasy. With one more hard thrust, a groan tore from him as he joined her in release. He held himself inside of her, both of them gasping for breath and pulsing as their hearts pounded.

As she drifted back down to earth, he withdrew from her.

"Did I hurt you, lass?" he said, brushing the backs of his fingers against her cheek.

"Not by the end," she said breathily. A deep contentedness was seeping into her limbs. She felt like she was made of warm honey.

"It is only like that the first time. After that, it is all the pleasure with none of the pain," he said.

She quirked a smile. "Really? I suppose I'll have to

experience it to believe it."

"That can be arranged," he said with a devilish lift of one eyebrow.

She longed to stare at his ruggedly handsome face, drink in the sight of his perfectly honed body, but suddenly, her eyelids felt heavy.

He pulled her into his arms, settling her head on his chest. "Rest now, lass."

The last thing she remembered was his calloused fingertips stroking her hair and bare shoulder.

Chapter Twenty-Nine

When Jossalyn woke, she was disoriented for a moment. The cave's dimness prevented her from knowing how long she had slept or what time it was. But Garrick's warm, strong arms were still around her, which made her feel at ease. He was absently playing with a strand of her golden hair. They were both still naked, their legs intertwined, though he had pulled up part of his plaid to cover them.

"How long did I sleep?" she said, lazily stretching.

"A few hours."

She sat bolt upright. "A few hours? Don't we have to keep moving?"

He looked up at her from his position on his back. "Aye, but I didn't want to wake you. You seemed so content."

She smiled softly at his words, feeling warmed by the memories of why she felt so languid and pleased. "I appreciate that, but I'm sure Burke has begun to worry."

He waved a hand dismissively, but slowly sat up next to her. "Aye, you're probably right." Even still, he didn't make any moves to get up. Instead, he let his eyes roam over her naked body.

She forced herself to rise despite the fact that she longed to wrap herself around him again and sleep for another few days. She went to the pile of her clothes a few feet away, but when she bent to pick up her chemise, she felt a twinge of pain between her legs. She must have winced, for Garrick stiffened.

"What is it, lass?" he said, his voice filled with concern.

"Oh, I'm just a little sore," she said lightly. The pain wasn't great, but she could certainly tell she was no longer a maiden.

Suddenly, he was standing in front of her, his hands cradling her cheeks. "I swear I'll never hurt you again," he said quietly, his eyes searing into her.

She felt her eyes widen slightly at the seriousness in his tone. "Thank you," she replied, feeling a surge of emotion at his protectiveness.

He let his hands drop, but he watched her closely as she pulled the chemise over her head, followed by her dress. He must have been satisfied, for after helping her with the laces on her dress, he turned to re-pleat his kilt and belt it around his hips, then donned his shirt and stuffed the ends into his kilt.

He went out of the cave in front of her, holding back the branches that blocked the entrance. The sun slanted toward afternoon but was still strong and bright. She had to shield her eyes after the dimness of the cave. A warm breeze played with the trees, and the air was full of the smells of the forest. The combination of the bright sun, the warm air, and the smell of pine and soil mixed headily, and she felt intoxicated by life.

She glanced back one more time at the dim interior of the cave. She was truly reborn now. She was her own woman, no longer a girl under her brother's control. She had now tasted freedom and the joy of shared pleasure. There was no going back, and she was glad.

Garrick guided her to a small stream nearby. They both cupped their hands and splashed water on their faces, then drank from the cool, fresh stream. She took a moment to re-plait her hair, though Garrick frowned crossly as she wrangled the golden waves into a braid. She only smiled back at him, relishing his enjoyment of her appearance.

Once they were refreshed and tidied up, they made their way back toward where they had left the horses. They found Burke sitting on a rock, whittling a stick idly. When he saw them approach, he raised an eyebrow at both of them. Jossalyn doubted very much that Burke missed the relaxed air about them, or the rosiness she could feel in her cheeks, but she didn't mind. She wasn't going to hide her happiness.

"All sorted out, then?" Burke said.

"Aye," Garrick said simply. He walked past Burke to his waiting horse.

As Jossalyn brushed past Burke, he said in a low but

merry voice just for her, "No leaves in your hair this time."

She felt her cheeks heat at his playful teasing, but she enjoyed Burke's conspiratorial tone and the fact that he seemed happy for them. "Not this time," she replied, not denying what Burke could clearly infer about what she and Garrick had been up to.

"We had better get moving," Garrick said over his shoulder to them. "Might as well use the rest of the daylight to get as far north as possible."

Burke nodded and tossed his stick aside. As he walked to his horse, he casually swiped a foot over the words that Garrick had scrawled in the dirt of the forest floor. "Clever," he said as he passed Garrick.

The two exchanged quirked smiles, and then mounted.

Jossalyn approached Garrick and Fletch and extended her hand up to him, ready to be pulled atop his giant warhorse once again. But when he hoisted her up, instead of straddling the horse, he arranged her so she was sitting sidesaddle. She suddenly had a vision of bouncing against the saddle on her now very sensitive privates, and felt a flood of relief at his thoughtfulness. She shot him a quick look, silently thanking him for saving her the discomfort. He didn't say anything, but his eyes softened slightly, and she knew he understood.

With a nudge of his legs, they were riding north once more.

Chapter Thirty

They traveled northward together for four more days. Without realizing it, the three of them slipped into a comfortable routine, or as much of a routine as was possible given the rough conditions and their ever-shifting sleep and travel schedule. Whether they were traveling day or night, though, Jossalyn and Garrick stayed pressed together atop Fletch's back, occasionally whispering something to each other, which often resulted in a blush from Jossalyn.

When they would stop, they would eat a simple meal, usually something Burke or Garrick managed to catch, or that Jossalyn foraged. Her knowledge of plants and herbs was proving quite useful, though the farther north they traveled, the more she saw flora she didn't recognize. Frequently, Garrick or Burke was able to fill in the gaps in her knowledge, since they had spent so much time working in the field on various missions.

After a meal, they would catch whatever sleep they could, regardless of the time of day. Jossalyn noticed, though, that after the first day of traveling north following the scene in the glen, they began to sleep more during the night and travel during the day.

Garrick and Burke were both visibly more relaxed now. She guessed they had determined that they had put enough distance between themselves and her brother's men, or perhaps it was just that they were more familiar with the terrain farther north.

Either way, she was grateful not to have to spend so many of her nights in the saddle. Though she and Garrick slept apart out of a sense of propriety in Burke's presence, he always gave her an extra length of his plaid to use as a pillow or to wrap around herself. Being enveloped in his warm scent was almost as good as sleeping in his arms. Almost.

Despite the fact that there was little time for anything besides eating, sleeping, and ever-more riding, Jossalyn and Garrick did manage to slip away from Burke one more time. Jossalyn had decided to bathe and wash her dress and chemise in a nearby loch. The sun was warm and the air was still, and her skin had begun to itch after so many days of riding. She still had her spare chemise and dress stuffed into the bottom of her satchel, and she decided to indulge herself in a clean body and fresh clothes.

When she informed the two men that she would be at the nearby loch for a little while and requested privacy, Garrick had grabbed his bow and quiver and said he was going hunting. Burke didn't comment, only raised an eyebrow at his cousin, which was met with a scowl from Garrick.

Jossalyn puzzled on this as she strolled toward the loch, but let it slip from her mind as her clothes slid from her body at the shoreline. She was sore, though not from Garrick and her lovemaking a few days previous. Instead, it was the long hours on horseback that had her muscles aching and her bottom sore. She wasn't used to such grueling conditions, and even with Garrick to lean against, she found it exhausting. Neither one of the men seemed to be affected at all, she thought with annoyance. They were clearly used to a rougher life.

She waded into the loch, its waters surprisingly cool despite the warm summer day. She half-sighed, half-shivered as she eased herself deeper, one step at a time. When the enjoyable torture was too much, she dunked her head beneath the water's still surface in one movement, feeling the refreshing rush envelop her. She held her breath underwater for a moment, scrubbing her fingers through her hair and letting the cool silence seep into her. When she broke the surface again a moment later and blinked open her eyes, she gasped at the sight before her.

Garrick stood on the shoreline, half-naked and in the process of undressing further. His eyes were locked on her, and even from the distance of more than a dozen yards, she could feel the heat radiating from his stare.

When he was fully naked, he stalked slowly toward

the water. She drank in the sight of his perfect body, all hard lines and rippling muscles. Her eyes lingered on one particularly hard part of his body, which plainly spoke of his desire and his intentions for her. Suddenly, the water felt too cold against her heated skin, and she shivered in anticipation as he waded toward her.

Just before he reached her, he too dunked his head underwater for a moment. When he reemerged, the water sluiced down from his dark hair and over the chiseled planes of his chest and torso. Without further ado, he closed the distance between them and took her in his arms.

"I can't wait any longer, lass. I have to have you," he whispered in her ear. His voice was tight with desire, his manhood pressing into her stomach.

In response, she wrapped her arms around his neck and stretched up to press her lips to his. He made a low growling noise in his throat and slipped his tongue inside her mouth. His hands cupped her breasts, and then slid below the waterline to grip her bottom, pressing his hips into hers. Then his hands slid lower to the backs of her legs, and he lifted her up, one hand behind each knee, to wrap her legs around his hips.

She could feel the head of his manhood pressing against her entrance. The cool water mixed with the contact of his heated skin. She could already feel herself pulsing, aching for him to fill her. She arched her back, pushing her taut breasts against his chest and giving him more access to enter her.

It was all the invitation he needed. He thrust fully inside her, causing her to gasp and moan at the tight sensation. He ground their hips together in agonizingly slow circles. It was all she could do to hold on to his neck as he brought her closer and closer to the edge of ecstasy. Even as her body shuddered and spasmed in release, she felt his muscles tense and his hips jerked hard as he joined her.

They floated for a few more minutes, sharing a tender kiss that was still edged with passion despite the fact that they had just found pleasure together. Then they slowly made their way to the shoreline, where Garrick dried both of them with his plaid and she donned a fresh chemise and dress.

"I had better go find something to shoot, else Burke will spread word that I'm a sorry shot at hunting," he said with a mischievous smile.

She watched him go, his bow and quiver slung casually over his broad shoulders, and his red kilt flashing through the trees. She lingered at the loch, scrubbing her old dress and chemise as best as she could, and then laying them out on a rock in the sun to dry. By the time she returned to their temporary camp, Burke and Garrick were roasting a rabbit over a small fire. Burke sent her an amused look, and Garrick shot her a surreptitious wink that almost caused her to giggle.

On what would be their last day traveling together, Jossalyn checked on Burke's stitches. The wound was healing rapidly with no lingering sign of infection, so she removed the stitches, declaring that as long as Burke continued to go easy on the leg for a few more days, he would be fine.

Only a few hours into their ride that morning, the two men halted their horses. The area looked identical to the terrain through which they had been traveling for the last few days, at least to Jossalyn's untrained eyes. The dense woods had thinned slightly, and there were increasingly more open swaths of land filled with rocky outcroppings and clumps of heather between the stretches of forest. Setting aside the general changes in landscape since they had been traveling north from the Borderlands, Jossalyn didn't recognize anything different about this place.

Both men dismounted, and after helping Jossalyn down, Garrick clasped arms with Burke.

"Travel safely," Garrick said, his voice a little more gruff that usual.

"And you as well," Burke replied.

Jossalyn looked back and forth between the two men. "What's going on? Where are you going, Burke?"

He smiled at her confusion. "I have a different mission to complete, lass. I am needed by my Laird back on Sinclair lands." He turned to Garrick and went on. "I'll give your best to your brother and Lady Alwin."

"And I'll tell the Bruce that you nearly gave your life to complete this mission," Garrick said seriously.

Jossalyn felt her jaw slacken, her thoughts a jumble. Garrick had a brother? Had she heard right that this mystery brother was the Laird of his clan? And there was some lady named Alwin—but wasn't that a boy's name? And Garrick had the personal ear of Robert the Bruce, enough to pass on a good word about Burke? And Burke was leaving them, meaning that they would be alone…

Garrick watched as Jossalyn's features clouded with confusion. She opened her mouth, and a flood of half-formed questions began to tumble out, but he held up a hand to still her.

"We can discuss all this later, lass," he said firmly, "but right now Burke must be on his way, and we on ours."

He could tell she wasn't happy about it, but she managed to clamp her jaw shut and cross her arms over her chest. He was about to clasp forearms with Burke one last time and turn back to his horse, but Burke grabbed him by the shoulder and pulled him several paces away from Jossalyn.

"What are you—"

"You two had better be married the next time I see you," Burke said quietly.

Though he was normally good at reading people, Garrick couldn't quite measure out the mixed quantities of amusement and warning in Burke's voice.

Garrick raised an eyebrow at his cousin. Even though he knew Burke was a good and honorable man, and that his advice was sound, it irked him to be told what to do.

"You're not her father, Burke, nor are you some saint yourself," he said dryly.

"Nay, I'm neither, but take the word of a man who regrets not being able to follow his own advice," Burke replied darkly.

Garrick frowned but remained silent. He had a vague memory of a boyhood love of Burke's being married to another, but he didn't want to pry if the memory was still painful. He didn't have to, for Burke went on.

"I once found a lass that I looked at the way I see you looking at Jossalyn. I missed my opportunity with her, though, and I regret it to this day. It is not only the honorable thing for you to wed Jossalyn, but the wise thing if you ever hope to find happiness in your life."

Normally, Garrick would have bristled at the way Burke was being so forceful with his advice—or at least he would have teased him for being so philosophical—but Burke's serious tone gave him pause.

What was stopping him from asking Jossalyn to marry him? They clearly cared for each other, and they had a spark between them like nothing he had experienced before. He was also starting to truly believe their lives might be compatible. He wanted to use his skills to help the Bruce and the rebellion, and so did she.

Was it that he still didn't fully believe that he deserved a lifetime of happiness? Perhaps, though he was coming to trust in Jossalyn's affection for him, despite his doubts about whether or not he deserved her. The thought of extending his heart to her and being rejected terrified him. Yet taking a shot and missing the target was better than never aiming at all.

One thing he wasn't sure of was how the Bruce would respond to the idea of his best marksman getting married. What if he prohibited it on the grounds that it would take Garrick away from his missions? Or forbade it because she was English, and Raef Warren's sister to boot?

His struggle must have been visible on his face, for Burke smiled a little and said, "You'll figure it out, I'm sure. When a Sinclair puts his mind to something, nothing can stop him."

Garrick returned his attention to his cousin. "You're a Sinclair, too, Burke. Perhaps you can find happiness as well." Though he had been outright hostile over having Burke join him on this mission at first, then only grudgingly accepting of his presence, his cousin had become not only a trusted companion but a friend over the course of these past several weeks. He truly wished him well and hoped he was able to resolve the lingering pain from his mysterious lost love.

Burke snorted wryly. "Mayhap, though I sometimes fear that we only get one chance at it. Don't waste yours."

The last was spoken seriously, and Garrick nodded soberly in response.

The two strode back to where the horses and

Jossalyn stood. Burke gallantly took Jossalyn's hand and swept a bow over it, which caused her to smile girlishly. For some reason, this made Garrick frown, but on seeing his dark face, Burke only chuckled and clasped arms with him once more before mounting his horse.

"Farewell!" Burke called over his shoulder as he urged his horse on, leaving them behind. He still had a few days' ride ahead of him to get to the farthest northeast corner of the Highlands, where the Sinclairs made their home. Garrick and Jossalyn, on the other hand, were only a few hours away from Inverness. Though the exact location of the Bruce's camp was not only top-secret but also ever-changing, Garrick knew it would be hidden nearby.

Garrick mounted Fletch and then helped Jossalyn up, suddenly sensing their aloneness. Should he speak what was on his mind regarding what Burke had said about marriage? He rejected the idea, deciding he would need to speak to the Bruce first. That would also buy him more time to chew on Burke's words. Besides, they would be at the Bruce's camp by the end of the day.

Jossalyn turned slightly in the saddle. "Now will you answer my questions?"

He smiled a little at her impatience, but also relished the thought of getting to talk more with her alone. "Aye, go ahead lass."

"You have a brother?"

"Two, actually."

She waited for him to say more, but he was enjoying goading her too much. Finally, she sighed and half-twisted in the saddle to glare at him for a moment.

"Care to say more?"

He chortled in amusement but held up a hand for peace when she narrowed her eyes.

"I have an older brother, Robert, and a younger brother, Daniel. We are all close in age, about a year apart each, which made for a…lively boyhood."

"What did Burke mean when he mentioned the Laird of the Sinclair clan?"

"Robert is the Laird. He was the one who sent Burke and me to gather information around Dunbraes—with the Bruce's blessing, of course."

Garrick didn't often talk about the fact that his brother was a Laird. He didn't want the other soldiers in the rebel camp to think he had risen in the Bruce's ranks because of nepotism. But he was nevertheless proud of his heritage as the descendant and brother of the Laird of a Highland clan. It was perhaps part of the reason he felt so strongly about being a part of Scotland's fight for independence—he wanted his clan to choose their own destiny and live freely.

"And what about this 'Lady Alwin'? What kind of name is that?"

Garrick tried to suppress a smile. Was that a hint of suspicion—or even jealousy—in Jossalyn's voice? Of course, he had told her next to nothing of his life or his family, so he shouldn't hold it against her that she would feel uncomfortable at the mention of a lady who lived back at his home in Roslin.

"She is my brother's wife." He sensed the slightest shift from her in front of him as she relaxed a hair's breadth. Then a thought occurred to him. "She's English, like you."

Somehow, his brother and Alwin seemed to make it work, despite their differences in nationality. But there was more to it than that, and suddenly, he felt uncomfortable with the next piece of information, unsure of how Jossalyn would react to it.

"In fact, she was betrothed to someone else before she married Robert. She was engaged to be married...to your brother."

She inhaled sharply and twisted around in the saddle again, pinning him with her green eyes, which were wide with shock. "I had heard rumors, but I never knew...Then she would have been...my sister?" Several emotions flitted across her face. Garrick was only able to pick out surprise, sadness, hope, and confusion from the bunch.

"What sort of woman is she? Is she kind? Does she love your brother? Why didn't she marry my brother?"

"Hold on, lass, one at a time! I've only met her once, but I can tell you everything I know."

She took a steadying breath and gave a little nod, turning back around in the saddle to face forward so she could listen more comfortably.

"The circumstances under which Robert and Alwin came to be married are…unusual," he began. Though bride-stealing and the dissolution of political unions in favor of love matches wasn't entirely uncommon in the Highlands, he wasn't sure how she would take it, given her English sensibilities.

"Alwin was on her way to meet your brother, when Robert…intercepted her and took her for ransom. Your brother gave chase but wasn't able to take her back. Robert had them wed, and now they are expecting their first child."

"So they are happy?"

Garrick could remember very distinctly how his brother had looked at Lady Alwin, how he doted on her and didn't seem to mind Garrick's teasing about what a moon-eyed whelp he was being. *Someday, you'll understand.* Robert's words floated back to him. Perhaps he was coming to comprehend his brother's behavior.

"Aye, very much so. Though it was an unusual union to begin with, they are made for each other. She's as strong and smart as a whip, and he's become a better Laird for it."

She exhaled and slumped slightly in the saddle.

"What is it, lass?" he said, suddenly confused by her reaction.

"I'm happy for them, really," she said, her voice sounding pinched. "In fact, I thank God she didn't have to marry my brother. Who knows what would have happened to her." She shivered, but then went on. "It's just...I didn't know for sure until you just mentioned it, but I could have had a sister. I know it's silly, since I never had her in the first place, but now it feels as though I've lost her."

Unbidden, a thought struck Garrick's mind like lightning. Jossalyn could still have Alwin as a sister—if he were to marry her. He shook himself a little, trying to get control of his thoughts. But despite his best efforts, the idea of bringing Jossalyn into his family tapped into something deep inside him.

"Maybe someday you'll get to meet her," he said, trying to ease her sadness.

"Yes, perhaps," she said, her voice slightly less strained. She gave herself a little shake, then switched topics. "What of your younger brother—Daniel, you said?"

"I haven't seen Danny in several years," he replied with a rueful smile. Despite the fact that his younger brother was the smallest and weakest of them growing up, he always fought the hardest, and sometimes even bested his older brothers. Though Garrick hadn't gotten to see him in quite some time, his younger brother had already turned into a skilled warrior and powerful leader.

"He is helping our uncle William run his keep until William's son can take over. We were all trained to be Lairds, in case something happened to Robert. Danny—Daniel—took to it far better than I did. Perhaps someday he'll get the opportunity to lead. Not the

Sinclairs, of course," he said quickly, sending up a prayer for Robert's good health and long reign. "But any other clan or holding would be lucky to have him."

She chewed on his words silently for a while, and the quiet of the woods stretched between them peacefully. But Jossalyn apparently had one more line of questioning to put to him.

"You mentioned that you would tell Robert the Bruce about Burke's actions. Do you truly have the Bruce's ear? I mean, I know that he is your commander, but you know him personally?"

This line of inquiry was a bit harder for him to answer. He still hadn't told Jossalyn the full extent of his work regarding his close relationship with the Bruce. He wasn't sure how she would react to learning that he wasn't just some soldier in the rebellion's army—he was one of the Bruce's most trusted and important advisors and marksmen. Garrick was the one the Bruce entrusted with the most dangerous, secretive, and internal missions and information. He wasn't just some bowman—he was known as the *best* shot, and a close confidante of the man leading Scotland toward freedom.

Just as he was about to open his mouth and fumble for an answer, Garrick noticed the forest around them had suddenly gone quiet. It had been peaceful before, but now he couldn't hear a single bird chirping or fluttering in the trees. He felt his stomach twist.

Something was very wrong.

Chapter Thirty-One

Jossalyn was waiting patiently for an answer from Garrick, but he was slow with his words. She didn't mind that trait at all—in fact, she liked that he thought about what he wanted to say, and then said it in a plain way. But her curiosity was getting the better of her, and she was growing impatient.

Suddenly, he pulled up hard on Fletch's reins, his body tense behind her.

"What is—"

Before she could get her question out, his hand clamped down over her mouth, silencing her. He leaned in very close to her ear.

"Shhh."

She nodded her understanding, and his hand eased away from her mouth. He slipped quickly and quietly from Fletch's back, but left her perched atop the large warhorse. Then he reached into his saddlebags and withdrew his bow and quiver, smoothly nocking an arrow and half-drawing it.

"Show yourselves, lads, or get an arrow apiece in the throat for your trouble," he said loudly into the woods.

She jerked this way and that, suddenly flooded with terror at the prospect of some unseen and unheard villain lurking nearby—or surrounding them.

Abruptly, a whistle pierced the air off to their left. Like lightning, Garrick swung his bow toward the whistle, drawing the bowstring all the way back to his cheek. But instead of letting the arrow fly, he sent another whistle of his own back, all the while keeping the arrow trained on a clump of dense trees and shrubs a little way off.

The shrubs rustled slightly, and from them emerged, to Jossalyn's horror, a fierce-looking, kilted warrior. He had a large sword strapped to his hip, and though he was still some distance off, she could tell that he was a giant of a man, both tall and broad.

Garrick kept the tip of his arrow trained on the man, but a rustle from behind them sounded, and he jerked his bow toward the new noise. Another large warrior in a different colored plaid emerged from the branches of a densely foliated tree. He swung down from a tree limb and landed with a thump on the forest floor.

As if from a nightmare, a third man appeared in front of them, his sheathed sword swinging at his hip as he walked slowly toward them. Jossalyn felt a scream rising in her throat. Even though she knew that Garrick was an excellent shot, it was three against one, and these savage-looking men appeared battle-hardened and deadly.

The sound of Garrick's laugh snuffed out her terror like a bucket of water over a fire. The sound startled her, for she had never heard him fully laugh before—he would chuckle, or snort, but never all-out laugh. That is, until they were surrounded by Scottish warriors looking murderous.

To her shock, the other men moving in on them also broke out into hearty laughter.

"Garrick! Garrick Sinclair! We were expecting to see that sorry, red-plaided arse of yours a week ago! What took you so long?" bellowed the giant who had revealed himself first.

Garrick finally lowered his arrow and released the tension on the bowstring. He replaced the arrow inside his quiver and slung the quiver, along with his bow, over one shoulder.

"Sorry to keep you waiting, Angus," Garrick said lightly.

When the giant had reached Garrick, he thumped him heartily on the back, a blow which should have sent Garrick flying, but he braced himself for it.

"Apologies for the welcoming party," the man approaching from behind said with a boyish grin. "Can't be too careful these days."

"I was expecting to ride several more hours before reaching camp," Garrick replied, turning to grasp forearms with the sandy-haired young man who had just spoken.

"We moved," the third man said tersely as he halted in front of Fletch.

Garrick only exchanged quick nods with this man, whose dark eyes continually darted between Garrick and Jossalyn.

Apparently, he wasn't the only one who had noticed her.

"And who is this radiant vision of a lass with you?" the one called Angus said in a hushed tone.

He was gazing up at her with wide eyes, and for some reason, Jossalyn had to suppress a giggle rising in her chest. No one as fierce-looking as the giant warrior in front of her should attempt gallantry or genteel manners. It was too incongruous.

"This is Lady Jossalyn—" Garrick cut off abruptly before saying her last name.

She noticed that he had spoken for her, and wondered if he didn't want these men to know that she was English. Well, she wasn't going to stay silent forever, so she might as well get it over with.

"I am Jossalyn Warren," she said in the most serene voice she could muster.

All of the warriors' eyes widened, and the sandy-haired one who had come up behind them sputtered into a coughing fit. The dark one who had approached from the front, and who had been looking at her suspiciously, narrowed his eyes slightly.

"As in, *Raef Warren?*" he said as he continued to hold her with his narrowed gaze.

"He is my brother," she said simply, trying not to crack under his scrutiny.

"You captured Raef Warren's sister? Good on you, laddie!" Angus bellowed, clapping Garrick on the back again.

This time, though, Garrick wasn't prepared for it, and the blow sent him stumbling forward a step.

"What's the plan, then? Ransom? I heard that that didn't work out so well for your brother, so I'd suggest—"

"Hold, Angus!" Garrick said firmly. "She is not my captive, and I do not plan to ransom her back to her brother."

Angus furrowed his bushy, reddish-brown eyebrows at that. "Then why did you drag a wee English lassie with you all the way to the Bru—"

"Stop your chattering, Angus, before you say something foolish," the dark-haired man glaring at Jossalyn hissed.

"It's all right, Finn," Garrick said. "She is loyal to the cause and wants to join us."

The man Garrick had just called Finn shifted his narrowed stare from Jossalyn to Garrick. "Just because you rut with a lass doesn't mean that she's trustwor—"

Before he could finish his insult, Garrick drew the dagger he kept in the top of his boot and closed the distance between them in a flash. He pressed the point of the blade into the little hollow at the base of the other man's neck lightly. Amazingly, Finn didn't even flinch.

"Disrespect her again, and I'll kill you," Garrick said quietly.

Finn only stared back silently, his unreadable dark eyes boring into Garrick.

"Easy, lads," the fair-haired man said cautiously. "We're all on the same side, remember?"

The group remained tense as Garrick slowly pulled his dagger back from Finn's throat and resheathed it in his boot.

"I'm sure you will be most welcome back at camp," the young man went on, turning to Jossalyn with a forcibly light tone to his voice. "I am Colin McKay, at your service, my lady. That brute is Angus MacLeod, and the one who forgot his manners is Finn Sutherland." He swept a bow at her, and she was suddenly reminded of Burke's smooth gallantry. "But if I may ask, what is a fair English lady such as yourself doing getting involved with Garrick Sinclair and the rebellion?"

She hadn't thought about how she might explain their circumstances or her desire to join the Scottish fight for freedom to others yet. She hesitated for a moment, but then decided there was no point in dipping her toe in cautiously. She might as well jump all the way in.

"I was trying to escape my brother, so I stowed away with Garrick and his cousin Burke while they were scouting Dunbraes. The long and the short of it is that we all ended up fleeing my brother, and I managed to convince Garrick to let me join him on his way to Robert the Bruce's secret camp. I am a healer, and I want to offer my skills to your cause."

Colin whistled softly, his sandy eyebrows arching above his bright blue eyes. "That's quite the adventure, lass. But if one of the most suspicious and unwelcoming men in all the Highlands trusts you, then I'm sure we can too." He clapped Garrick on the back playfully as he spoke, but also shot a meaningful look at Finn as well.

Angus, apparently missing the laden exchange, rumbled his approval at Colin's words. "Let's be on our way, then!" the ruddy giant said merrily.

Finn didn't say anything, but even without looking at him, she could feel his dark eyes on her again.

Garrick mounted behind Jossalyn but kept the horse at a walk so as to keep pace with the three warriors striding at their side. Jossalyn had to keep reminding herself that these men were apparently friends—or at least allies—and not enemies.

She could suddenly understand Garrick better now that she saw him surrounded by other Highland warriors. It explained a lot of his gruffness, his hardened exterior, and his honed fighting skills. Nothing about these men was soft.

Then again, she suspected that once she got to know them better, Angus would prove tender-hearted, and she sensed Colin was a mischievous and people-loving sort. Finn, however, didn't strike her as anything but cold and hard.

Despite being in the company of his fellow soldiers, Garrick seemed slightly more on edge that normal as well. He kept one hand on the reins, but he wrapped the other protectively around Jossalyn's middle, holding her close to his chest. The tension she felt from Garrick, plus her own nervousness, both in the company of strange warriors and in anticipation of reaching the Bruce's camp, made time stretch. How much farther could this camp really be?

It was likely only an hour or so after they had encountered the three warriors that she got her answer. At another indiscernibly different point in the forest through which they were walking, Colin sent out a loud whistle, which was immediately called back by some unseen watcher in the surrounding trees. Then the woods thinned slightly, and Jossalyn caught a glimpse of canvas between the trees ahead.

As they kept moving forward, she saw more and more splashes of off-white canvas. They were tents, set up in the open spaces between the pine trees. She also saw movement between the trees and the tents.

At first, her eyes registered dozens of men, all clad in different colored plaids, many with fearsome weapons strapped to their hips, backs, or over their shoulders. But once they were moving among the tents, she realized there must be hundreds of men here. Those who noticed them nodded or waved, and many seemed to know Garrick by sight. They would call a greeting to him or welcome him back, often sending curious looks in her direction.

The deeper they went into the sea of tents and men, the more Jossalyn was struck by the scale of it all. This wasn't merely some thrown-together camp—this was a mobile village. Off to one side she saw several pens filled with livestock, and behind them, a row of carts and wagons, presumably to be able to transport all these tents and gear for the men quickly if the need arose.

But how could such a large and well-run operation stay secret and hidden for so long? The English had heard rumors of the Bruce's headquarters and sought it with fervor. Perhaps it was the Scots' superior knowledge of the surrounding area.

But that wasn't enough. Jossalyn realized that there were at least two rings of scouts and security around the camp. The three warriors they had met were the outer layer, and whoever Colin had whistled to as they approached the heart of the camp would be another level of protection. If anyone approached, either on foot or on horseback, the camp could be alerted and either prepare for battle or disassemble and moved, potentially with several hours of notice.

Jossalyn was in awe of the scale and order of the rebel camp. Everywhere she looked, men were practicing with their weapons, or were leaning over a map spread on a stump, or even preparing food. She caught a glimpse of a few women as well. She assumed that they were the camp's lemans, but they also appeared to be helping out with washing, cooking, and generally keeping the camp running smoothly.

The group weaved their way through the maze of tents, seeming to know where they were going, though Jossalyn was already thoroughly lost. Eventually, they stopped next to a small tent that looked like all the others, except for the fact that it was adjacent to the largest tent she had seen yet.

"We got you all set up after our most recent move, since we were expecting your return last week," Colin said to Garrick.

Garrick nodded his thanks as he dismounted, and then wrapped his hands around Jossalyn's waist and pulled her down to the ground next to him. She suddenly realized that all four of the warriors surrounding her towered over her. Burke and Garrick were both tall and broadly muscled, but to be inside a circle of four such hulking, battle-hardened men was rather intimidating. She could see why the English spoke of the Scottish rebels as monstrously large barbarians.

"We'll let you get settled," Colin went on, "but then the Bruce would probably like to see you."

"I'll see to Fletch," Angus said, his attention suddenly focused solely on the horse. He stroked its mane and whispered something into his ear.

Colin only smirked at the display of affection toward the animal. To Jossalyn, he said, "Angus had a special place in his heart for beasties of all sorts, lass. It's probably why he likes Garrick so much."

Garrick rewarded Colin for his teasing with a wry smile and one raised eyebrow. Finn didn't say anything, and instead, simply strode off to another part of camp without even a farewell.

"Don't mind him, lass," Colin said as he watched Finn walk away. "He's a sourpuss, but he's not a threat to you."

"If you say so," she said under her breath.

Colin and Angus bid them farewell and departed also, with Angus leading Fletch behind them. Garrick turned to the tent and held its flap, which functioned as the door, open for her. She slipped under his arm and entered.

It was small and simple, but also surprisingly clean and orderly. There was no floor, only the four canvas walls and a sloping roof. In one corner, there was a cot with a straw mattress and a blanket folded at the foot, and a few feet away on the other side, there was a simple wooden table with a pitcher of water and a basin. There was only one other piece of furniture, a wooden shelf with a few essential items on it like a cup, bowl, a bar of soap, and the like.

Garrick entered after her and was watching her closely. "It's very simple, I know, but—"

"But all the essentials are covered, I'd say," she said lightly. She didn't want to give him a chance to start thinking she was somehow looking down her nose at the accommodations. It was far more basic than her life had been at Dunbraes, but she wouldn't trade it for the world.

He was still looking uncomfortably around the small space, though. "If you'd like, I can arrange to sleep somewhere else."

She turned to fully face him, capturing his jaw between her hands. "Now why would I want you to do that?" she said, a slight tease in her voice.

He relaxed under her touch. "Very well, lass, but you can't say I didn't try to protect your reputation—and protect you from my lust."

She smiled up into his handsome face. His jaw was bristly with dark stubble. It could almost be called a beard, given how long it was. She could feel his jaw clench under her touch, and she watched as his gray eyes lit with fire as they roamed over her face. He leaned in slowly, placing a soft, intimate kiss on her lips. He lingered there for a moment, but then sighed and pulled back from her.

"We shouldn't keep the King waiting," he said, though the look he was giving her said he wanted to do otherwise.

He approached the pitcher and basin, and then poured some water over his hands and quickly scrubbed them over his face. He held out the pitcher to her and poured the water in a slow stream as she rinsed her hands and face as well. It wasn't much, but it was the least they could do in preparation to see the man who had crowned himself King of Scotland.

The thought sent Jossalyn's already-taut nerves pulling even tighter. She re-plaited her hair as neatly as she could, and then smoothed her wrinkled and dirty dress with her hands, though it did little to help. What if the Bruce sent her away, refusing the help of the sister of their English enemy? What if he did worse? What if he believed her to be a spy or a traitor? What if…?

She forced herself to take a deep breath and stop the spinning of her mind. She would have her answers soon enough.

When they were as ready as they could be, she turned to exit the tent, but his hand on her arm stopped her. She turned back to him and watched as he removed both the dagger and its scabbard from his boot, then extended it toward her. She looked up at him in confusion.

"I want you to have this," he said simply.

"Why? Do you think I'll need it?" The memory of that very blade pressed against Finn's neck chilled her inside. What she unsafe here?

"Nay, lass—or, probably not, anyway," he replied with a frown.

She guessed he was thinking about the same moment that had occurred less than two hours ago as well.

"I would just feel better knowing that you have it, that's all."

For some reason, she didn't entirely believe his intentionally casual tone, but she took the dagger anyway. She didn't have anyplace to put it, though, so after searching a bit, Garrick found a strip of leather on the tent's shelf, and then bent and took her ankle in his large, warm hands. As he tied the dagger and sheath to her ankle with the piece of leather, she let herself be calmed by the feel of his hands on her skin.

"We need to get you some boots, lass," he said at her feet as he finished up fastening the leather. "These slippers aren't made for the woods, and they are nearly falling apart."

She chuckled, remembering how rushed she had been when she was preparing to sneak out of Dunbraes and stow away with Garrick and Burke, the two kindly blacksmiths from a few miles north whom she had just met. Yes, her footwear choice had been wrong, but she never would have guessed that she would be standing in the middle of Robert the Bruce's secret camp in the Highlands of Scotland less than two weeks after she escaped Dunbraes. So much had changed.

Garrick held the tent flap for her again as they exited, but they didn't have far to go. The large tent practically right next to theirs was apparently Robert the Bruce's meeting and strategy headquarters. They stopped in front of the tent, and a fierce-looking warrior poked his head inside the canvas.

"Garrick Sinclair and the lass he arrived with are here to see you, sire."

Jossalyn's stomach twisted with nervousness, and her heart pounded in her ears.

"Come in!" came a deep voice from within the tent.

The guard pulled back the canvas flap, and they stepped inside.

Chapter Thirty-Two

It took a moment for Jossalyn's eyes to adjust to the relatively dim interior of the tent compared with the bright summer day outside. She slowly took in the carpeted floor, several heavy upholstered chairs, and the large wooden desk in the middle. Behind the desk sat a man who appeared to be slightly older than Garrick, handsome and well-built. His dark brown hair was pushed back from his forehead, and he had a neat beard on his face that had a faint tint of red to it. When she met his brown eyes, she saw that he was scrutinizing her.

She immediately lowered her head and dipped into a deep curtsy, as she was used to doing in her brother's presence. She silently cursed herself for staring into the King's eyes. Her brother would have beaten her for a lesser offense toward anyone of noble blood.

"Nay, lass, rise, rise!" the Bruce said, standing quickly from his chair and walking around to the front of the desk.

She dared a glance up at him from her crouched curtsy and was surprised to see a kind expression on his face. Garrick extended a hand to her and helped her stand, then went directly up to the Bruce and clasped arms with him.

"It's good to see you again, Garrick," the King said warmly.

"Aye, it's good to be back," Garrick responded with genuine heartiness.

She felt her eyes widen at the exchange, but couldn't tamp down her surprise. Then the Bruce turned back to her, and her pulse hitched again.

"And who have you brought with you?" he said to Garrick, though his dark eyes surveyed her with curious scrutiny.

"This is Lady Jossalyn Warren," Garrick replied.

She registered in the back of her mind that he hadn't tried to hide her last name this time. Perhaps since she had already shared it with the three warriors who had greeted them in the woods, he figured she wouldn't mind him telling the Bruce.

But her bluster and courage from the forest seemed to have left her, and her pounding heart was nearly deafening in her ears. She almost dropped into another curtsy out of habit when Garrick said her name, but then she realized she would be disobeying a King and jerked herself upright halfway through.

She saw a little smile playing at the corner of his mouth at her awkward movements, but then she watched as her name registered and his face darkened slightly. "You wouldn't happen to be a relation of Lord

Raef Warren, would you lass?" he said with a frown.

"Y-yes, my lord," she said shakily. "He is my brother."

The King's frown deepened slightly, and he shot a look at Garrick.

"Why don't you take a seat and explain things to me, lass," the Bruce said, motioning toward one of the finely upholstered chairs nearby.

Her knees shook slightly as she walked over to the chair and sank down into it. The Bruce walked back around his desk and resumed his seat, gesturing for Garrick to take a chair as well.

She registered in the back of her mind that there was a partially drawn curtain behind the desk at which the Bruce sat, and she caught a glimpse of a bed. So this was not only the Bruce's strategic headquarters, but also his private living space. She swallowed hard, more intimidated than ever to be here. But the Bruce was looking expectantly at her, waiting for her to speak. She swallowed again and took a deep breath.

As Jossalyn launched into her story, she decided to hold nothing back, hoping that her motivations and earnestness would be clear to the King. She told him of what life had been like under her brother, his cruelty and controlling ways, and the freedoms she would steal whenever she could. She explained how her brother had gone to Cumberland to meet with King Edward, who was rumored to be ailing, and how her brother had hoped to ingratiate himself and gain a Barony from the sickly King.

She described meeting Garrick and Burke while she had snuck to the village to lend her healing skills to those in need, and how she had decided to stow away with them in the hopes of escaping her brother's cruelty. But the two men had taken her back to Dunbraes, just as her brother was returning. A battle had broken out, and the three of them fled.

She told of how she had helped heal Burke's leg, and how they had almost been discovered by her brother and his men, but Garrick had saved them. She did her best to explain her realization that she wanted to join the rebellion and offer her healing skills, and how Garrick and Burke finally agreed to her request. She spoke of their journey east, then north, and finally, their parting with Burke and their arrival at the Bruce's camp. She left out Garrick and her lovemaking, since even the thought of mentioning something like that to a King made her blush.

"It has been an adventure to say the least, sire," she said, her voice steadier after sharing her story. "I only hope you will allow me to aid your cause in the best way I know how—by lending my healing skills to your warriors."

He rubbed his bearded chin in thought for a moment, absorbing what she had said. He turned to Garrick with a sharp eye. "What do you think of the lass's request, Garrick?" he said, leaning forward slightly.

Garrick considered the Bruce's question for a second, then gave a little nod. "I think we would be incredibly lucky to have her skills," he said honestly.

"And what of the fact that she is English, and one of our fiercest enemy's sisters, no less," the Bruce prodded, keeping a keen eye on Garrick.

"I believe her to be in absolute earnest and veracity when she says she supports our cause. She is to be trusted."

Jossalyn felt a swell in her chest at Garrick's words. She knew he trusted and believed in her—enough to bring her here, at the very least. But to hear him speak so sincerely and straightforwardly on her behalf to the King sent a flood of emotion through her. She gave him a look that was full of everything she was feeling. His gray eyes met hers, and she saw her emotions mirrored back in his gaze.

Robert the Bruce glanced from one to the other of them, seeming to gather all that passed between them in the quick exchange. He steepled his fingers in front of him, considering for a moment.

"How about this, lass? Why don't you stay on with us for a few weeks, or even months if you like, and see how you find the work."

He didn't have to state his intention; it was plain to Jossalyn. She was getting a probationary trial period, and not just for her benefit to make sure that she enjoyed working in a war camp. The Bruce wanted to make sure he could trust her fully, and even with

Garrick's word of approval, he wanted to see for himself. She understood his shrewdness and need for complete certainty. Even one traitor in their midst could mean the ruination of the entire rebellion.

She nodded. "Thank you, sire. I look forward to being of use."

He stood, and she followed his example. Garrick stood as well, but the Bruce turned to him and motioned for him to stay. He walked her to the front flap of the tent and held it open for her.

"I shall look forward to learning more about you, Lady Jossalyn Warren," he said mysteriously.

She didn't know exactly what he meant, but her thoughts were too jumbled to sort it out just yet. She walked the few paces back to Garrick's tent and entered. She sat down on the corner of the cot, suddenly realizing she was alone in the middle of Robert the Bruce's secret war camp.

Taking a deep breath, she waded into the swirling pool of her thoughts and emotions, trying to untangle her lingering fear, her elation at Garrick's words, the King's reaction to her story, and her chance to stay here at the camp for at least a few weeks. She only wondered how much of it she would have sorted out by the time Garrick returned from his private meeting with the King.

Chapter Thirty-Three

The Bruce turned back from the tent flap to face Garrick. "She is certainly a remarkable woman," he said appreciatively.

"Aye, Robert, she is." The Bruce insisted that when they were alone, Garrick should call him by his given name. At first it had been a struggle, but now he truly felt comfortable enough with him to do so. He didn't want to strain their relaxed relationship, so he tried to keep his voice light even though he felt a twinge of something at the Bruce's tone—was it jealousy? Territoriality?

He must not have hidden his annoyance very well, for the Bruce broke out into a hearty laugh. "Stand down, man, I wouldn't dare cross you on this matter. But I now know where things stand between the two of you."

No matter how long Garrick spent in the Bruce's company, he was always struck by how sharp and shrewd the man was. There was no point in trying to deny it.

"I have come to...care for the lass," Garrick said,

running his hand through his hair.

"And you truly believe she can be trusted?" the Bruce said, all mirth leaving him as he pinned Garrick with a serious stare. "Is there anything you couldn't or wouldn't say in front of her that I should know?"

"Nay, Robert, I would trust her with my life, and you know that's not something I say lightly," Garrick replied, holding his King's gaze.

The Bruce arched his eyebrows at his words, nodding to himself in thought. "Truly remarkable indeed," he said almost to himself.

"I do not worry *about* her," Garrick went on. "But I do worry *for* her. Though she is a healer, she is less familiar with the wounds of war. She may not be prepared for the more grisly aspects of warfare," he said, remembering her reaction to the horrific scene in the glen. "I am also concerned about how she will be received."

"You think the men will turn on her because she's English, or because she's Raef Warren's sister?"

"Perhaps. It may be hard for some of them to accept her." *And her safety is paramount to me.* He didn't speak the last part, but he guessed by the Bruce's sharp eye on him that the man had gathered the unspoken thought.

"I suppose some of them might be a bit…resistant at first. If she is as good a healer as you say, she shouldn't have any problems for long, though." The twinkle returned to the Bruce's eye. "If I were you, I'd be more worried about the men falling head over heels for her, not shunning her."

Garrick cracked a wry smile, which the Bruce found amusing enough to laugh at again. When his King's mirth finally died down, Garrick turned serious once more.

"I do have some news for you, Robert. It wasn't relevant to Jossalyn's tale, so she didn't mention it, but you need to hear this."

"Out with it, man."

Garrick took a deep breath. "Longshanks is dead."

The Bruce exhaled sharply and sat down in one of the chairs next to Garrick's.

"That was why Warren was returning to Dunbraes from Cumberland. Edward II has likely already been crowned."

"The Hammer of the Scots. Dead," the Bruce breathed. "And we know nothing of his son's desire for either war or peace." Already the shock was wearing off, and the Bruce's incisive, calculating side was kicking in.

"Aye, but you know the news before the rest of Scotland, and likely before many parts of England as well."

"You've done well, Garrick," the Bruce said, turning to him once more. "We will have to be prepared for the worst, of course, but at least we have time to ready ourselves. In fact, this may prove a good time to fully commit to our shift in strategy…" He rubbed his beard as he thought for another moment.

"To what would you attribute our success at the battles of Glen Trool and Loudoun Hill?"

Garrick considered the Bruce's question. The man had a mind designed for strategy, and he often liked to pose these kinds of questions to his inner circle, either looking for weaknesses in their tactics or strengths that could be developed for future engagements.

"We fought on our terms," Garrick said finally. "We didn't play by the English army's rules. Instead, we used the landscape, the element of surprise, and the chaos of battle to our advantage."

The Bruce nodded, his eyes bright with excitement at the memories of victory. "And you were central to our success as well, Garrick—don't forget that. It was you who was firing arrows on horseback rather than in a straight line among the other archers, you who suggested that some of the men lie in the heather or in the surrounding forests rather than stand before the English waiting to get hacked down."

Though he remembered his role clearly, his chest swelled at his King's praise. Those two battles, where they had finally tried something other than acting like a lesser version of the English army, had been the turning point in the rebellion. Garrick was with the Bruce when they had been forced to flee, first to the Hebrides islands and then to Ireland just last year. They had all been near giving up, but the Bruce wanted to make one more push for his claim to the Scottish crown and independence from England.

During their flight and exile, the two of them, along with a few of the Bruce's closest confidantes, devised a strike-and-retreat strategy, which used their knowledge of the Scottish landscape and harnessed the element of surprise, to attack the English. It had worked, both at Glen Trool in April and Loudoun Hill in May. Suddenly, Scotsmen from all corners of the country were joining the rebellion and pledging their allegiance to the Bruce and his cause.

It had seemed like a foolhardy, last-ditch effort at the time, but their guerrilla tactics had led them to two small victories, enough to keep the cause alive. Now they were poised to finally tip the scales of war one way or the other. On the one hand, Longshanks's death could mean the perfect time to strike, sealing their claim to independence. On the other, Edward II was an unknown entity who very well might redouble his father's efforts to bring Scotland to heel. Edward II could even change his father's tactics, making the Bruce's recent success moot.

The Bruce stood again, pacing across the carpeted floor of the tent absently. "I have been thinking that those victories should be our guide on how to proceed with the English. You have been the one to spearhead this stealth fighting strategy. You have clearly proven its effectiveness on the solo missions I have sent you on. You have been able to strike quickly and quietly, leaving the English no target to attack."

He halted in his pacing and turned to Garrick, the full force of his dark stare leveling him. "I want you to train all of our men in such tactics. We will be an entire army of silent, invisible warriors who strike quickly then dissolve back into the landscape. We will harry the English until they are so frustrated, so exhausted, so depleted, that they'll have to leave Scotland alone. We will be a thorn in their side."

"Or a thorn in their hand," Garrick said, subtly reminding the Bruce of their motto, "No one attacks me with impunity," and the image of the Scottish thistle that resulted in a handful of thorns if a person tried to grab hold of it.

The Bruce's eyes lit with an ambitious fire. "That's exactly it!" He took a step toward Garrick so that he stood over him in his chair. "What do you think, Garrick? Will you train the men in this new style of warfare?"

"Aye, Robert, I will." Of course, Garrick would have agreed no matter what—the Bruce was his King, and he was loyal to him until death.

But it was more than that. He had seen for himself how effective their new strategy had been at both Glen Trool and Loudoun Hill. And of course, there was a reason he had risen so rapidly among the Bruce's ranks to be one of his closest advisors: his skill at stealth attacks had proved invaluable to the cause. Even though he was only one man, his work had helped level the playing field for an otherwise outnumbered and out-trained Scottish rebel force. The thought of the entire rebel camp being educated in evasion, stealth, and surprise attacks sent a surge of hope through him that they might truly claim their freedom.

There was another aspect of the Bruce's plan that made his chest squeeze in optimistic anticipation, too. If his main task was to train the rebels in the art of guerrilla warfare, that would mean he could no longer spend weeks or months in the field working alone. Though he had always been proud of his work and grateful to serve in the rebellion, he found himself wanting something else now—or someone else. This new scheme could mean he would be at camp more often. Suddenly, the idea of having a loved one—a wife or even a family—didn't seem so impossibly incongruous with his life and work.

The Bruce was watching him closely, and must have been able to perceive something of these thoughts on his face, despite the fact that Garrick prided himself on being unreadable. But the Bruce was not only a warrior trained in surveillance—he was also a sage observer of men.

"You have worked in the field for many years, Garrick. Perhaps it is time for a new chapter in your life. Though I know you do not think of yourself in this way, I sense you will be an excellent leader and teacher. Plus, you might enjoy the...connections that such work allows you to make."

Garrick didn't miss the knowing twinkle in the

Bruce's eyes as he spoke. He didn't need to convince Garrick of the benefits of such a course of action—he could have simply commanded him, and Garrick would have acquiesced. But the Bruce was showing Garrick that he understood very well the fact that Garrick would be able to pursue Jossalyn in this new role. This appointment was not only a strategically smart move for the rebellion, it was also a reward for Garrick's loyal and steadfast service. Damn, but the Bruce was a clever man, Garrick thought with admiration.

Garrick was about to stand and excuse himself from the Bruce's company when one more thought struck him. "And if such a...connection should prove stronger than any other?" His chest squeezed at the thought, but he needed to know if the Bruce would allow one of his top warrior-advisors to marry.

The Bruce smiled faintly, sadness touching his eyes. He was likely thinking about his own wife and daughters, who had been kidnapped and imprisoned by the English the year before. It had been the start of their dark time together, when all hope seemed to be lost for the cause. As far as they knew, the Bruce's women were still alive, but Garrick knew that for the Bruce, this fight was deeply personal.

Seeing his King's deep anguish at the loss of his wife and children had always made Garrick silently swear not to make such attachments, so as to avoid the potential pain of losing them. But now he realized that a life without love was meaningless. Instead of shying away from love to avoid its potential loss, he suddenly understood that he would fight to the death to protect it—to protect *her*.

Was it love with Jossalyn, then? Aye, what else could it be? He was drawn to Jossalyn like no other, was fascinated by her, and longed to know more about her. She fired his blood like nothing he had ever experienced, and he was in awe of her beauty, grace, skill, and strength. Even the mere thought of her not being in his life—or worse, being taken from his life—made him blind with rage and grief. He could only imagine what the Bruce had gone through—and was still living through—at the loss of his wife and daughters.

The sadness flitted away from the Bruce's dark eyes, though, to be replaced by a knowing light of approval. "Sometimes, for all that we maneuver and strategize, Fate makes her own plans, eh, man?"

But then the King turned more serious. "I will give you the same suggestion I gave the lass. Why don't you view these next few weeks as an information-gathering mission? If in that time your connection proves a solid one"—and he didn't say it, but Garrick thought, *and if Jossalyn proves herself to be loyal and trustworthy, Englishwoman that she is*—"then who am I to stand in the way of Mistress Fate's plan for you two?"

Garrick's pulse surged. The Bruce would allow him to marry Jossalyn. He was being cautious, as always, when it came to the safety of the larger cause, but nevertheless, Garrick had an opportunity to secure the King's blessing on a union with the English sister of one of Scotland's greatest enemies. And with Garrick's newly designated role as a trainer of the rebels, marriage suddenly seemed more possible—and more desirable—than ever before.

In truth, he wouldn't even consider marriage if it weren't for Jossalyn. He wouldn't just be getting married, or acquiring a wife, he would be binding himself to *her* forever. The thought send a jolt through him. How greatly life had changed since he met her only a couple of weeks ago outside Dunbraes.

Garrick stood, exchanged a firm forearm grip with the Bruce, and turned to exit the tent. He had to remind himself that the Bruce had only given him permission to explore the possibility of marriage with Jossalyn. He still needed to secure his final approval. And, of course, he had to ask the lass! Though she had given herself physically to him, and had proclaimed her feelings for him, they had not spoken of the future, or of love.

He forced away the voice inside his head that told him she would reject him, that a fling didn't mean she would want to be tied to him for the rest of her life. The old misgivings about his unworthiness still haunted him, but he reminded himself of his word to her that he wouldn't doubt her. He would have to learn to trust her feelings for him. For if she could come to love him, anything was possible.

Chapter Thirty-Four

The days passed smoothly as Garrick and Jossalyn formed a new routine within the Bruce's camp. They each spent the days working on their own tasks, and then came together in the evenings to share a meal. More often than not, when they would retire to their tent, a simple brush of the hand or kiss on the cheek would turn into passionate lovemaking. When the metal frame of their small cot began to squeak too much after a week of use, they pulled the straw mattress to the floor and entwined their limbs, taking each other to the heights of pleasure, then sleeping deeply in each other's arms.

When Garrick had returned from his private meeting with the King, he had explained his new role as a trainer of the men to Jossalyn. He spent much of his days in a nearby glen with rotating groups of a dozen Scottish soldiers, teaching them what he had learned on his missions about weaknesses in English fighting styles, armor, and weaponry.

Meanwhile, Jossalyn began to make the rounds through the camp, seeing to its residents, doling out herbs and roots and introducing herself. Though she was often met with surprised stares when she opened her mouth and spoke for the first time—her English accent no doubt jarring in this setting—most people she encountered were quick to welcome her, especially when she was able to help with a persistent cough or an achy joint. A few of those she met remained reserved or even openly suspicious of her, but she didn't try to push them too hard into trusting her. She would just have to let her work speak for itself.

She grew more comfortable after the first week in the camp, not only with being surrounded almost entirely by giant, burly warriors in kilts, but also in her role as the camp's healer. She wasn't afraid to gather medicinal plants in the thinner parts of the surrounding forest, for she knew her brother wasn't going to catch her at any moment and strike her for her disobedience. She was sometimes aware of the scouts around the outskirts of the camp, but quickly realized they were protecting her and the others in the area, not trying to prevent her from practicing her healing.

The only time she felt the itch of discomfort was when she would be crouched to gather some flower or root, or in conversation with a warrior who needed a new poultice for a minor cut, or just wandering through the mazelike camp, and then suddenly, she would catch a glimpse of Finn watching her. He didn't try to hide, but he kept his distance, staring silently at her from several dozen yards away. Though his dark eyes were unreadable, his gaze would often send a shiver through her, for she felt his suspicion and distrust of her palpably.

When she would catch him watching her, she would level her chin and go about her business, though her internal impulse would be to scurry away under his sharp eye. She didn't mention it to Garrick; she figured she was just being overly sensitive, and she didn't want to behave like a worrywart. Nevertheless, the sight of Finn lurking nearby always sent the hairs on the back of her neck up.

On a particularly warm late-summer day nearly two weeks after they had arrived at the camp, Jossalyn was in need of more dandelion and decided to stroll toward the practice field to gather some. One of the older soldiers was complaining of gallstones, so Jossalyn had suggested a dandelion tea to ease the discomfort and help dissolve the stones. The glen where the men often practiced and trained with Garrick was one of the few grassy areas nearby, and she thought she remembered seeing some of the cheery yellow flowers there.

As she approached the field, she noticed that while a group of more than a dozen men were practicing their aim with bows and arrows, another group of a similar size stood waiting for their turn on the outskirts of the glen. She recognized Colin and Angus among those standing along the edge of the field and approached.

When Colin noticed her, he waved her over to them. "Fine day, isn't it, lass?"

The warm weather had caused many of the men to shed their shirts and practice only in their kilts. She blushed as she took in the sight. She wasn't quite used to so much male flesh on display.

Then she caught sight of Garrick, and suddenly, she was grateful for the hot sun overhead. Like many of the others, he had stripped to the waist, and sweat glistened off the hard planes of his torso. Though all the men present were warriors, his physique seemed especially honed and magnificent—at least to her eyes, she thought with another blush.

Garrick hadn't noticed her standing on the outside of the glen yet, and she relished the opportunity to watch him work. He was explaining to the group of men on the field how English bowmen would normally make a long line and fire a round or two of arrows to create cover for foot soldiers to move forward.

"This is incredibly ineffective and inaccurate, though," he said as he strolled around the group of men. "And even when they are lucky enough to hit something, why would we simply stand there and make their job easier for them?" The men rumbled their agreement.

"So instead of standing around like a bunch of scarecrows waiting to let an Englishman get lucky"—at this the men chuckled—"we're going to make their target smaller, harder to spot, and harder to hit. We'll learn how to shoot from a crouch."

Those on the practice field remained silent, but several of them shot skeptical glances at one another.

"You should all be able to hit the same target standing up—" Garrick snatched his bow and an arrow off the ground and stood, firing smoothly at a target on the far side of the field, hitting it dead in the center "—as you can from a crouch." He knelt down, one knee on the ground and the other bent at ninety degrees. He took another arrow into his bow, aimed, and let it fly. It thunked into the center of the target, nearly overlapping with the first arrow. The men murmured their approval.

"We will begin practicing shooting from a crouch tomorrow at the same time," Garrick said, dismissing the group on the field and turning to the waiting men.

Just then, he spotted Jossalyn, and she felt warmth suffuse her whole body—and it wasn't from the sun. He strode over to her, his eyes locked on her and a little smile playing around the corners of his mouth. He had shaved a few days ago, but dark stubble already dusted his handsome face, which was made more enticing by the quirk of his lips. She watched him approach, letting her eyes drop from his face to his bare torso, mesmerized by the movements of the muscles.

"What brings you to the practice field today, lass?" Then he leaned in and whispered just for her "Couldn't wait for the sun to go down to see me nearly naked again?"

She was sure that none of the other men around her, including Colin and Angus standing right next to her, had heard his suggestive tease. Nevertheless, she had to repress the desire to gasp in shock and swat him for the comment.

"I'm only gathering dandelions for a tea," she said instead.

"But I have something for you in the tent."

This time she did swipe his shoulder, but it only made him chuckle. "I mean it, lass. I have something I wish to give you that I think you'll enjoy greatly."

The men heard that well enough, and several of them chortled or murmured a bawdy response.

Turning to the group, Garrick said in an authoritative voice, "I'll return in fifteen minutes. I expect you all to have run twenty laps around the field by that time as a warm-up to our training session."

There was a collective groan from the men.

"Fifteen minutes sounds like an awfully long time, Garrick. Are you sure you'll take that long?" Colin's ribbing remark drew more chuckles from the men.

"Make that thirty laps, then," Garrick replied with a lifted eyebrow, not taking Colin's teasing bait.

There were more lighthearted grumbles from the group, but they started trotting around the field. He slid into his shirt, which had been tossed on the ground nearby, then took Jossalyn's hand and led her back into the camp.

Jossalyn shot a wide-eyed look at Garrick as he led

the way back to their tent.

Catching her stare, he smiled. "Don't believe the filthy minds of that lot, lass," he said. "I merely want to give you something. A...present."

"A present?" She could feel a smile spreading across her face to match his. What a decadent thing to receive a gift from her lover. She had begun to allow herself to mentally use that word to describe Garrick, for what else was he? It felt very wanton of her to have a lover, but she also relished the thought that she had chosen him of her own free will and shared her body and her passion with him willingly. Not many women—especially ladies—had that kind of freedom.

But the word wasn't the perfect fit—or maybe it was just that she would like another word even more. *Husband.*

She was completely content with their arrangement as it was now. She was savoring her newfound confidence and the freedom to openly practice her healing art. Their hungry desire for each other only seemed to grow with time, no matter how much they sated their passionate appetites, she thought with an internal thrill. She was coming to care for and respect him more and more, and she sensed his growing and deepening affection as well. Then why did she want to introduce the idea of marriage into their lives?

She knew Garrick had once thought himself incapable of marriage, or perhaps more accurately, incapable of predicting the future to know if he would ever be settled sufficiently to have a family. She also knew he feared that she wouldn't accept him as he was, though her affection these last few weeks should show him otherwise. She supposed she was greedy, but she wanted more with him—she wanted his love, for she now realized that she loved him.

Though she had never loved a man as a woman before, she knew with certainty that this was it. She simply couldn't imagine life without him. The mere sight of him simultaneously set her at ease and sparked something inside her that made her want more of his company. She admired his kindness and thoughtfulness toward her, his command and confidence with the men, and his deep sense of honor. He had already given her the one thing she had longed for her entire life—freedom. And at the same time, her freedom would mean little to her without him in her life.

She knew she could be content with life the way it was. She could keep working as a healer, and they could keep enjoying each other's company. But a small part of her—which was admittedly growing by the day—longed to publicly proclaim to all who would listen that they were committed to each other. Of course, the future could not be known, but she hoped to always face it with him—together.

She would never pressure him into it, though, so she brushed the thoughts—which were become increasingly frequent—aside as they arrived at their tent. He held back the flap for her to enter, and he joined her in the dim interior. Sitting on the bed was a package wrapped in canvas. She eyed him for a moment, but when he gave her a little nod toward the package, she pulled the canvas back.

Sitting in front of her were the finest leather boots she had ever seen. She gasped as her fingers brushed against the leather. It was soft, yet thick, perfect for moving around in the outdoors—which was the only place she went anymore. There were ties running up the front of them, and they looked like they would rise to mid-calf.

"Try them on, lass," Garrick said over her shoulder.

She sat on the bed and kicked off her tattered, threadbare house slippers, then slid one of the boots onto her foot. She sighed at the feel of the soft leather as it encased her foot and ankle perfectly. He knelt in front of her, taking the other boot in his hand. He lifted the hem of her skirt up to her knees, then slowly slid the other boot onto her foot. The sensation sent little tendrils of heat up her legs.

"How did you manage to get these?" she said, her voice filled with awe.

"After I saw what a sorry condition your slippers were in, I had a chat with the camp's tanner. He has spent the last week on these."

She stared at him for a moment. His gray eyes, normally hard and sharp, were gazing at her with a mixture of anticipation and—was that worry?

"Do you like them, lass?"

Without speaking, she launched herself into his arms, sending them both toppling backward onto the floor of their tent. "I love—" She stopped herself just in time. She didn't want to potentially spoil the moment and make him uncomfortable if he didn't feel the same as she did. She didn't doubt his affection, but also didn't want to push him. "I love them."

Though she thought she had caught herself in time, he had clearly heard the declaration she had almost made, for he rolled over so that she was lying on her back and he was leaning over her. He pinned her with an intense gaze.

"Good, because I love you and want you to be happy."

She felt all the air gust out of her in a whoosh. "W-What did you just say?"

He smiled down at her but took a breath that hinted at his nervousness. "I love you. I want you to be happy. I'll bring you a thousand pairs of boots if that's what it takes."

A wild giggle escaped her. She felt like she was going to burst with joyous energy. "I love you too. Even without the boots."

A rumble of laughter shook his chest. But then his face went serious, and he pulled her upright and placed her on the edge of the cot. He remained kneeling on the floor in front of her. He took both of her hands in his and met her eyes.

"Marry me, Jossalyn."

If she had thought she would explode with excitement and happiness before, then now she was bursting into a thousand pieces of pure elation.

"Yes." Her voice sounded distant and garbled to her ears, and she realized that tears of joy had formed in her eyes and were blurring her vision of his handsome face. It didn't matter, though, because the next moment he had closed the distance between them and was capturing her mouth in a searing kiss.

Before she registered how or when they had moved, they were lying next to each other on the narrow cot, mouths locked together. One of her legs rose up to wrap around his hip, and she used it to pull their bodies even closer, pressing their hips together. His hands skimmed over her hips and bottom, her waist, her breasts, her hair. She had already undone the tie holding his hair in its dark queue, and her fingers tangled in it, holding his mouth to hers as their tongues teased each other.

A distant thought tugged at the back of her mind, and she pulled her lips back a little. "What about your men? They are waiting for you."

"Let them wait," he breathed, rejoining their lips. One of his hands was working on the ties at the back of her dress, and she arched to give him more access.

In short order, they had stripped each other of their clothes, except for Jossalyn's new boots. Jossalyn didn't think she would ever grow tired of the intoxicating feel of their bare skin pressed together. Just as Garrick was rolling on top of her, the cot screeched loudly. They froze, staring at each other, then simultaneously burst into laughter.

"Perhaps my next gift to you will be a new bed," Garrick said play-sourly. Then his eyes lit with an idea, and before she knew what was happening, he had scooped her up, wrapping her legs around his hips and hoisting her into the air. She shrieked and giggled.

"You're louder than the cot, lass," he said as he carried her from the bed to the wooden table with the pitcher and basin for water. "Hold on."

She entwined her arms around his neck, squeezed her legs against his hips, and locked her booted ankles behind his back. He kept one arm under her but used his free hand to move the pitcher and basin off the table. Then he set her down on the table so that her bottom rested on the wooden surface but her legs were still wrapped around his hips. He pulled back a little, then guided his swollen, hard manhood inside her.

She shivered and gasped at the feeling of his cock filling her. He took hold of her hips and began moving in and out, building the slow, achingly torturous pleasure for both of them. Her breathing increased despite his steady pace, which was driving her mad as the pressure grew.

She released her arms from his neck and leaned back, placing her hands on the table. His eyes followed her, devouring her hungrily. She watched him drink in the sight of her breasts, bobbing in rhythm with his thrusts, and noticed that a muscle in his jaw was clenched and twitching. The sight of him straining so hard to maintain control sent her hitching even higher.

She moaned and moved her hips, wordlessly begging him to go faster. He obliged, thrusting into her harder and more rapidly. With just a few more strokes, she was sent careening over the edge into pure ecstasy. She tried to muffle her cries of pleasure but didn't care if she succeeded or not. He followed her almost immediately, groaning out his release and grinding into her.

As they both came back down to earth, he leaned forward and claimed her mouth in another heated kiss. They disentangled themselves slowly, and his eyes lingered on her as she went about picking up her clothes, which were strewn all over the inside of the tent. Reluctantly, he reached for his shirt and kilt, donning both.

"I had better go see about that training session," he said grudgingly.

"They might tease you to death if you don't return soon," she replied, her merriment barely contained.

He raised an eyebrow at her. "Are you mocking me, my bonnie bride?"

She wished she could come up with some clever retort, but the way he called her his bride overwhelmed her. Instead, she threw her arms around him again and buried her face in his shoulder.

"I'll be back this evening, lass. I'll talk to the Bruce tonight, and then we will be able to truly celebrate."

His words held a promise, not only of their pleasure to come, but of everything that awaited them in the future—together, just as she had dreamed.

Chapter Thirty-Five

Garrick strode out of the tent toward the practice field, but he might as well have been walking on air.

He hadn't planned on proclaiming his love for Jossalyn or asking her to marry him. Yet the way she had almost let her words of love slip out, and then tried to cover them up, had made him realize he was being a damn fool for not speaking his mind. What a rare gift and treasure the love of such a woman was. He didn't want to wait a second longer to let his feelings for her be known, else he lose the opportunity, as Burke had warned him.

And now he was to be a married man. The thought was strange, but pleasantly so. He thought back to his last visit with his older brother Robert. He had always assumed Robert would marry, since he was the Laird of the Sinclair clan and it was his responsibility to produce legitimate heirs. But he had known his brother for so long as a single man, a warrior and leader, that it had been strange to suddenly see him completely entwining his life with a woman.

Garrick had thought Robert was daft at first, given the way his eyes followed Lady Alwin and how aware he seemed to be of her. But now, Garrick realized that he, too, had become like that with Jossalyn. Like his brother, he had fallen in love. And now he would marry—against all odds—the woman who both humbled him and filled him with pride to have her at his side.

A married man! He had thought of himself as a lone wolf for so long, and had devoted his life to his work so completely, that he had begun to discard the question of marriage and a family out of hand, assuming such joys would never be his to know. He had thought this way for so long that he had nearly convinced himself that he didn't *want* any of those things.

But Jossalyn had changed all that. She had cared for him and reminded him that he wasn't an irredeemable man who was nothing but a killer. She had believed in him even when he hadn't believed in himself. Damn, but he was the luckiest man on earth.

Lost in his joy, he made his way to the practice field. When he reached its edge, the men had already finished their laps, and Angus had taken charge, which was fitting, given the fact that he was one of the most senior and seasoned warriors in the camp. He was leading the men through a bladework drill in pairs.

"Thank you, Angus," Garrick said when he reached the giant warrior's side.

"Aye, of course, laddie. We couldn't *all* wile the afternoon away with a bonnie lass." The man's bushy red eyebrows wriggled with merriment.

He spoke loud enough for several of the men nearby to hear, including Colin, who doubled over laughing.

Garrick only smiled in response. He was a lucky bastard indeed.

By the time he had wrapped up the final training session for the day, Garrick was sweaty and tired. Even still, he felt like a giddy lad at the thought of seeing Jossalyn again—and speaking with the Bruce.

He forced himself to take a quick dunk in the nearby loch so as not to smell like a boar, and then hustled back to the camp. As had become their routine, they would dine with the Bruce and several others in the King's inner circle shortly. Garrick hoped to have a private word with the Bruce during the meal, then, assuming he could get his blessing, he and Jossalyn could share a quick toast with those present before retiring to their tent once more.

Despite the cold loch waters in which he had just dunked, his cock stirred at the mere thought. He guessed that because of his delay, Jossalyn would already be at the King's dining table, which was kept out in the open near his tent during the fine summer months, so he went straight there.

When he reached the open area on the other side of the Bruce's tent, where the dining table was set up, he spotted her instantly. She was talking to Angus and Colin on the other side of the table, waiting for the Bruce to indicate when to sit. There were a few other men gathered around the table between them, so she hadn't caught sight of him yet. After scanning the remaining men, he spotted Finn a few paces away, and noticed that the man kept glancing at Jossalyn out of the corner of his eye.

Garrick frowned. He had never been close to Finn, despite the fact that they had worked together with the Bruce for several years now. Like him, Finn was someone whom the Bruce trusted more than the others. Though Garrick found the man to be overly suspicious, and didn't entirely trust him, the Bruce seemed to enjoy having disagreements and different points of view among his circle of advisors, so as to balance each other.

He could live with the man, but twice now he had noticed that Finn seemed overly interested in watching Jossalyn, and it wasn't to appreciate her appearance. He looked at her like she was the enemy, and despite the fact that nearly everyone else in the camp had already come to trust and respect her, Finn remained guarded—and watchful of her.

"Garrick!"

His thoughts were pulled away from Finn at the sound of the Bruce calling him. When the Bruce reached his side, they exchanged a shake.

"How goes the training?"

"Very well. The men are taking to it, and they relish the idea of not having to act like the English, standing in rows to do battle," Garrick replied.

"I imagine so. I brought together a few of the advisors, as well as some newer members, to discuss this change in strategy," the Bruce said, motioning with his head toward the men gathering around the table.

The Bruce had indeed gathered a well-balanced group. Angus was respected for the fact that he was a seasoned warrior, though he was slower to adopt innovative approaches when it came to battle. He would be a more cautious voice. Colin had only just started to be groomed to join the Bruce's inner circle. He was newer to the rebellion and a few years younger than Garrick, but he had proven himself both on the battlefield and in training, and seemed to take to the stealth strategy quickly and eagerly. Most likely, the Bruce wanted his energy and fervor in discussing their new approach. And Finn would be the critical one, always thinking about how things might go wrong so they could plan around their weaknesses.

It was a sign of trust that the Bruce had allowed Jossalyn to stay for such a meal. Though they likely wouldn't delve too deeply into strategy, it was an indication that he had confidence in her loyalty even to be in the presence of a handful of inner-circle advisors.

Several servers began putting platters of food on the large wooden dining table, so the Bruce broke off further discussion of tactics and moved to take his seat at the head of the table. Garrick was honored with the seat directly to the King's right, and Jossalyn moved next to him, sitting on his other side. To his displeasure, though, Finn silently took the seat to her left.

As the others took their seats, one of the servers brought out a special platter and placed it in front of the Bruce. While all the other dishes were filled with simple but hearty fare, the King's steaming platter contained what appeared to be a mincemeat pie.

The server leaned in. "'Tis a pheasant pie, sire, your favorite."

The Bruce's eyes lit up. "And what is the occasion?"

"The new cook, sire. He as just arrived from the Lowlands and would like to please you especially," the wench replied.

"My compliments to him," the Bruce said, then raised his fork with a nod to those around the table.

As the others began to dish and eat their food, Garrick leaned in toward the Bruce.

"Robert, there is something very particular I wish to discuss with you."

The Bruce closed his eyes for a moment as he savored a bite of the pheasant pie. Then he turned to Garrick and raised an eyebrow, that knowing look in his dark eyes again.

"Is there?"

"Aye. It involves what we discussed a few weeks ago upon Jossalyn's and my arrival—the matter on which you advised me to...gather information?" For some reason it was proving harder than he had anticipated to speak with the Bruce about his desire to wed Jossalyn.

The King wasn't helping him out any, either, of course. He merely stared back at him, a half-smile on his face.

Garrick pressed on. "I am certain now that I have all the information I need. I hope that you will give us your blessing to..."

The Bruce frowned and cleared his throat. He took a sip of his ale, but that only caused him to cough more.

"Are you all right, Robert?" Garrick said quietly.

The Bruce tried to take a gasp of air, but it sounded thin and reedy. Garrick pulled him to his feet and pounded on his back several times, but it didn't seem to help. By this time, the rest of those seated at the table had stopped eating or talking and were looking at them with growing concern.

The Bruce's chest jerked again as he tried to suck in a breath, but this time, Garrick didn't even hear a thin wheeze to indicate that he was getting any air.

"Is he choking?" Jossalyn said anxiously at Garrick's side. The Bruce's eyes darted between them, and he grabbed his throat, but then reached for his face. Jossalyn pushed past Garrick to stand next to the Bruce. She touched his face where he had indicated, but didn't find anything. Then her eyes widened, and she pried his jaw open.

Inside the Bruce's mouth, his tongue had swollen to more than three times its normal size. It looked to be blocking his entire throat and pushing against the back and roof of his mouth. The Bruce's eyes began to droop, and his lips were starting to turn bluish.

"Poison!" Jossalyn said with frantic horror.

The entire table erupted.

Chapter Thirty-Six

"Who did this?"

"How do you know?"

"Do something, lass!"

"Silence!" Garrick bellowed over the desperate shouts of the others. "Lay him on the table."

Instantly, several hands were helping to clear the table and spread the King's limp body on it. Garrick turned to Jossalyn, whose breath was coming fast as she stared at the Bruce's form in concentration. He spoke quietly to her, like he would a scared animal. "Jossalyn, what do you recommend we do?"

"Horehound," she muttered to herself. Then she raised her eyes to Garrick. "My satchel. It is in the tent."

Before she had finished speaking, Colin had darted out of sight toward their tent.

"I need a feather. Like a quill, with a long hollow shaft."

Angus didn't bother to find the door-flap to the Bruce's tent, which was right next to the dining table. Instead, he lifted the bottom of the canvas wall straight up, tearing some of the material and toppling two of the corner poles. He returned with a quill in his hand just as Colin sprinted back to the table with Jossalyn's satchel.

"Cut the feather's shaft so that it is a few inches long, and make sure the hollow interior is clear," she said to Angus.

Then she turned to Colin. "Find some boiling water, and put all of this—" she grabbed the satchel from his hand, rummaged through it, and pulled out a grayish plant that looked like mint, but with smaller leaves "—into it. Boil off as much of the water as you can to distill it, but we won't have much time."

Colin nodded and bolted off in the direction of one of the camp's fires.

Then she turned to gaze at the Bruce, who lay motionless and blue-lipped, for a fleeting second. "Heaven help me," she murmured, then reached toward her ankle. When she stood upright, she had Garrick's fletching dagger in her hand and was moving it toward the Bruce's throat.

Instantly, Finn shot to her side. He clamped a hand over her wrist and jerked the blade away from the Bruce's throat.

"What the bloody hell are you doing, you English witch?" Finn shouted as he twisted her wrist farther back.

She yelped in pain as her wrist torqued. Suddenly, all the remaining men had their swords drawn, but none seemed to know at whom to point them.

Garrick darted to the two of them but held up his hands so as not to startle Finn. "Let her go, Finn. She is with us, remember? She is trying to save the King," he said in a low voice.

"Like hell she is. She put a knife to his throat!" Despite his vehement words, Finn repositioned her arm so that he was no longer twisting it painfully, but he still held firmly to her wrist, not letting the dagger move an inch.

"Garrick, do you trust me?" Jossalyn said, completely ignoring Finn and locking her gaze on him. Her wide greed eyes pinned him with a searching look.

"Aye, with my life, and with the life of the King," he said without wavering.

"I need to make a small cut in his throat to let air in. It is dangerous, but he'll die in a matter of minutes if I don't act now," she said with calm certainty.

"Finn, unhand her now, or the King's death will be on your head just as much as it is on the poisoner's," Garrick said, shifting his gaze to Finn.

Finn met his stare, a battle waging silently between the two of them. Finally, he released Jossalyn's wrist, but said darkly, "And if the Englishwoman slits our King's throat, you will be responsible, Garrick."

The moment Jossalyn's wrist was free, she blocked out everything around her and let herself be completely consumed by the task at hand. She had never done this operation herself before, but had seen her old teacher Meg perform it successfully on a man who had suffered a stroke.

She stepped to the Bruce's side and raised the dagger to his throat, just below his Adam's apple. She made a small vertical incision in the soft flesh of the King's throat, then another horizontal one inside the first cut. She left the tip of the blade inside the flesh, and without taking her eyes off the incision, she extended her free hand toward where Angus had been standing. "The feather."

He placed the trimmed and hollow quill in her hand. She brought it in front of her and gave it a cursory glance. It was the right shape and size for the task. She slid the shaft of the quill along the dagger's blade, pulling open the incision slightly with the tip of the knife. Then she inserted the quill into the incision and removed the blade, positioning the quill so that it was inside the cut but stuck out several inches from the Bruce's neck.

Just as she had prayed, she heard a gust of air through the quill, and the Bruce's chest rose slightly. Almost as if in echo of the Bruce's inhalation, a gasp swept through the men surrounding her. She felt all her breath leave her as relief swept through her.

"Christ, lass," Garrick whispered. "You did it. You saved the King."

His words brought her back to reality. "That was only the first step," she said grimly. "The poison caused his tongue to swell and blocked his airway, even to his nose. Now he has an airway, but the poison is still inside him. Someone fetch Colin."

Within moments, Colin was at her side, holding a pot of steaming water and boiled plant matter.

"Help me get the King upright," Jossalyn said. Several men lifted the Bruce's still-limp torso so that he was reclined but more vertical. Jossalyn grabbed one of the stray spoons left on the table and scooped up some of the liquid brew. She forced the Bruce's jaw open and poured the tea inside. Most of it dribbled out, since his tongue was still so swollen, but she thought some of it managed to slide down his throat.

"Er, lass, forgive me, but won't that liquidy stuff just come out of the hole you made in his throat?" Angus said softly. He was one of the men propping the King up, and he looked worriedly between the spoon in her hand and the quill sticking out of the Bruce's neck.

She kept her eyes on her task, but said, "Different tubes," as a simple reply. She continued to slowly spoon the brew into the Bruce's mouth. Even if he didn't swallow much, just coming in contact with the brewed horehound should take the swelling down in his mouth and tongue, she reminded herself for reassurance.

Somewhere in the back of her mind, she registered the sound of the serving wench sobbing.

"I did not know, you must believe me!" she wailed

to someone.

"I believe you, lass, but think. Did you see anything unusual?" Finn asked urgently.

"I didn't think it strange at the time, but the cook insisted on making something special for the King," she said through her sobs. "I thought it was an attempt to get into the King's good graces, since the cook was new. He only just came up from the Lowlands a few days ago."

"How did he know where to find the camp? Who admitted him?" Finn's voice was tight with frustration.

"I don't know, I don't know!" the woman moaned.

Garrick, who was also holding up the Bruce, shot a look behind him to where the server and Finn were talking. He motioned for another man to take his place at the King's shoulder, then joined the two out of Jossalyn's line of sight. She could still hear them as she continued to spoon the horehound brew into the Bruce's slack jaw, though.

"Where is the cook now?" Garrick said.

"I haven't seen him since I took the King's tray from him," the server said frantically.

"I'm going after him." Though she couldn't see his face, Garrick's voice was steely and hard, just as his eyes would be now.

He strode to her side, and she paused in her ministrations.

"How does he fare?"

"I think the swelling is going down slightly, which

means I may be able to get more of the horehound into his system. It's an antidote to some poisons, and it is also used to reduce swelling and help with breathing, but since I don't know what the King was poisoned with, I can't be sure it will work."

"I'm going after the cook," he said heavily.

"I'm going with you," Finn said as he approached the two of them.

"And so am I," Colin interjected.

"You two will only slow me down," Garrick said tightly through clenched teeth. "I work better on my own."

"There is no way I am letting you leave without me," Finn responded flatly. "You need someone to watch your back."

"And I can track better than both of you," Colin said.

Garrick ran a hand through his hair in frustration. "I don't have time to argue with the two of you. I am leaving as soon as I can get Fletch saddled. Either you are with me when I ride out of here or you're not, but the man already has a lead on us, and I don't plan on letting him live through the night."

The other two men simply nodded and disappeared into the falling twilight of evening. Garrick turned back to Jossalyn, his eyes tight with worry.

Before he could say anything, though, she gave him a quick kiss on the lips. "Go. Find him. We will be here when you get back."

A flood of relief washed over his features before they settled back into their hard, determined lines. Without further ado, he turned and headed to their tent for his bow and quiver, and then toward the stables.

She sent up a prayer for his safety, and another for Colin and Finn. They would be traveling hard through the night, and who knew what awaited them in the dark woods.

She forced her attention back to her patient. The King of Scotland's life was in her hands. She raised the spoon to his mouth yet again, pleading silently for the medicine to work, one painfully small drop at a time.

Chapter Thirty-Seven

Garrick pushed Fletch into the darkening forest, urging his loyal horse on despite the uneven footing. They couldn't play it safe, though. They had to find the man responsible for poisoning the Bruce.

Colin and Finn were fanned out several yards away on either side of him, somehow managing to keep up with his grueling pace. They had departed the stables together without a word, grim determination on all their faces.

After a quick query with the guards and scouts on the edge of camp, they discovered that a slight man on horseback had left about a half an hour before, headed south. No one recognized him, but a man leaving the camp was far less worrisome than a man trying to enter, so they had let him go unquestioned.

Another hour later, they reached the outer circle of scouts. One of the men in the area had seen a solo rider heading south, and at a reckless pace given the falling darkness. It would likely be the last piece of information they would get before they caught up to the assassin posing as a cook.

If they caught up to him, Garrick thought darkly. If the man was somehow able to outpace them, he could potentially make it all the way back to England to spread word of the death of the pretender King of Scotland, Robert the Bruce.

The thought sent Garrick spurring Fletch once more, though he knew the animal was giving him everything he had. The one small saving grace was that a nearly-full moon hung in the dark sky, giving them at least some light by which to see.

For the thousandth time, Garrick scanned the stretch of dark forest ahead of him, looking for any sign of movement or the trace of a trail left by the killer.

A flicker caught his eye in the distance. He blinked, fearing that his weary and straining eyes were playing tricks on him. But no, he saw it again. A rustle in the foliage far off ahead of them, and then—was that a flap of cloak?

"There!" Garrick shouted to the others, pointing.

Finn and Colin, already on the alert, jerked their heads in the direction of Garrick's hand. They must have seen it too, for at the same moment, all three spurred their horses, digging for every last drop of energy from the animals. They fell into a single line so they could move faster, with Colin in the front, followed by Garrick and Finn.

Like its rider, Colin's horse was young and spirited. Colin leaned over the animal's neck, stretching out the distance between him and Garrick little by little. Even still, the three of them were gaining ground on the fleeing rider. Now Garrick could fully see the solitary cloaked figure atop a horse, riding hard.

The fleeing man must have heard them crashing through the forest behind him, for he shot a quick look over one shoulder, then kicked his horse to try to gain distance.

"Halt!" Colin shouted.

The man didn't slow or even look back. He kept barreling forward through the woods. All four of them, the fleeing man and his three pursuers, were at the mercy of the dark forest. An unseen fallen log or a branch at the right height, even a rock or slight dip in the ground could potentially kill one or all of them.

As Garrick realized this, he whistled to Colin, who was several strides ahead of him but only marginally closer to the assassin. He reined Fletch in, forcing Finn to halt behind him as well. Colin turned over his shoulder, and when he saw that his two companions had halted, he reluctantly slowed his horse.

"What are you doing?" Colin shouted at Garrick, his voice loud and tight with adrenaline.

"We'll never catch up to him like this," Garrick said, more to himself than in response to Colin's angry question.

He swung his bow off his shoulder and smoothly nocked an arrow. He took a deep breath, trying to slow his pounding heart so that his pulse wouldn't throw off his aim. His eyes locked on the lone rider, who was still crashing through the forest several dozen yards ahead of them, the distance growing with each pound of Garrick's heart.

Colin said something, but Garrick didn't register it. His mind was blank, his vision narrowed so that the only thing he perceived was the man, whose cloak hood had fallen back in his flight. Moonbeams flitted across him and his horse as they moved. He aimed at the soft, exposed neck, but then thought otherwise. He wanted the man to be able to talk. Shifting slightly, he targeted the man's shoulder.

He exhaled and let the arrow fly. Time seemed to slow as the arrow sliced through the air, whizzing past the trees toward its target.

It found its mark. The shaft sunk into the man's shoulder, slightly more toward the center of his back than Garrick had intended, but it had the desired effect. The man jerked at the impact of the shot and lost his balance, first slumping forward, then falling backward off his horse.

Finn and Colin surged forward, leaving Garrick behind to take one more steadying breath before slinging his bow back over his shoulder and following them to where the man had fallen. When they reached his crumpled form on the forest floor, they dismounted and moved in on him. He was reaching feebly behind him, trying to grasp the arrow shaft, but the fall had driven it farther into his back.

"Tell us what you know, and we will make this

quick," Finn said flatly.

The man sneered, a half-cough, half-laugh escaping him. "Go to hell, you cock-sucking rebels." He spoke in a Lowland accent, but that didn't mean he wasn't allied with the English. Not all Scots supported the Bruce and his campaign. Many lived in the pockets of the English and openly opposed the rebellion, and a few even worked as spies—or assassins.

"Who do you work for?" Colin demanded.

When the man didn't answer, Finn leaned down and grasped the arrow shaft protruding from the man's back, giving it a twist. The man bellowed in pain. Garrick longed to turn away, to have it over with, but he knew this had to be done. Yet still the man wouldn't break.

"You can torture me all you like, you shit-eating savages. There will be plenty more like me to cut you down soon enough."

The three men exchanged a silent look. Garrick shook his head slightly. They wouldn't get anything out of him. Without speaking, Finn drew a dagger from his boot. As the blade flashed in the moonlight, the assassin smiled faintly, likely relieved he wouldn't be tortured or put to a traitor's death of handing, disemboweling, drawing, and quartering.

"Long live the King," he sneered under his breath.

Before Finn's blade could reach the man's throat, Garrick said, "You've failed. The King of Scotland lives. Our healer has already given him an antidote to your poison." He couldn't be sure if the Bruce still lived, and he prayed Jossalyn's brew was working, but he feared the worst. However, he wasn't going to give this bastard the satisfaction in the last moment of his life of thinking that he had succeeded.

The man's face shifted from condescending resignation to surprise, then horror. Finn's blade descended on his throat, and likely the last thought the man had was of his own failure.

Garrick turned away from the scene of the would-be assassin's lifeblood leeching from him, his eyes going blank and frosted. He walked back to Fletch's side and mounted.

"What should we do with his body?" Colin asked.

"Leave it. The crows can have his eyes, and the rats his heart," Garrick said coldly.

The other two mounted as well, and Colin collected the reins of the dead man's horse. Though he was exhausted, Garrick was suddenly determined to get back to camp and be at his King's side, even if it was the Bruce's death bed that awaited him. He reined Fletch northward and pushed him forward with his heels.

Jossalyn rubbed a shaky hand over her face, pushing some of her loose hair out of the way. The sun was just cresting the horizon, and the King still lived, though barely. She had managed to get all the horehound brew into his system, which took the swelling in his throat and tongue down enough that she had been able to remove the quill that was serving as his airway and stitch closed the hole in his neck.

She also had another batch of the horehound tea brewing. Luckily, she had found one more stalk of the short, leafy plant in her satchel. Once this batch had been steeped and spoon-fed to the Bruce, though, she would have to scour the area for more of the plant. Blessedly, it wasn't particularly rare or hard to find. At least the sun would be up to help her search.

The Bruce lay on his back now, still strewn across his large wooden dining table. Word had spread through the camp like wildfire that an attempt had been made on the King's life with poison, and many had gathered to watch her work or offer to help. She had more boiling water and brawny men to hold the King upright than she knew what to do with, but she was touched at how so many had wanted to come to her aid as she had worked through the night to try to keep the Bruce alive.

She wouldn't let herself worry about what would happen if she failed. Even though the swelling had gone down, the Bruce was still unconscious, and the poison must be lingering in his system, for although he breathed shallowly on his own now, his lips were still faintly tinged blue.

She also wouldn't allow her mind to run wild with fears for Garrick. It had been growing dark when the three men had set out, and they hadn't returned yet.

She had seen the tight urgency in his body as he left, and she feared the pace they would set in rough conditions. She understood his imperative to find the disappeared cook, but she longed to see him safely returned.

Just as she stood wearily to set out for more horehound, she heard a shout that had her jerking her head up. Riding right through the center of the camp toward her was Garrick, along with Finn and Colin, and an ominously riderless fourth horse. Suddenly her knees were weak as relief crashed into her. His gaze locked onto hers as he approached, and his eyes were hard and flat.

"How does he fare?" he asked without preamble before he had even brought Fletch to a halt.

"He's breathing on his own, now. The swelling has gone down, but the poison is still in his system. He hasn't woken up yet," she replied wearily.

Garrick strode to her side to gaze down at the Bruce, worry and exhaustion tightening his jaw. He searched over the Bruce's prone body with his eyes for a moment, watching his chest rise and fall weakly. Then he turned to her, and without speaking, gathered her in his arms and pulled her against his chest.

She hadn't realized it until that moment, but she was hanging onto her composure by a mere thread. At Garrick's wordless act of kindness, she nearly came undone completely. But she forced the tears that were threatening to choke her back down, reminding herself that she still had work to do, and that all these men were counting on her.

The sight of Colin and Finn dismounting behind Garrick tugged her attention back to her fears for what they all had been through.

"What happened?" she said, pulling back a little so that she could look up into his face.

"We caught up to the man," Garrick said, his tone clipped. "He fled, so I brought him down."

"I wouldn't have believed the shot if I hadn't seen it with my own eyes," Colin said, respect tinging his voice.

"He admitted his guilt, but he wouldn't speak more." There was something else that Garrick wasn't saying, and Jossalyn felt an internal chill sweep through her.

"And so you...?" She dreaded the answer, but felt compelled to ask.

"We gave him a traitor's burial," Finn said coldly.

Her eyes shifted to him, and she feared his suspicious stare, but as he met her gaze, his dark eyes were unreadable. He approached, and she held her breath, a fleeting thought that he might still think her a traitor as well flitting across her mind. But to her shock, he knelt before her and grasped one of her hands, lowering his head in contrition.

"Forgive my suspicion, Lady Jossalyn," he said, his head bowed. "I doubted you at first, wrongly assuming that because you are English and the sister of our enemy, that you were not to be trusted. But I value loyalty above all else, and you have proven yourself ten times over with your actions tonight, and in the past weeks. I only hope you will accept my apology and my unwavering fealty from this moment onward."

She was frozen in shock for a moment, and he raised his head with a worried expression on his face. She came back to herself with a little shake and pulled him up to his feet by the hand. "Of course I accept your apology, Finn. I understand your suspicion and am grateful for your friendship."

Satisfied, Finn gave a little nod and retreated a few steps. The swell of relief and gratitude at Finn's words almost pushed all the worries and fears from the last night away. But her eyes returned to the Bruce's limp form, and she remembered the task at hand.

"I must go search for more horehound," she said to Garrick.

"Nay, lass, you need to rest," he said gently but firmly. "Is this a fresh batch of the brew?" He picked up the warm pot of horehound water from the table.

She nodded.

"Gregor!" he called.

A large warrior stepped forward from the group of men gathered nearby.

"Give Gregor your instructions. Then you'll rest," Garrick said.

She began to protest, but he stopped her.

"Only for a few hours. And Gregor will come get you if anything…changes with the King's condition."

Gregor nodded in agreement with Garrick, so she sighed and explained how to spoon the brew down the Bruce's throat every few minutes. Gregor listened intently, likely grateful to have something to do to help his King.

When she was done giving the warrior her instructions, Garrick took her by the hand and began leading her toward their tent. Colin and Finn were also wandering tiredly toward their cots. Just as Garrick veered toward Fletch, Angus appeared before all four of the horses. He produced an expensive and rare lump of sugar from his pocket for each of the animals. "I'll see to them, laddie. You need rest just as badly as the lassie does."

Jossalyn reached out and wordlessly squeezed the giant's hand. He had been her shadow throughout the entire night, helping her lift and lower the Bruce, keeping the throngs of shocked men at bay, and even soothing the hysterical serving wench as she hovered around the table in tears. He smiled back at her and gave her a nod, bobbing his ruddy head slightly.

Leaving the horses in Angus's care, Garrick led her to their tent. Without bothering to undress or even take off her new leather boots, Jossalyn went straight for the cot and curled up on her side. Garrick followed her, settling himself behind her and pulling her back snugly against his chest. His warmth and strength surrounded her. No matter what happened, she could count on him. That thought soothed all her fears, and exhaustion and sleep claimed her almost immediately.

Chapter Thirty-Eight

The next week passed in a blur for Jossalyn. She slept and ate when she could, but mostly, she stayed by the Bruce's side. After that first night, he was moved into his tent and placed in his own bed. Jossalyn set herself up at his bedside, giving him more horehound tea and watching for any signs of change, for better or for worse.

Men from the camp came and went, sometimes bringing her food, other times refreshing her supply of horehound or boiling water. She had described the medicinal plant to a few of the men, and before she knew it, they were bringing her armfuls of the stuff. Just as she had suspected, it wasn't rare here, for which she was grateful.

Garrick stayed nearby as well, though he occasionally disappeared to brief those in the camp about what had happened or update them on the King's current condition. He also ran a few training sessions in an attempt to burn off some of the men's anxious energy and sense of uselessness. She suspected that it helped him feel useful to have a task like training to complete as well.

Garrick also called a few meetings of the Bruce's advisory circle over the week. The dozen or so men would gather in the Bruce's tent a few feet away from where Jossalyn sat at his side to discuss their plans. Though they never openly talked about what they would do if the King were to die, the air was always heavy with unspoken worry during these meetings.

A week after the night of the poisoning, Garrick called Colin, Finn, Angus, and a few others to the Bruce's tent for a discreet meeting.

"I've been thinking on what the Lowland assassin said, though he didn't give us much to work with," Garrick began in a low voice. "He mentioned there would be more coming."

"Another assassination attempt? More planted traitors?" Finn said, his brow furrowing.

"I doubt it would work a second time," Garrick replied.

"I have spoken with the serving lass again," Angus offered. "She didn't have much new information, but she remembered that the man passing himself off as the new cook claimed to be the cousin of the old cook. The old cook was called back to Inverness to see to his ailing father. A few days after he returned to his village, the body of his cousin was found floating downstream in the River Ness."

"Then that bastard would-be assassin has at least one death on his hands," Finn said bitterly.

"Aye, and he's paid for it." Garrick's voice was grim. "But now that his plot has been discovered, no one has been allowed to enter or exit the camp. Besides the poisoner, everyone here has been with the cause for months and has already been vetted and proven themselves."

"So what did the bastard mean when he said that more like him were coming?" Colin asked.

"That's just what's got me fashed, Colin," Garrick said, running a hand through his hair. "I think he may have let slip more than he intended. Could he have been alluding to an attack?"

"He said, 'there will be plenty more like me to cut you down soon enough,'" Finn said quietly. "Lowlanders?"

"Or Scots who have sided with the English against the Bruce. The Comyns have been openly hostile to the Bruce for more than a year," Garrick responded. "Either way, we need to be ready. There could be an attack mounting, and even if they don't know the exact location of the camp, they may be gathering nearby."

"I'll warn the scouts," Colin said, his normally easy features tight with concern.

"And I'll increase the men's training, especially in covert archery. If there is going to be a battle in the area, we'll need to use the forest as an advantage rather than a hindrance. There likely won't be any open-field fighting if we are attacked."

The circle of men all nodded and began dispersing.

Garrick came to Jossalyn's side and sat on a stool next to her.

"Will we really be attacked?" She tried to keep the edge of fear from her voice but didn't succeed. She wanted to be brave, but the thought of being in the middle of a battle terrified her. She knew all the men in the camp, most of all Garrick, were capable and skilled warriors. Even still, she hated the idea of them clashing with men who were bent on killing them.

He ran a soothing hand over her back. "The scouts will give us plenty of warning if it comes to that, lass. More likely, they'll be able to detect the movements of a large group in the area, and we will be able to meet them on our own terms."

"And you think they might be Scotsmen? Why would your own countrymen fight against the cause for freedom?"

Garrick shook his head slightly. "Some have found it more profitable to remain aligned with the English. Others dislike the Bruce and his tactics. He didn't exactly make friends when he killed the Red Comyn last year." A rueful but tired smile touched the corners of his mouth. "Perhaps having the entire English army to battle wasn't enough of a challenge for him."

Just then, the Bruce sighed and muttered something. Both Garrick and Jossalyn jerked, suddenly alert, their eyes locked on the Bruce. He muttered and rolled his head from side to side a little. It was almost as if Garrick's sarcastic comment had penetrated into the

Bruce's mind and roused him somehow. His eyelids cracked open slowly.

Garrick seized the Bruce's hand. "Robert, can you hear me?"

The Bruce blinked a few times, then croaked out a whispered "Aye."

Relief flooded through Jossalyn. She grabbed a cup of water that sat on the table nearby and handed it to Garrick, who gently lifted the King's head and gave him a few sips.

When he was settled back onto his pillow, the Bruce said, "What happened?" This time is voice was a bit stronger.

Garrick launched into an explanation of the poisoning, Jossalyn's life-saving operation and her antidote to the poison, the cook's flight, Garrick and the others' pursuit of him, and their most recent suspicions that an attack could be mounting against them. As Garrick spoke, the Bruce went from dazed to shocked to serious.

"We must be ready for this attack," he said, trying to prop himself up on his elbows. "We must—" He suddenly closed his eyes and swallowed, looking nauseated.

Jossalyn gently pushed him back down to lie flat on the bed. "You are still weak, sire. You may be through the worst of it, but you have a long way to go to recover your strength."

"But I must be able to lead my men!" he said, frustrated. "I cannot ask them to go to battle for me when I cannot stand at their side and lead by example."

"Instead of snapping at the lass for the fact that you are still recovering, I should think you owe her thanks for saving your life," Garrick said with one raised eyebrow.

At first, Jossalyn was shocked that Garrick would speak to his King in such a way, but then the Bruce gave a faint chuckle.

When the chuckle died down, he sighed. "I owe you my life, Lady Jossalyn," he said, all the bluster and intensity leaving him for a moment, to be replaced by earnest humbleness. "I thank you. But I warn you that you'll find me an exceedingly difficult patient. I want to be able to stand in front of my men and lead them into battle, if it comes to that."

"Then we'll just have to work together to get your strength up again," Jossalyn replied with a smile.

"You're a lucky man to have this woman as your bride, Garrick," the Bruce said, some of the old twinkle returning to his eyes.

Garrick's eyes widened. "Then…you give us your blessing?"

"Of course, man! How could I deny it to one of my most trusted warriors and advisors and the woman who saved my life? I'll do the ceremony myself if my healer will allow me." He turned his shrewd gaze on Jossalyn.

"I'm—I'm sure we can find a way," she stumbled,

overwhelmed by the surge of excitement inside her. They would officially be wed—and soon, as long as she thought the Bruce was well enough to preside over a ceremony. Her heart hitched, and she sought out Garrick's gaze. His eyes mirrored her excitement and joy, and she thought she would burst with happiness at that moment.

"Then we'd better get started on my strength-building right away," the Bruce said, interrupting their moment. "I'll start with some food—I'm famished."

Chapter Thirty-Nine

Robert the Bruce was glaring at her. The King of Scotland was giving her a sour look as if she had just taken away his favorite toy. Jossalyn had to repress a smile at the thought.

"My suffering amuses you, lass?" he grumbled.

Apparently, she hadn't repressed it as well as she imagined. "No, sire," she said, trying to straighten her face.

"For the hundredth time, lass, call me Robert!"

She nodded, though she didn't think she would ever get used to the idea of calling the King by his familiar name.

He tried to push himself off his bed and onto his feet once again, but like the ten times before, he only made it halfway before collapsing back down onto the mattress.

"That's enough for today, I think," she said.

He tried to stand again, but she put a gentle hand on his shoulder to stop him. Even her light touch was enough to force him back down. Though he had been awake for a week, his strength was slow in returning.

And no wonder. It was a miracle he was even alive. Being unconscious for a week and bedridden for another was a blessing, but the Bruce was impatient to be up and about again.

The rumors about an impending battle didn't help matters, of course. Though the scouts had yet to substantiate the speculations, the mood around the camp was serious and tense.

Garrick had been training with the men harder than ever before, putting them through their paces and running seemingly endless archery drills. Though the men were showing great improvements when it came to shooting on the move, among obstacles like trees and shrubs, and from different positions, Garrick kept on them, demanding their full dedication.

In fact, she had barely seen him this past week except at mealtimes and after the sun had set, when he would drag himself, exhausted, into their tent. Despite the fact that he didn't speak much about it, she sensed that, like the others around the camp, he was tense and on edge for the battle that seemed to be looming in all of their minds. Though the enemy hadn't shown himself yet, he was a palpable presence in the camp.

Just as she was settling the Bruce back onto a stack of pillows and reaching for a bowl of stew for him, she heard a piercing whistle. She froze mid-motion, her insides chilling as she heard the whistle echoed again and again all around them. Suddenly, the Bruce was alert, his sharp eyes darting around the room.

The canvas flap at the other end of the shelter was ripped back, and Garrick burst inside. She gasped and jerked to her feet.

The Bruce simply said, "Speak," as if he were waiting for such a startling interruption.

"It's the Comyns. Along with a smattering of men from other clans, they are moving in toward us. We are believed to outnumber them, but we only have a preliminary report from the scouts."

The Bruce's eyes scanned the carpet at Garrick's feet in thought. "We should move now, while they are still positioning themselves," he said quietly.

"I agree. The men are preparing themselves."

Jossalyn felt her stomach drop to the floor. The moment had come. They were going into battle. Garrick could be wounded or—or killed. She made herself finish the thought, and it sent panic stabbing through her.

As if sensing her distress, Garrick shifted his eyes to hers, and though he stayed rooted in place, his gaze communicated silently his understanding of the grave situation.

"I must be with the men," the Bruce said in a pained voice as he tried to push himself up off the bed.

"Nay, Robert. You aren't well enough," Garrick said, striding to his side.

"Damn you, man! Don't tell me what I can and cannot do!" Even as he ground out the words through gritted teeth, the Bruce fell back onto the pillows. He pounded a fist into the mattress in frustration.

"Garrick, I need to be out there," he said, this time his voice low with desperation. "I'm not so great a fool to think I can fight, but I am the King and leader of this rebellion. I need to let the men know that I stand with them in spirit, that their King is still strong and very much alive."

Jossalyn exchanged a look with Garrick, shaking her head slightly. Though the entire camp knew the Bruce had survived the attempt on his life, very few had actually seen him due to his enfeebled condition. There was no way he would be able to stand in front of his men, let alone walk out of his tent under his own power.

A light flashed into Garrick's eyes, though. "I have an idea."

An hour later, all the able-bodied warriors in the camp had gathered in the practice field, which was serving as their launch point for the battle. As Garrick looked out at the sea of men, who were bristling with weapons and covered in a variety of plaid colors, he felt his chest squeeze. Partly it was the heat of the anticipated battle seeping into his blood. These men were prepared, well-trained, and determined. Though he didn't relish the thought of killing, and dreaded the fact that some of their own would surely fall, the adrenaline of the fight was coursing through him, and he was ready for it.

But another source of the squeeze in his chest was

the fear of leaving Jossalyn at the camp. The rebels absolutely couldn't be bested today, for if they were, their enemies would do their worst to the few who would remain back at camp. And though he had never feared death, he realized now that he was terrified at the idea of leaving Jossalyn if he died. The thought of living without her was worse than any fate he could imagine. He had realized, as he had prepared himself to depart for battle, that if she felt the same way about him, she was likely twisting in pain and fear inside at the thought of losing him.

As if summoned from his mind, he caught a glimpse of her moving toward him from behind the sea of warriors in front of his gaze. She was walking next to a litter carried by two burly soldiers. Inside the litter lay Robert the Bruce. A few of the men at the back of the crown began to notice the small group, which included their King reclined in the litter, and parted for them. A murmur ran through the gathered crowd as the Bruce was carried to the front of the group where Garrick stood.

When they reached the front, the two men carrying the litter halted, and Garrick and Jossalyn helped prop up the Bruce so that he was sitting upright. A hush fell over those gathered.

"Scotsmen!" the Bruce began in a loud, clear voice. "We stand at the precipice of either a gory end or a victorious beginning. Now is the day—now is the hour—to battle for our lives and our freedom. Edward would have kept us in chains, slaves to do with as he pleased. And Edward II will prove himself Longshanks's son, in name and in deed."

The crowd rumbled in response.

"Who among you will die the death of a traitor today?"

The men exploded with shouts of, "Not I!"

"Who among you will die the death of a coward today?"

Again, the crown shouted their denial heartily.

"Now, who among you will fight and die for Scotland, for your King, and for your freedom?"

A cacophony erupted. The shouts of the men's ayes mixed with the rumble of their feet stamping the ground and the clang of their weapons beating against their shields.

"Today, you will stand as freemen, and you may fall, but you will fall as freemen also. Your freedom is in every stroke of your sword, every arrow you let fly, every swing of your mace or axe. No tyrant or usurper can stand against us. Let us take our freedom, or die trying!"

The response of the men was deafening. A whistle was sent up, and the warriors bellowed their battle cries, and then began marching southwest toward where the Comyns were gathering.

As the men moved out of the field, the Bruce collapsed backward into the litter, completely spent. Garrick lifted his limp arm and clasped it in his hand, locking eyes with him. The Bruce gave him a little nod in response.

Then Garrick turned to Angus, who was waiting a few paces away. "Guard the King with your life," Garrick said to him solemnly. He leaned in slightly and said more softly, "And Jossalyn."

Angus clasped arms with him firmly. "Aye, I will, Garrick."

It was time. The moment he hoped he would never have to face had arrived. He had to say goodbye to Jossalyn, potentially for the last time. Their eyes met, and he feared he would come undone before he could say everything he wanted to. Her eyes shimmered with tears, and he felt like he would drown in their emerald-green depths. She was trying to keep her emotions in check, but her rosy lower lip was beginning to quiver.

He closed the distance between them in one long stride, slamming their bodies together in a hard embrace. He buried his nose in her hair and inhaled deeply, locking away the intoxicating scent of wildflowers and sunshine in his mind forever.

"I love you, Jossalyn," he whispered into her hair.

"I love you too, Garrick," she choked out.

Suddenly, he forgot everything that he wanted to say to her. He could only think of how much he loved her at the moment, how much he admired and respected her, how humbled and honored he was to be the recipient of her love.

Pulling back from her was one of the hardest things

he had ever done, but he forced himself to do it. He turned before he could see the tears streaming down her beautiful face, for he feared he wouldn't be able to leave if he didn't go now. Though his feet felt like they were made of lead, he kept one moving in front of the other as he caught up to the tail end of the swarm of warriors headed to battle.

He willed himself not to look back, instead holding the image of her in happier times in his mind. After several minutes, though, he cracked. He turned to look behind his shoulder, but she was already out of view. He spun back around, ready to face the battle ahead.

Chapter Forty

Once she had gotten the King settled in his bed, fed him some soup, collected a few herbs and roots along the outskirts of the camp, and tidied both her own and the Bruce's tent, there was nothing for Jossalyn to do but wait. And pace. And worry.

The King had fallen into an exhausted stupor after overextending himself to give the rousing speech to his men. Except for eating, he mostly slept, leaving Jossalyn alone with her thoughts and fears. Angus was like her silent shadow, pacing outside the Bruce's tent or trailing a few yards behind her when she moved around the camp.

The midday sun sloped toward the west, and the afternoon stretched into evening, then darkness fell, and still there was no word or sign of what was happening on the battlefield several miles away. Jossalyn tried to tell herself that no news didn't mean bad news, that Garrick and the men were well prepared, and that their new stealth tactics would serve them well. But despite the tight rein she was keeping on her thoughts, every once in a while, the image of Garrick lying broken and bleeding somewhere in the forest flashed into her mind, unbidden.

She tried to sleep briefly. The camp was quiet, the few remaining women and the non-warrior men who helped run the camp having hunkered down for the night to wait, but despite her fatigue, she couldn't quite manage to crawl into the cot she shared with Garrick. His clean, masculine scent lingered on the pillow and in the blanket, and it made her heart ache. So she lit a candle and went back to the Bruce's tent, plunking herself down in one of his upholstered chairs as the minutes passed painfully slowly.

When the pre-dawn sky finally began to lighten, Jossalyn roused herself from her torpor and the swirling thoughts that consumed her and went out to one of the camp fires. She stoked the fire, and then hung a pot of water over the flames to boil. She wasn't even sure why she was doing it, but at least it was something to do. By the time she was done, the sun was just inching its way over the horizon.

Suddenly, her ears pricked. Were those voices in the distance? She shot a look at Angus, who stood a few yards away. He was also alert all of a sudden, his eyes fixed on the southwest end of the camp. A whistle went up from afar in that direction, a noise that Jossalyn was becoming familiar with. Angus recognized it as well.

"They return, lass!" he said, his voice urgent, though he didn't say how many of them were out there or if they were victorious. For all they knew, based on the whistle, only one of the rebels had escaped and had made his way back to camp. Jossalyn's heart squeezed, dread and anticipation mingling sickeningly in her stomach.

Just then, she caught a glimpse of a flash of red through the tents and the outlying forest. Her breath caught as she strained to see whose plaid she had spotted. Other colors began to emerge from the forest behind the red one. More and more of the men were materializing from the forest. But Jossalyn's eyes were locked on the splash of red at their front. She finally got a clear line of sight. Before she knew what she was doing, she was sprinting as hard as she could toward the red-clad figure.

Garrick was alive and running toward her too.

As soon as he spotted her, he had broken into a run ahead of the others. As the distance between them finally closed, she launched herself into his arms, laughing and crying at the same time. He held her so tight she didn't think she would be able to breath, but she didn't care. He was saying something to her, words of love and reassurance, but she didn't register them. All she was aware of was his arms squeezing her hard, his body enveloping hers.

She opened her eyes, blinking past the tears, and noticed a smear of red on his neck a few inches from her face. Suddenly realizing that he might be injured, she pulled back and scanned him, worry creasing her brow.

"Are you hurt?" There was dried blood on his neck and hands, and his shirt underneath the studded leather vest he wore was dirty and blood-smeared as well.

"Nay, lass. Only minor wounds."

Angus arrived next to them just then, huffing a little. "What news, Garrick?"

"We are victorious!" he said loudly, which caused the men tromping back into the camp around them to cheer noisily. Though they appeared tired and a bit bedraggled, their spirits were high.

He turned his attention back to Jossalyn. "I must get to the King and tell him of the battle."

She nodded and turned back toward the Bruce's tent, but he tugged her back to face him, his voice serious. "We didn't sustain very many losses, but there are several wounded men who are being helped back to camp as we speak. They will be arriving shortly."

She swallowed but gave him another nod, steeling herself. This would be her true test. She had already proven herself to the Bruce and the camp of rebels with her healing skills, but now she had to confirm for herself that she was able to be a battlefield healer. In a few minutes, she wouldn't just be seeing to one man's toothache or a case of indigestion. She would be responsible for overseeing and tending to all those wounded in battle. She was nervous, but she realized she didn't want to turn away and flee from such a task. She knew she could help and was honored to be able to lend her skills to aid these brave men.

Garrick took her hand, and they strode quickly toward the Bruce's tent. Apparently the whistle and the sound of the men filtering back into the camp had roused him, for he had managed to prop himself up when they entered the tent.

Before the Bruce could ask, Garrick said again, "We are victorious."

The breath rushed from the King in relief even as his eyes lit up with excitement. "What happened?"

"Once we got closer to the Comyn camp, we spread out to flank them. Though they were preparing to move on us, we caught them by surprise. We were able to keep our distance for much of the battle."

"And that must have allowed our archers to use their training in shooting from cover and in obstructed conditions," the Bruce said.

Garrick nodded, his face showing traces of his pride. "Aye, the training paid off. We lost very few of our men. We were able to take cover, and their archers were at a loss for how to fire back through the forest. They haven't let go of the English style of fighting."

"It worked," the Bruce said quietly, almost to himself. Turning his attention back to Garrick, he said, "And what of the Comyns? Have they been adequately quelled?"

Garrick sobered slightly. "They took a hit, but they fled when our victory was clear. I doubt this is the last we will see of them. And Robert—a few other clan colors were visible in their midst. Others may be joining the Comyns to oppose you and stand with the English."

The Bruce's face darkened. "Then we will have to show them, once and for all, that they cannot crush this rebellion." He took a breath and schooled his dark features. "But today, we are victorious. We have proven ourselves and our tactics yet again. Any man, English or Scottish, who dares attack our freedom, can challenge us and see for himself what we are capable of!"

Garrick laughed, a sound of relief and joy. Just then, a distant shout went up, and Garrick jerked his head around. "The wounded are arriving. I must see to the men."

"And so must I," Jossalyn interjected.

The Bruce waved them away, and they strode out of the tent together. Just as Garrick had said, the wounded from the battle were arriving back at camp, being aided by their fellow warriors. Some hobbled in, leaning on the shoulders of their comrades, while others walked on their own but gripped broken arms or bleeding wounds.

"Bring those with the most serious injuries over here," Jossalyn shouted to the approaching men. "The remaining can gather over there." She turned to Angus and Garrick, who were waiting for her word. "Boil as much water as you can. I'll also need thread and a needle, which should be held over a flame for a full minute. Someone fetch me my satchel!"

She rolled up her sleeves as a man with a serious gash on his calf was brought over to her. Just before she became completely engrossed in her work, a thought flitted across her mind. Not long ago, she had been a scared girl under the control of her cruel brother. Now she was a respected healer for the Scottish rebellion. She was loved by and loved in return a good-hearted, brave, and passionate man, who never tried to restrain her work or deny her skills. She had arrived into the future that she could have only dreamed of a few months earlier.

She brought her attention back to the man with the leg wound. She could contemplate her blessings later. Right now, she was needed.

Epilogue

"Before we get to the joyous events of the evening—"

Garrick felt Jossalyn's eyes on him, and he gave her a sideways glance, taking her hand in his and giving it a little squeeze.

"—I have some news, and a few things to discuss with you," the Bruce finished.

Jossalyn began to excuse herself, but the Bruce waved his hand to halt her. "Nay, stay, Lady Jossalyn. This involves you as well. We'll get this business taken care of, then get on with the real reason you're here."

The two of them stood before the Bruce in his tent. He had managed to walk under his own power from his bed to a large chair that was pulled out in front of his desk. It was a major accomplishment—yet another milestone in the King's recovery. His progress was slow, frustratingly so to the Bruce, but in the week since the battle, Garrick had noticed his color was returning. And though his body was still weak, the Bruce's mind had resumed its normal sharpness.

The Bruce withdrew a folded piece of paper from

the silk vest he wore. "I have received a missive from your brother," he began.

Garrick felt his eyebrows rise. "Is all well? Lady Alwin and the child and—"

"Aye, aye, all is well. In fact, Robert sends me news that felicitations are due to your cousin Burke."

"Felicitations? Of what manner?" Jossalyn asked.

"Apparently he has gotten married. It seemed that he beat you two to the punch!" the Bruce replied with a mischievous smile.

"Married! I didn't even know Burke was looking for a wife!" Jossalyn turned to Garrick for confirmation, her green eyes wide with surprise and joy.

"Nor did I," Garrick said, just as baffled as Jossalyn. A snippet of conversation with Burke flitted back into his mind. His cousin had said there had been someone special once, but that he had lost his opportunity and didn't believe to find such happiness again. He hoped Burke had been wrong, that the opportunity had perhaps re-presented itself and that he could indeed experience happiness in marriage.

The Bruce's tease about his cousin beating them to wedded bliss finally registered through his surprise at the news of Burke's marriage. "And how much longer do you suppose it will be before we join my cousin in married life?" Garrick said to the Bruce with a raised eyebrow.

The Bruce roared with laughter at Garrick's thinly veiled impatience. When the King finally caught his breath and wiped the tears from the corners of his eyes, he said, "Unfortunately, you'll have to wait a few minutes longer." He cleared his throat, sobering further. "Your brother also mentioned that the Comyns have been active near Sinclair lands, trying to stir up trouble and recruit others to join their resistance against me."

Garrick's mood instantly darkened. Just as he had suspected, the Comyns wouldn't go quietly. If they had already been moving through the Highlands trying to gain support against the Bruce and the rebellion, then the battle a week ago was only the beginning. Now the Bruce would have to worry about not only Edward II and his English army, but also the resistance of fellow Scotsmen who were allied with the English.

The Bruce was watching him closely. "Edward II's role remains to be seen. Only time will tell if he will choose to take up the mantle of Hammer of the Scots from his father. But now we'll need to devote ourselves to winning over our own countrymen," he said, seeming to read Garrick's thoughts. "An uphill battle, to be sure."

Garrick raised an eyebrow. "And by 'winning over' you mean…"

The Bruce smiled ruefully. "As you well know, Garrick, we are gaining more support by the day. Yet if Laird Sinclair's report is accurate, and I'm sure it is, our success is only galvanizing those who oppose us. It isn't just the Comyns anymore. The MacDougalls and

Argylls have sided with the Comyns, and the Southerlands and Rosses have only given me a temporary truce. Like many others, they are merely waiting to see who will emerge as the stronger force, and then ally themselves with the victor."

Garrick ran a hand through his hair. "What do you propose?"

Knowing the Bruce, he would likely have already hatched some stratagem to both hold off the English and confront his Scottish opponents, either forcing them to join him or be met with his guerrilla army of rebels.

"We will continue to battle those who would oppose us within the country. This most recent battle against the Comyns will give them and others much to think about before they stand against us again," the Bruce said, bringing his hand up to rub his bearded chin. "But we must also secure the Borderlands, both against the English and our Scottish enemies who would collude with them."

"Isn't James Douglas already doing just that?" Garrick asked. Douglas was one of the Bruce's most trusted friends and allies. From what Garrick had heard, Douglas was currently making his way through the Borderlands, razing English-held castles and garrisons so they couldn't be recaptured and used against the Scottish again.

The loss of heavily fortified castles that could potentially be held by the Scottish rebels was hard to swallow, but Garrick understood the Bruce's motivations. Too often in this war for independence, the Scots would capture a castle or town, only to have the English recapture it, using their own structures against them.

The English couldn't hold their location without a large fortress or castle in which to fortify themselves, but the Scottish rebels could. They were learning how to dissolve into the forests, hide in the heather, and take cover in the mountains. This was their home, after all. They would rebuild someday, once their freedom was secure, but for now, the rebels had to use their knowledge of the landscape, paired with the English army's immobility and need for the protection of a castle, against their enemies.

"Aye, Douglas is making progress in the south," the Bruce responded. "But he has only been tasked with destroying those castles and fortresses that could be recaptured and used against us. We need a holding of our own."

This surprised Garrick, as it represented a shift in the Bruce's tactics. Again, the Bruce seemed to anticipate his thoughts. "Douglas will continue on as before," he said, "but we will need a base from which to operate if we are to recapture and destroy the more…impervious locations."

Here the King's eyes flickered to Jossalyn, trying to gage her reaction, but her brow was furrowed in confusion. Garrick tried to untangle the Bruce's implied meaning. Then it dawned on him.

"You mean to destroy Dunbraes, and you need a base of operations nearby from which to attack it."

"Aye."

Jossalyn's eyes widened slightly. Her lips parted as she tried to find words, but the only sound was a gust of breath as she exhaled. The Bruce remained silent, watching her closely.

Finally, Jossalyn was able to speak, though her words came haltingly. "I-I don't know what to say. You are going to raze Dunbraes?"

"Aye, lass," the Bruce said quietly. "It has been held by the English for years and has never fallen to Scottish attacks. It served Longshanks well as a holding and a launch-point for the English army. Strategically, we must capture it if we hope to stem the flow of English soldiers into the country. And it would be a moral victory for the rebellion as well."

The Bruce paused for a moment, seeming to choose his words carefully before going on. "Taking Dunbraes would also give us the opportunity to deal with your brother. He appears to have been forced to turn back in his search for you and has returned to the Borderlands. My scouts and messengers got word that there is no longer English movement in southwest Scotland, where you said he was hunting you. Raef Warren has brought much death and suffering to Scotland. We cannot simply ignore him. Though he has evaded us several times over the years, we *will* end this."

Jossalyn nodded absently, her eyes drifting to the floor. Garrick watched as a barrage of emotions played out on her face. He saw her shame for her brother's actions, her shock at the thought of her former home being destroyed, and also fear and sadness, likely for the people of the castle and village whom she had come to know and care for.

"We wish only to defeat your brother and the English army, lass," the Bruce went on. "Our war is not against villagers and farmers. But this is warfare."

She nodded again, blinking back the tears that had sprung into her eyes. The Bruce's words seemed to reassure her slightly. "I wish your campaign well," she said simply.

"Then you do not wish to make a case for your brother?" the Bruce asked carefully.

She didn't hesitate. "No, I do not. He has brought much suffering into this world. I have managed to survive him, but I know all too well that others have not been so fortunate. He has earned his own fate."

As she spoke, Garrick took her hand again. He stood in awe of her strength and fortitude. She had been through so much, and yet she still carried herself with grace and integrity.

"Very well, then. I appreciate your honesty, lass, and I give you my word to do right by the people of Dunbraes," the Bruce said, a light of respect in his eyes.

"Thank you, sire—Robert."

The Bruce turned back to Garrick. "The last piece of news from Laird Sinclair is regarding your younger brother. Apparently, he has been helping your uncle run his keep these past few years?"

"Aye. My uncle William has been ailing, and his son is but fifteen and unready to take over for his father. Daniel has been helping out in the training of young Will to prepare him to be a Laird."

"How convenient," the Bruce said, almost to himself.

"Dare I ask what plan you are hatching now?" Garrick said wryly.

The fire that the Bruce got in his eyes whenever he was strategizing flamed now. "You remember Loch Doon, don't you?"

"Aye, of course." When the Bruce and his men had been forced to flee the previous year, first to the western islands and then to Ireland, they had stopped for refuge at Loch Doon Castle for a brief time. It was the Bruce's family holding. In fact, the Bruce had built the enormous eleven-sided curtain wall by hand with his father. Amazingly, they had built the entire holding on a small island in the middle of the loch. When Garrick had first seen it, he had been stunned by its beauty, then awed by its strategic location. It would be nearly impossible to siege, or even approach unseen. It was exactly the kind of castle that the Bruce would build and reside in.

"Then you'll remember that it is in the western

Lowlands, near the border, and also near Dunbraes."

The Bruce's plan began unfolding in Garrick's mind. "So you hope to take Loch Doon Castle and use it as the base from which to attack Dunbraes."

"Exactly. Though Loch Doon is mine by birthright, it is currently being held by Laird Gilbert Kennedy. I entrusted the castle to him when I began my campaign, but he was set upon by the English. He allied himself with them rather than have the castle destroyed in a siege, or so he claims."

"You don't believe him?"

"I'm not sure what to make of the man. Now that we've defeated the English three times in the last year, he has sent me a missive proclaiming his unerring loyalty to me despite his formal alliance with the English. I trust him about as far as I can throw him," the Bruce said, raising an eyebrow sardonically. "But I want Loch Doon back under my control—and in one piece."

"So you won't raze it like the other Borderland castles," Garrick finished.

Jossalyn tapped her index finger against her lips as she, too, pieced together the Bruce's plan. "But how do you expect to wrest it from this Gilbert Kennedy and hold it while you're here?"

The Bruce smiled a little. "That is where the third Sinclair brother comes in," he said, clearly pleased with himself.

"You're sending Daniel?" Garrick realized that after

the words were out, his shock sounded more like disapproval. He tried to temper his tone somewhat as he went on. "He's certainly more than capable of running a castle. He surpassed me in our training to potentially become Laird, and he has handed down that training to our cousin Will. I suppose I'm just surprised that you would select him above all others, Robert."

"The Sinclairs have stood with me from the beginning, despite the hardships they have endured because of it." Though he didn't name him, the Bruce was referring again to Raef Warren and the bloody and costly battle at Roslin he had brought to Sinclair lands.

"Both you and Laird Sinclair have done more than almost anyone else to help the cause. You have both risked your lives and done much for the rebellion, and for that I am grateful. I figured that the youngest Sinclair brother should have an opportunity to prove himself." The Bruce quirked a smile, but then grew serious once more.

"In truth, I consider it a reward for your family's loyal service. There is no one I can think of whom I trust more with my ancestral holding at Loch Doon than a Sinclair."

Garrick's chest swelled with pride at the Bruce's words and at the honor that was being bestowed on his younger brother. He could think of no one better for the job of holding the castle against the English, keeping it running smoothly, and setting the stage for a siege against Dunbraes than Daniel.

"Oh, and there is one other reason I'm sending your brother," the Bruce said, a twinkle of mischief in his dark eyes. "Laird Sinclair's missive was in answer to my question regarding whether or not your younger brother is married."

"He isn't," Garrick said cautiously, suddenly unsure again of what the Bruce was plotting.

"Which works out perfectly for me. Laird Kennedy has a daughter who is of marrying age. I still have my doubts about the man's loyalty, so I plan to force his allegiance to me by marrying his daughter to someone I can trust. Daniel Sinclair will do nicely."

Garrick tried his best to mask his shock and misgivings about such a plan, but the Bruce's merry eyes missed nothing. "Do you object, Garrick? Is there some reason your brother shouldn't enter a marriage alliance for his King?"

"Nay, Robert, it's only….Daniel was always a stubborn lad growing up, and it has only increased with age. He is a natural-born leader, but acquiescing to the will of others has never been a strong suit of his."

"He sounds like just the man for the job, then. He won't take any of Kennedy's shite—beg pardon, Lady Jossalyn—and he'll get Loch Doon back in line with the Scottish cause."

Garrick had to admit that the Bruce was right, but he didn't want to imagine how Daniel would respond to being told—nay, *commanded*—to leave the Highlands to marry some Lowland, English-sympathizing Kennedy lass, sight unseen.

"Perhaps you feel sorry for your brother, since he hasn't had your good fortune to make a love match in marriage?" the Bruce prodded gently, a small smile still on his lips. "If it makes you feel any better for him, I have heard rumors that the Kennedy lass is bonnie—and spirited. Perhaps even such an arranged marriage can prove to be a good match—or at least an interesting one," he said with a chuckle.

"I'm sure Daniel will be honored to oblige his King's plans," Garrick said diplomatically.

"I truly hope he is as lucky in love as his brothers have proven to be," the Bruce said cheerfully. "That's enough business for now. Let's turn to the real reason you two are here."

The Bruce called to the guard standing outside the tent, and the canvas door-flap was pulled back. Several of the Bruce's advisors, including Angus, Colin, and Finn, filed in and stood next to Garrick and Jossalyn. As Angus moved to Garrick's side, Garrick caught a distinct whiff of whisky emanating from the men entering the tent. He raised his eyebrow silently at Angus, who merely shrugged and smiled, his bushy red eyebrows wiggling.

"We started the celebration without you," he said on a whisky-filled breath.

"I think our witnesses are drunk," Jossalyn said to Garrick in a faux-horrified whisper loud enough for everyone in the tent to hear.

Her words brought on a rumble of laughter, which only further filled the tent with the scent of whisky.

"Kneel before me," the Bruce said, and despite his merriment, his voice was filled with gravitas.

They stepped toward the King's chair and knelt. Jossalyn's hand brushed against Garrick's, and he intertwined their fingers.

"We are gathered here today…"

Garrick tried to focus on the words that the Bruce spoke, which joined him to the beautiful woman kneeling next to him, but his eyes kept tugging toward her, longing to drink in the sight of her. She looked up at the Bruce with earnest joy in her emerald eyes as he spoke of the commitment she and Garrick were making to each other, in front of their King and in the eyes of God.

He noticed that her breath was coming faster, and he realized that his pulse was racing, but not in fear. Not long ago, he had thought himself irredeemable in the eyes of someone as compassionate and good-hearted as Jossalyn. He had imagined the happiness he had seen in his brother after marrying Alwin and starting a family would never be his. Though he believed in the cause he was fighting for, he had thought himself unworthy of a woman like Jossalyn. But despite all that stood between them and should have kept them apart, she had come to love him. Out of all the men in the world, she had chosen him. He was humbled by her choice, and even more, he was redeemed by her love.

He didn't remember most of what was said during the ceremony, but suddenly, he was kissing her, her scent surrounding him, and her soft lips melting into his. A cheer went up from their slightly inebriated group of witnesses. He leaned in and whispered his love for her into her ear over the riotous cheering, and then stood and helped her to her feet.

"There's a happy ending, if I ever saw one," Angus said, delivering a powerful slap to Garrick's back.

"Nay, Angus," Garrick said over the din, locking eyes with Jossalyn. "It's only the beginning."

The End

Author's Note

Though this is a work of fiction, several events, locations, and characters were based on historical record.

Dunbraes is a fictitious castle and village, though the English did hold several castles in Scotland during the Wars of Independence, especially in the Borderlands.

King Edward I, called Longshanks for his remarkable height and the Hammer of the Scots for his merciless suppression of the Scottish people (whom he viewed as rebellious subjects in need of punishment), did indeed die on July 7, 1307 in the farthest northwest region of England formerly known as Cumberland. He is rumored to have asked that his heart be taken to the Holy Land, and for the flesh to be boiled from his bones so that his skeleton could be taken into Scotland on future campaigns to suppress the rebellion. Eventually, he was buried at Westminster Abbey.

The battles of Glen Trool and Loudoun Hill did in fact happen in April and May of 1307, respectively. Robert the Bruce and his army had been routed in the Battle of Methven in 1306, and were forced to flee to the Hebrides and eventually Ireland, where they regrouped and developed a new strategy for battling the English. When the Bruce and his army returned to

Scotland, they tried out their new guerrilla tactics at Glen Trool and Loudoun Hill. The Bruce's success in these two battles proved to be a turning point in the rebellion.

The Bruce and his rebels did relocate near Inverness in Aberdeenshire in the summer of 1307, where the Bruce fell ill. Likely, though, he was exhausted from his difficult and lengthy campaign—a bit less dramatic that poisoning. The final battle in the novel is based on the Battle of Slioch, which occurred on Christmas Day, 1307, but which I have shifted to late summer for continuity. The Bruce's opponent was John Comyn, Earl of Buchan, whose cousin, John "The Red" Comyn, the Bruce had killed in 1306. It was largely an archery battle, which the Bruce's forces won after an initially inconclusive engagement. The rousing speech that the Bruce gives in the novel just before the battle is adapted from Robert Burns's 1793 poem "Scots Wha Hae," which was itself an adaptation (or an invention by the poet) of a speech the Bruce gave before the Battle of Bannockburn in 1314.

The Latin motto *Nemo me impune lacessit* (roughly translated as "no one attacks me with impunity") was used by the Stewarts of Scotland, and appeared on coins minted in 1578 and 1580 under the reign of James VI of Scotland. It was also adopted as the motto of the Order of the Thistle and several Scottish units of the British Army, including the Royal Company of Archers. Of course, my inclusion of this motto in the novel would place its use in Scotland centuries before these historical records indicate, but the motto's origin story may hint at earlier uses of the phrase. According to legend, the Scotch thistle (or "guardian thistle") helped save ancient Scotland from a Viking attack. When one Viking invader stepped on the thistle, he cried out in pain, thus alerting Scottish defenders to the attackers' presence, and thus linking the image of the thistle with the Scotland's history of resistance to invasion.

Garrick's recurve bow could indeed have come from the Holy Land and would have been an immense improvement over the English longbow, which was inaccurate and cumbersome. The recurve bow, by comparison, is smaller and more accurate, but more difficult to make, and so would have been hard to come by.

Jossalyn's use of medicinal herbs and plants is based on medieval understandings and uses of such flora. The emergency tracheotomy (or more accurately, cricothyrotomy) she performs in the novel on Robert the Bruce is incredibly dangerous, but was actually recorded as having been used as far back as 124 B.C.E.

Garrick and Jossalyn themselves are both fictitious characters (though their love is real to me!).

Thank you!

Thank you for taking the time to read Highlander's Redemption! Consider sharing your enjoyment of this book (or any of my other books) with fellow readers by leaving a review on sites like Amazon and Goodreads.

I love connecting with readers! For book updates, news on future projects, pictures, newsletter sign-up and more, visit my website at www.EmmaPrinceBooks.com.

You also can join me on Twitter at:
@EmmaPrinceBooks

Or keep up on Facebook at:
facebook.com/EmmaPrinceBooks.

Teasers for the Sinclair Brothers Trilogy

Go back to where it all began—with **HIGHLANDER'S RANSOM**, Book One of the Sinclair Brothers Trilogy. Available now on Amazon!

He was out for revenge...

Laird Robert Sinclair would stop at nothing to exact revenge on Lord Raef Warren, the English scoundrel who had brought war to his doorstep and razed his lands and people. Leaving his clan in the Highlands to conduct covert attacks in the Borderlands, Robert lives to be a thorn in Warren's side. So when he finds a beautiful English lass on her way to marry Warren, he whisks her away to the Highlands with a plan to ransom her back to her dastardly fiancé.

She would not be controlled…

Lady Alwin Hewett had no idea when she left her father's manor to marry a man she'd never met that she would instead be kidnapped by a Highland rogue out for vengeance. But she refuses to be a pawn in any man's game. So when she learns that Robert has had them secretly wed, she will stop at nothing to regain her freedom. But her heart may have other plans…

Burke's story continues in **HIGHLANDER'S RETURN**, a Sinclair Brothers Trilogy BONUS novella. Available now on Amazon!

First love's flame extinguished...

Burke Sinclair and Meredith Sutherland want nothing more than to be married, but ancient clan hostilities tear them apart. When Meredith is forced to marry another to appease her father and secure an alliance, the young lovers think all is lost.

Only to be reignited...

Ten long years of a stifling marriage nearly crush Meredith's spirit. But when her unfeeling husband dies and Burke, now a grown man and a hardened warrior, suddenly reappears in her life, the two may get a second chance at first love—if old blood feuds don't rip them apart once and for all.

Follow the thrilling conclusion of the Sinclair Brothers Trilogy with **HIGHLANDER'S RECKONING**. Available now on Amazon!

He is forced to marry...

Daniel Sinclair is charged by Robert the Bruce to secure the King's ancestral holding in the Lowlands—and marry the daughter of the castle's keeper to secure a shaky alliance. But the lass's spirit matches her fiery hair, and Daniel quickly realizes that the King's "reward" is more than he bargained for.

She won't submit without a fight...

To protect her secret—and illegal—love of falconry, Rona Kennedy must keep her new husband at arm's length, no matter how much his commanding presence and sinfully handsome face make her knees tremble. But when an all-out war with Raef Warren, the Sinclair clan's greatest enemy, finally erupts, will their growing love be destroyed forever?

Teaser for Enthralled (Viking Lore, Book 1)

Step into the lush, daring world of the Vikings with **Enthralled (Viking Lore, Book 1)**!

He is bound by honor...

Eirik is eager to plunder the treasures of the fabled lands to the west in order to secure the future of his village. The one thing he swears never to do is claim possession over another human being. But when he journeys across the North Sea to raid the holy houses of Northumbria, he encounters a dark-haired beauty, Laurel, who stirs him like no other. When his cruel cousin tries to take Laurel for himself, Eirik breaks his oath in an attempt to protect her. He claims her as his thrall. But can he claim her heart, or will Laurel fall prey to the devious schemes of his enemies?

She has the heart of a warrior...

Life as an orphan at Whitby Abbey hasn't been easy, but Laurel refuses to be bested by the backbreaking work and lecherous advances she must endure. When Viking raiders storm the abbey and take her captive, her strength may finally fail her—especially when she must face her fear of water at every turn. But under Eirik's gentle protection, she discovers a deeper bravery within herself—and a yearning for her golden-haired captor that she shouldn't harbor. Torn between securing her freedom or giving herself to her Viking master, will fate decide for her—and rip them apart forever?

About the Author

Emma Prince is the Bestselling and Amazon All-Star Author of steamy historical romances jam-packed with adventure, conflict, and of course love!

Emma grew up in drizzly Seattle, but traded her rain boots for sunglasses when she and her husband moved to the eastern slopes of the Sierra Nevada. Emma spent several years in academia, both as a graduate student and an instructor of college-level English and Humanities courses. She always savored her "fun books"—normally historical romances—on breaks or vacations. But as she began looking for the next chapter in her life, she wondered if perhaps her passion could turn into a career. Ever since then, she's been reading and writing books that celebrate happily ever afters!

Visit Emma's website, www.EmmaPrinceBooks.com, for updates on new books, future projects, her newsletter sign-up, book extras, and more!

You can follow Emma on Twitter at:
@EmmaPrinceBooks

Or join her on Facebook at:
www.facebook.com/EmmaPrinceBooks

Made in the USA
Lexington, KY
03 January 2019